Praise

"A slam dunk for those . . . surprising twists and turns."

—*Kirkus Reviews*

Praise for *All Murders Final!*

"There's a lot going on in this charming mystery, and it all works. The dialogue flows effortlessly, and the plot is filled with numerous twists and turns. Sarah is a resourceful and appealing protagonist, supported by a cast of quirky friends. Well written and executed, this is a definite winner. Bargain-hunting has never been so much fun!"

—*RT Book Reviews,* 4 Stars

"A must read cozy mystery! Don't wear your socks when you read this story 'cause it's gonna knock 'em off!"

—*Chatting About Cozies*

"Just because Sherry Harris's protagonist Sarah Winston lives in a small town, it doesn't mean that her problems are small. . . . Harris fits the puzzle pieces together with a sure hand."

—Sheila Connolly, Agatha- and Anthony-nominated author of the Orchard Mysteries

"A thrilling mystery. . . . Brilliantly written, each chapter drew me in deeper and deeper, my anticipation mounting with every turn of the page. By the time I reached the last page, all I could say was . . . wow!"

—*Lisa Ks Book Reviews*

Praise for *The Longest Yard Sale*

"I love a complex plot and *The Longest Yard Sale* fills the bill with mysterious fires, a missing painting, thefts from a thrift shop and, of course, murder. Add an intriguing cast of victims, potential villains and sidekicks, and interesting setting, and two eligible men for the sleuth to choose between and you have a sure winner even before you get to the last page and find yourself laughing out loud."

—Kaitlyn Dunnett, author of *The Scottie Barked at Midnight*

"Readers will have a blast following Sarah Winston on her next adventure as she hunts for bargains and bad guys. Sherry Harris's latest is as delightful as the best garage sale find!"

—Liz Mugavero, Agatha-nominated author of the Pawsitively Organic Mysteries

"Sherry Harris is a gifted storyteller, with plenty of twist and adventures for her smart and stubborn protagonist."

—Beth Kanell, Kingdom Books

"Once again Sherry Harris entwines small-town life with that of the nearby Air Force base, yards sales with romance, art theft with murder. The story is a bargain, and a priceless one!"

—Edith Maxwell, Agatha-nominated author of the Local Foods mystery series

Praise for *Tagged for Death*

"*Tagged for Death* is skillfully rendered, with expert characterization and depiction of military life. Best of all Sarah is the type of intelligent, resourceful, and appealing person we would all like to get to know better!"

—*Mystery Scene Magazine*

"Full of garage-sale tips, this amusing cozy debut introduces an unusual protagonist who has overcome some recent tribulations and become stronger."

—*Library Journal* on *Tagged For Death*

"A terrific find! Engaging and entertaining, this clever cozy is a treasure—charmingly crafted and full of surprises."

—Hank Phillippi Ryan, Agatha-, Anthony- and Mary Higgins Clark-award-winning author

"Like the treasures Sarah Winston finds at the garage sales she loves, this book is a gem."

—Barbara Ross, Agatha-nominated author of the Maine Clambake Mysteries

"It was masterfully done. *Tagged for Death* is a winning debut that will have you turning pages until you reach the final one. I'm already looking forward to Sarah's next bargain with death."

—Mark Baker, *Carstairs Considers*

I KNOW WHAT YOU BID LAST SUMMER

Also by Sherry Harris

Agatha-Nominated Best First Novel
TAGGED FOR DEATH

THE LONGEST YARD SALE

ALL MURDERS FINAL!

A GOOD DAY TO BUY

AT

LAST SUMMER

Sherry Harris

KENSINGTON PUBLISHING CORP.
http://www.kensingtonbooks.com

KENSINGTON BOOKS are published by

Kensington Publishing Corp.
119 West 40th Street
New York, NY 10018

All Kensington Titles, Imprints, and Distributed Lines are available at special quantity discounts for bulk purchases for sales promotions, premiums, fund-raising, and educational or institutional use. Special book excerpts or customized printings can also be created to fit specific needs. For details, write or phone the office of the Kensington special sales manager: Kensington Publishing Corp., 119 West 40th Street, New York, NY 10018, attn: Special Sales Department, Phone: 1-800-221-2647.

ISBN-13: 978-1-4967-0753-6
ISBN-10: 1-4967-0753-2
First Kensington Mass Market Edition: March 2018

eISBN-13: 978-1-4967-0754-3
eISBN-10: 1-4967-0754-0
First Kensington Electronic Edition: March 2018

10 9 8 7 6 5 4 3 2 1

Printed in the United States of America

To Bob
In your words:
You can thank me for always
keeping murder on your mind.

Chapter 1

"I need your help, Sarah," Angelo said to me.

I'd rushed over from the Ellington High School gym, where I was in the throes of setting up an athletic equipment swap meet for the school board. The swap was in the morning, and I'd been up to my ears in ski poles when Angelo sent me a text asking me to stop by. Angelo never sent texts, so I had literally dropped everything and would have a mess of ski poles to clean up when I got back.

We sat in his restaurant, DiNapoli's Roast Beef and Pizza, at one of the wooden tables lining the far right side of the room. It was just after nine-thirty, and Angelo had closed for the night. His deep brown eyes crinkled with concern.

"Anything. What can I do?" Angelo and his wife, Rosalie, who sat next to him, had done so much for me that I'd gladly do anything this side of legal to help them. And maybe the other side of legal, if it was really important. They'd supported me when I'd moved to Ellington, Massachusetts, from nearby

Fitch Air Force Base during a personal crisis over a year ago. The DiNapolis encouraged me if I was down and celebrated my successes, like starting my Sarah Winston garage sale business. I leaned forward, shoving my glass of Chianti to the side.

Angelo looked at Rosalie. I thought I detected a slight roll of the eyes on Rosalie's part.

"You don't have to help," Rosalie said.

"Of course I will." In the past I'd found replacement tables and chairs for them if something wore out. This sounded more serious, and I was getting anxious. I wished they'd just spit it out. I looked back and forth between them.

Angelo cleared his throat. "Did you hear about the lasagna bake-off in Bedford next week?"

Bedford was the town next to Ellington. I nodded, mystified. While I was a whiz at setting up garage sales, my cooking skills were renowned for how awful they were. I hoped he didn't want me to enter. I thought the contest was open only to chefs at area restaurants.

"I signed up," Angelo said.

"That's great. You'll win," I said. "Do you need a sous-chef?" I could try, but it seemed like Rosalie or someone who worked here with him would be a better choice.

"I want to make sure I win," Angelo said. "I have to win." His hand fisted, but he refrained from pounding the table.

This time Rosalie definitely rolled her eyes. "You don't *have* to win. You want to win," she said with a shake of her head.

"So what do you want me to do?" My imagination was going wild. *Poison, sabotage, kidnapping?* What would making sure Angelo won entail? There were rumors his family was connected, that his uncle had more than just ties to the Mob. And I knew his cousin Vincenzo, an attorney, had gotten a few mobsters off racketeering charges. It seemed like Angelo had better options than me to make sure he would win. I grabbed my Chianti and took a big swig. Why did they call that Dutch courage—or in this case Italian?

"I need you to go to the top five competitors' restaurants and sample their lasagna and report back." Angelo leaned back in his chair.

That was it? He wanted me to eat pasta? Relief made my body feel like an overcooked piece of lasagna, saggy and limp. "I can do that."

"And bring me back a sample, without telling anyone what you are up to."

"Of course." Jeez, how hard could that be?

An hour and a half later I roamed up and down the long rows of tables in the Ellington High School gymnasium, using a hockey stick as a baton, making sure everything was ready. I pictured myself as a drum majorette being cheered on by a crowd in a huge football stadium. I could do with someone cheering for me. I probably looked more suited to leading the band from *The Music Man*, with my hockey stick and crazy march. Slaphappy. Giddy. Punch drunk. I was all those things. Maybe it was the combination of the Chianti from earlier with the DiNapolis and the caffeine I'd consumed after in the form of coffee, lots of it, from Dunkin's.

My stomach rumbled, and I thought about the lasagna Angelo had mentioned. I hadn't had much of an appetite since my ex-husband, CJ, left me six weeks ago, despite the rekindling of our relationship last February. I still couldn't believe he had chosen a job in Florida over me. But I couldn't think about that now.

The lasagna project was something to look forward to, something to keep me busy. Busy had been my mantra since CJ left. I'd overbooked myself in the hopes that I'd be dead tired. But sleep, like my appetite, had all but disappeared. The lasagna would have to wait, though, because in nine hours the doors to the swap would open.

For the past week, people had been dropping off their gently used athletic equipment. Items they were tired of or that had been outgrown. Tomorrow other people would come and pick up what they needed. It was something that made everyone happy. The last of my helpers had left right after I returned from DiNapoli's around ten. Who could blame them? Some people had things to do on Friday nights. All the hard work getting ready for the swap was better than hardly working.

I twirled the hockey stick in my hand as I checked one last time to make sure all the equipment for the sports swap was at least somewhat organized. It hadn't taken long to learn that sports equipment didn't like to be arranged. It liked to roll or topple over. Baseball bats, lacrosse sticks, balls, pretty much all sports equipment. They were unruly and didn't lend themselves to neat arrangements. Except for the helmets. At least they cooperated by sitting proudly in rows.

I'd get zippo for doing this, so maybe it wasn't a smart business move. The last Saturday in June was primo garage sale season. I had turned down a lot of jobs, hoping that organizing this would up my profile in the town of Ellington and the surrounding suburban areas outside of Boston. It hadn't taken long to learn that sports equipment swaps were very popular in this area. Old and outgrown equipment was a big draw.

Most of the school board members had liked my idea of adding a silent auction to raise more funds for the school district. With all the sports teams in Boston, it had been easy to get items owned or signed by famous athletes and to prove their provenance. I'd even had a fan girl moment when I ran into Tom Brady the day I picked things up at Gillette Stadium, home of the Patriots. He was bigger in person and better looking. His smile almost melted my shoes.

I tossed the hockey stick up into the air as I twirled around, planning to catch it before it hit the floor. The lights went out, and I skittered to a stop mid-twirl. The hockey stick glanced off my shoulder and clattered to the floor by my feet.

"Ow," I said to the empty, silent gym. I felt around

for the hockey stick so I didn't trip myself. After I picked it up, I shook my head, hoping the power outage wouldn't prevent the swap from taking place tomorrow. I shuffled in the general direction of my purse and cell phone, not wanting to knock over one of the tables full of equipment. If I could find my phone, I could use the flashlight app. Footsteps echoed on the gymnasium floor and they weren't mine.

"Hello," I called. At least I wasn't alone. Slow, deliberate footsteps headed toward me. "Who's here?" I couldn't make out anything in the dark.

There wasn't a response except for the echo of steps. I whirled, still clutching the hockey stick, and hurried blindly toward my cell phone. I knocked my hip into a table. Balls of all sorts, from basketballs to golf balls, spilled, bounced, and rolled around me. I stutter-stepped around them, slipping, hoping that they would slow whoever else was in here, too.

Footsteps pounded across the gym floor, growing closer. I veered away from my purse. Sprinted toward the only light in the gym, one of the glowing exit signs. Something hooked around my foot. Another freaking hockey stick. I sprawled as I slid across the gymnasium floor and landed in a display of skis. They thundered down, battering and bruising me. I started to shake off the skis, to get back up, to get away.

Something whacked my lower back, my kidneys. Another blow hit the back of my thighs. I collapsed and curled into a ball, making myself as small as possible. I flung my left arm over my head, protecting it. My right hand clutched the hockey stick. My eyes were adjusting to the dark, and I could see the outline of a shadowy person bending toward me. The person grasped my arm, wrenching my left shoulder, and dragged me. I tried to trip him with the hockey stick. He stomped on my hand. I let go of the hockey stick as I cried out.

I heard a door open. Hinges creak. The only doors that weren't exits in the gym were to the equipment room or the locker rooms. The door to the equipment room was the one with the creaky hinges. He shoved me. The door banged shut. Something was dragged across the floor, and it hit the door.

I huddled on the floor, trembling. I knew I should move, but couldn't. Too scared. Too hurt. Noises sounded from the gym, bangs and bumps, and I wondered what the hell was going on out there. I pushed myself up to a sitting position and listened. After a while I didn't hear anything. I got to my feet and stumbled forward blindly. I bumped into some kind of shelving unit. It rocked madly, but nothing fell on my head. I fumbled around for the light switch, running my hand up the rough walls, where it seemed like it should be.

I finally found it and flicked it on, blinking as the fluorescent light came to life. One of the long tubes blinked sporadically, crackling and sputtering. It created the perfect setting for a horror movie. The equipment room was full of creepy shadows. The doorknob turned easily in my hand, but when I tried to push the door open, it wouldn't budge. And every part of my aching body seemed to protest the action. Whoever was out there had blocked me in. I cursed when I realized I was stuck for the night, because no one would miss me until the morning. But what if he came back?

Chapter 2

I couldn't just sit in here, waiting. I looked around the equipment room for something to protect myself with. Athletic equipment was locked in wire cages. A stack of dingy towels, lightbulbs, and a mop with no head were scattered around the room. *Throw the towels, break a bulb for something sharp, and whack the man with the mop handle?* I spotted a spray bottle filled with bleach. That was more like it. I gave it a couple of trial squirts. It had a strong, steady stream.

It would keep him at a distance. That should do as a weapon. I hooked it through a loop on my shorts so my hands would be free. I flipped off the light in the equipment room, hoping my eyes would adjust to the dark before I went back into the dark gym. Maybe it didn't make sense to worry about the light showing either, with all the noise I was probably about to make. Whoever was out there knew I was here. I pushed on the door. Was that a tiny bit of movement? I shoved again and again.

Whatever was blocking me in was making a lot of noise as it scraped slowly, painfully, away from the door.

I stopped once and listened at the tiny crack I'd created. Tried to look out. The gym was still blacker than the inside of a cave. Something banged, and I held my breath. Was it a door shutting? Was someone coming? Or going? The adrenaline that had gotten me this far seemed to flow out of my body like a hundred-year flood. It left me weak and a bit dizzy. I felt every painful blow that I'd been dealt. My hand throbbed. My back ached. I wanted to curl up in a corner and cry.

Instead, I threw my body at the door, widening the crack to a couple of inches. I went through my listening and peering routine again. Nothing. I took a deep, shaky breath, braced my legs against the floor, and shoved. This time whatever was blocking the door moved enough that I could slip from the equipment room back into the gym. But did I want to?

I squeezed out and raced toward the glowing exit sign nearest to me. It was my holy grail, my path to freedom. It seemed like it was a hundred miles away, even though it was only yards. My eyes had adjusted to the dark enough that I managed to leap over a pile of ski poles without slowing. Out the door and into the hallway.

I focused on the doors to the outside as I ran by lockers and trophy cases. I hoped the pounding in my ears was only my heartbeat and not someone chasing me. I was too scared to look behind me.

The bleach bottle slapped my hip. I slipped it off the loop and put my finger on the trigger. It wasn't much, but it was something.

The high school sat next to the library, which was perpendicular to the police station across the road. I kept that foremost in my mind as I banged through the doors and sucked in the warm, humid air. Focused on the police station, I didn't see the man right in front of me until I smacked into him. I stumbled back a couple of steps and aimed the bleach bottle. The man closed the gap and smacked the bottle out of my injured hand. I screamed. Maybe by some miracle, someone at the station would hear me. The man grabbed me by the shoulders and shook me.

"What the hell, Sarah?"

I blinked my eyes. "Pellner?" It was Scott Pellner, a police officer with the Ellington PD. After a tiny second of hesitation, my knees went liquid. I threw my arms around Pellner to keep myself upright or just to have some human contact. The most I'd had with anyone since CJ left. Pellner was solid, a few inches taller than me, and a happily married man with five kids. I dropped my arms, embarrassed. He led me over to a bench and sat next to me.

I stuttered out my story. Pellner talked into his shoulder mike and asked for an ambulance. *Why?* Then I realized he wanted the ambulance for me, and protested.

"I'm fine. I just want to go home," I said. Wailed. It was more of a wail than a statement. I tried to steady my voice, because if I went all hysterical female, he'd never let me go home.

"Stay here. I'm going to check out the gym."

I watched his back as he slipped through the door. No moon shone down, but the stars twinkled in the heat. No way I was going to sit out here alone, even though I knew other officers would arrive in minutes. So I followed Pellner and stopped just inside the gym doorway, the lights now on, looking at the carnage. Most of the sports equipment I'd worked so hard to organize lay haphazardly across the floor.

I gasped, and Pellner turned.

"I should have known you wouldn't stay put. What do you think went on in here?"

"Someone couldn't wait until eight-thirty for the start of the swap?"

Pellner's dimples deepened. On another man, they might have softened the hard angles of his face, but on Pellner, they only made him look menacing.

"Not funny?" I asked him.

"You being attacked isn't funny." He paused and looked around. "Can you tell if anything's been taken?"

I shrugged. *Ouch. No shrugging. No moving at all would be even better.* "It's not like I inventoried everything. It's a swap. People drop their old stuff off. Other people will come pick it up." I glanced up at the clock by the electronic scoreboard. Midnight. "I have eight and a half hours to get this place back in order."

Pellner was already shaking his head. "Someone maybe. Not you. You're going to the hospital."

Two more officers ran in. I recognized them but didn't really know them. They were followed by two EMTs.

"I'm fine." Every part of me seemed to ache, but I had work to do. I took a better look at the tables against the wall where the silent auction was set up. Pellner caught my frown.

"What?" he asked.

I walked over to the other side of the gym. The cops and EMTs trailing behind. "Someone took a lot of the silent auction items."

"Must be what went on here tonight. No one expected you to be here and came to steal this stuff. Who knows about the swap?"

"Almost everyone in the three surrounding counties. We've been advertising the heck out of this event." I turned to Pellner. "How did you happen to be here?"

"I saw your Suburban parked in the lot and thought I'd check on you."

There had been a time when I didn't trust Pellner, but I did now. He didn't look away under my scrutiny. "My car is in the side lot. You can't see it from the station."

Pellner pursed his lips. "I always drive through the parking lots on my way back to the station to make sure no one's lurking around the school. Do you have a problem with that?"

I shook my head.

"Okay, then. You are going with the EMTs to the

hospital. You can do it the easy way and walk with them, or I can cuff you and chain you inside the ambulance."

I frowned at Pellner. "Since you put it that way, I'll go with them. But what about the stuff that was stolen?"

"You can give me a list of what was stolen later. Let's make sure you're okay first."

"Thankfully, I kept the four most valuable pieces in the Suburban." I started to follow the two EMTs but turned back to Pellner. "As soon as I'm released, I'm coming back to get this place organized and ready to go for the eight-thirty opening."

Pellner ignored me, but I was fairly sure he muttered something about me being as stubborn as his fourteen-year-old.

I dragged myself back to the lobby of the hospital around two o'clock, with a clean bill of health. Not that I didn't ache all over; the ibuprofen they gave me only helped so much. Nothing was broken but a bit of my spirit. I'd napped in between tests while I waited for results. Just as I realized I didn't have a ride back to my car, my friend Laura Nicklas burst through the doors. Someone must have called her for me. I smiled as she glanced around worriedly.

"Laura," I called.

She blinked when she spotted me.

"How did you know?" we asked each other at the same time.

"Know what?" I asked Laura. People always told

her she looked like Halle Berry, but right now she just looked like worried.

"That Brody is here," she said.

Brody was Laura's oldest son, a high school junior. "I didn't. What happened?"

"He got a concussion playing baseball tonight."

"Oh no. What can I do?" I asked.

"Help me find out where he is. Mark is parking the car."

Mark was Laura's husband and was a colonel in the Air Force. I led Laura to the information window. Brody was still in the emergency room. We hustled over there. His high school coach and a couple of players were sprawled around the waiting room.

His coach jumped up. "He's fine. He was alert and talking. They're doing some scans. I don't know the results."

Laura nodded, but still looked panicked

"Come on, guys," the coach said to the players. "Time for us to clear out."

I followed them a few steps. "Excuse me. I just wondered how it happened."

The coach stifled a yawn. "Wild pitch. Nothing I haven't seen before. Brody leaned in at the wrong moment."

I nodded. "Okay. Thanks."

I went back to Laura, and we found the bay Brody was in. He was asleep. His dark lashes curled against his deep sandalwood skin.

"Isn't he supposed to stay awake?" Laura asked me.

"I think that's an old wives' tale. Rest is supposed to be good."

Laura hurried over to Brody and kissed his cheek. He snored gently.

I went to the nurses' station, told them that Laura had arrived, and asked if they could give her an update on Brody's condition. The nurse said she'd come down in a few minutes. When I went back to Brody's bay, Laura sat holding his hand. They were supposed to be moving today out to Joint Base Lewis-McChord in Tacoma, Washington, where Mark would have a new command. We'd said our goodbyes a couple of days ago.

"We stayed so he could play this last tournament with the high school team. Some silly all-night thing. Now I wish we'd said no and left earlier in the week," Laura said when she noticed I'd returned.

"No one could have foreseen this. The nurse will be here in a minute. Is there anything I can get you?"

"No. Thank you. I'm glad you were here."

Mark strode in.

"I'm going to leave," I said after greeting him.

"Why are you here if you didn't know about Brody?" Laura asked.

It didn't seem like the right time to share what had happened. "Just me being clumsy. I'm fine. I'll go. Let me know how Brody's doing."

Laura nodded distractedly.

Chapter 3

I woke with a jerk and straightened my stiff muscles as best I could in the front seat of my Suburban, still parked at the high school. I'd taken a taxi from the hospital to the high school. My plan had been to drive home for a couple of hours' sleep. I remembered leaning my head back and thinking I'd close my eyes for just a couple of seconds. Or maybe I hadn't wanted to face my empty apartment. I looked at the clock. That had been three hours ago. Dew had beaded on the top of the white hood of my car. The sun was rising and turned each dewdrop into a tiny prism, hundreds of rainbows to start my day. That must be a good sign.

I popped the locks, slipped out onto the pavement of the high school parking lot, muttering, "Ow, ow, ow." I circled my shoulders a couple of times before moving toward the gym. Every part of me seemed to ache, except for one spot on the back of my head.

I pulled out the key as I walked over to the gym. The sun hit my back. I reveled in the heat and the promise of a hot summer day. My hand shook a little as I stuck the key in the lock. The idea of going back into the gym alone scared me more than I cared to acknowledge to my conscious self. But I had to straighten the room, and I hoped there was still enough equipment for a decent swap. I had three hours to get my week's worth of work back in order.

A car door slammed and then another. I spun around. My best friend, Carol Carson, stood by her SUV, with a box in her hands. Even from here I could smell her delicious homemade cinnamon buns. Stella Wild, my landlady and friend, walked toward me with a tray full of Dunkin' Donuts coffee cups in her hands. Tears not only filled my eyes but also spilled over, and a few seconds later Niagara Falls had nothing on me.

Both Carol and Stella gave me one-armed hugs and scolded me for not calling them.

I finally got it together enough to speak. "What are you doing here?"

They exchanged a look.

"Pellner called me a little bit ago." Stella bit her lip. "I probably should have thanked him for the call, but instead, I yelled at him for not calling me sooner."

"He called me, too," Carol said.

I finished unlocking the gym door to hide my amazement. I was ashamed, thinking about that brief moment of suspicion last night, when Pellner was outside the gym so conveniently. When we first met, I'd been convinced he was a bad cop. Since then things had changed. Now he'd called my friends for me, knowing I was alone, since CJ had left. I yanked the gym door open and stepped inside. A chill hit me when I looked over the mess. It had nothing to do with the air, which was warm and stale.

Stella and Carol bustled in behind me.

"Coffee and food first," Carol said. "Then we start organizing."

I didn't think I was hungry, until I bit into the soft, still warm, and oh-so-cinnamony roll. I devoured it, and as I licked a bit of icing off my finger, I looked up. Carol and Stella stared at me.

I shrugged. "I didn't realize I was that hungry." I drank some coffee. The sugar and caffeine seemed to restore some of my determination. "Let's get to work. Would you two mind working on the swap stuff while I inventory what's missing from the silent auction?"

"It's fine with me," Carol said.

Stella nodded her agreement.

First, I had to figure out what had been stolen and what it was worth for the police report I knew I'd eventually be making. I took out my phone and made a list in the notes section. Ten sports jerseys were gone that had been signed by athletes from different area teams. Framed team photos of each of the Boston pro teams, gone. Also missing were an official Patriots football helmet, several signed Bruins hockey sticks, tickets to a Celtics game, a

Red Sox team pendant and baseball. Over twenty items were gone. Estimating the worth was difficult. I finally decided to go with what we used as the opening bid on each item, although we expected to make a lot more than that. So a low ball amount was around three thousand dollars. We could have easily doubled that.

By the time I finished the inventory, Carol had straightened the ski poles. I pushed back the memories of them falling on me in the dark. Stella had the helmets in gleaming rows. I started on the lacrosse equipment, then moved on to the baseball bats, working methodically around the room. There was a little bit less of everything. It was hard to tell what had been taken, and for the life of me, I didn't know why this had happened. As we worked, I realized that either Carol or Stella was near me at all times. It wasn't necessary. I'd convinced myself I was okay. But I appreciated their efforts.

By seven o'clock things were at least separated by type of equipment. It didn't look as good as it would have with more time, but it was good enough. I inventoried the remaining silent auction items.

"We are woefully short of silent auction items," I told Carol and Stella.

"Does it have to be sports-related stuff?" Carol asked.

I thought it over. "I guess not."

"Then I'll donate a group painting lesson," Carol said. "I'll even throw in the wine and refreshments." Carol owned a store called Paint and Wine, just down the street from DiNapoli's. She taught people how to paint. I'd been to several of her group parties, and they were a lot of fun.

"I can donate some private voice lessons." Stella taught voice at Berklee College of Music in Boston and gave private lessons, too. She'd traveled the world as an opera singer when she was younger, before some drug-related issues ended her career.

"Thank you," I said. "For being here, for donating."

"I'll make some calls to get other people to make donations, too." Stella had lived in Ellington for most of her life and knew a lot of people.

"Me too," Carol said.

"I'll send a note out to the booster club and the PTA," I said. Tears threatened again. Stella and Carol eyed me.

"Do you want to run home and take a shower?" Stella asked.

"Do I need to?" I asked.

Carol and Stella glanced at each other.

"If you're going for a messy, 'I slept in my car' look, you don't need to," Carol said.

I laughed. "Okay. I'm going."

"We'll stay here and keep organizing while you're gone," Stella said.

Ten minutes later I limped up the stairs to my apartment. I lived in an old Colonial house that Stella had converted into four apartments. Stella and another couple lived on the first floor. The couple were rarely around and seemed to use their apartment only to park a few things between travels.

Ryne O'Rourke opened his door as I hit the top landing. I jumped a little, still not used to his presence. He'd moved in about six weeks ago to help at his ailing uncle's antique store in Concord. He looked me over with his green eyes. A chunk of his wavy jet-black hair fell across his forehead. He had a cleft chin, the kind most women went nuts over.

"Rough night?" he asked.

I felt a hint of steam rising through my body. My typical irate reaction to this guy since I'd first met him at an estate sale. *Let him, and his cleft chin, think what he wants about me.* I tossed my head and smiled. "Very."

I slipped into my apartment and headed straight to the bathroom to see how bad it was. My blond hair looked like it had been styled by a tornado. There was a smudge of dirt on my cheek, and my blue eyes looked dull. My clothes were a wrinkly mess, so I stripped them off, stuffed them in the hamper, and jumped in the shower.

The hot water eased the aches and pains. I thought about Ryne and felt humiliated. He'd moved in right as CJ and I were falling completely apart. I was sure he'd heard more than one argument through the thin walls. He'd probably heard me cry myself to sleep more than once, too, since our bedroom walls adjoined. But I let the water wash away thoughts of him. I didn't have time to stay in the shower for more than a few minutes.

* * *

I made it back to the school a little after seven-thirty. It was amazing what clean hair and clothes did for a person. Fortunately, other than my bruised hand, my bruises were hidden under the knee-length sundress I'd put on. No one would guess what had happened to me. I juggled the four most important auction items, grateful I'd left them in my car, so they hadn't been stolen last night. A jersey signed by Tom Brady, a basketball signed by former Boston Celtic Kevin Garnett, and a hockey stick signed by the great Bruins player Bobby Orr. Stella's aunt Gennie "the Jawbreaker" Elder, a retired martial arts expert, had great connections within the sports world. She'd managed to get all of this for the auction. Plus, she'd donated one of her own tank tops from her illustrious career as a cage fighter.

I nudged the door open with my hip. Carol hurried over and took the basketball and hockey stick.

"I have to leave in a few minutes," she said.

"Thanks for coming over," I said as we walked across the gym. More volunteers had shown up, and things looked almost back to normal. The balls had been organized by type, and the baseball gloves were neatly stacked by size, position, and left or right hand.

"You look better," Carol said, studying me.

"The shower helped. Thanks."

After we finished setting up the silent auction, Carol gave me a gentle hug and left. Donations had poured in. Everything from a party at the hockey rink to weekends at lakeside and ocean-side houses to tickets to sporting events was available. One volunteer had set up a table with coffee, tea, and water. By eight-fifteen there was a line waiting outside the doors, and people surged in when the doors opened at eight-thirty.

I spent most of the morning over by the silent auction. The whole thing would be over by eleven-thirty, when I announced the winners. Some of the school board members hadn't thought a silent auction and a swap meet were a good blend. But the next chance to do an auction was in the fall, after school started, so they had agreed to give it a try now.

Judging from the number of people lingering around the tables and the way the bids were jumping up, it seemed to be going great. By eleven-twenty only the roughest-looking things were left stranded on the tables. The downside to this event was all the noise echoing around the gym. Excited kids squealing, parents reprimanding, neighbors calling out to each other all turned into a cacophony of noise that pressed in on my weary head.

People were still one upping each other at the silent auction tables. I worried about two men who hovered over the Brady jersey. As soon as one bid, the other immediately upped it. They stood side by side, pens in stiff hands, their posture more suited to a couple of boxers waiting to go a round than to participants in a school fund-raiser. I hoped a fight wasn't going to break out. As time ticked down to eleven-thirty, people noticed what was going on between the two men. Some started taking out their phones and staring at them. Ready to capture any action and post it on social media. Not what I wanted to have happen. A low murmur spread through the gym. Only the two men by the Brady jersey ignored the goings-on.

Chapter 4

The alarm on my phone went off just then. I called out in a loud voice, "The silent auction ends in one minute." People rushed the tables. The two men tried to elbow each other out of the way. One grabbed the other's shirt. I stared, horrified, as both pulled their fists back, but I wasn't about to get between them. Fortunately, someone else did. Ryne flipping O'Rourke.

"Gentlemen, I think we can resolve this without resorting to fisticuffs in front of the wee ones," Ryne said, gesturing to all the kids in the room, most of whom stared at the scene.

I shook my head at his Irish brogue. Half the time it sounded put on to me.

"How do you figure?" the bigger of the two men growled.

"Let me show you." Ryne stepped between the two men and placed a bid. He wrote with a flourish and grinned at me just as I yelled, "Time."

They both looked at him, jaws dropped. I took a

step back, not wanting to be collateral damage when they started beating on Ryne. But instead of beating him, they both broke into laughter. One man slapped Ryne on the back.

"Well played," he said.

"How about I buy you two gents lunch and a drink at Gillganins?" Ryne said to them.

Gillganins was an Irish Pub near Fitch Air Force Base. The men nodded, and all three left without a backward glance. I stared at their backs in astonishment.

Most people cleared out rapidly. The auction winners smiled as they paid, claimed their winnings, and carted them off. A crash made me jerk around. Someone had knocked over the coffee urn. Brown liquid spread across the floor. I hustled over to the woman.

"Everyone okay? No one got burned?"

"We're fine. Let me clean it up." Her son was crying, and her daughter pouted.

"It's okay. I've got it." I hurried to the equipment room to grab the stack of towels I'd spotted last night. I fished out my key, unlocked the door, yanked it open, flipped on the light, and stopped, staring in horror.

Melba Harper sat there with a vintage ski pole through her heart. I clapped a hand over my mouth to keep from screaming. There were still kids in the gym. I didn't want anyone out there to be frightened or to run over in response to a reaction from me. I stepped in and pulled the door closed behind me, making a little whimpering noise.

"Melba?" I asked, not expecting an answer. I quickly checked for a pulse, thinking I'd done this way too often recently. Her eyes were closed, as if she had just slipped in here to take a short nap. I felt nothing but cool skin. *Keep calm.*

I grabbed a grubby towel off a hook by the door before I stepped into the gym and closed the door. A few kids were shooting baskets as their parents laughed in a corner. I hurried over to the spilled coffee, dropped the towel, and stepped on it to encourage it to soak up the coffee. I hoped everything I was doing looked normal, because my mind was spinning in some kind of awful loop.

Melba, the school superintendent, is dead. Keep calm. Get everyone out of the gym. Call for help. I clapped my hands together as loudly as possible and felt a reverberation through my aching body. "Listen up. I need you to clear out of the gym so we can finish cleaning. Thanks so much for coming today."

There must have been something in my voice, because parents herded protesting children out. One woman threw a nasty look in my direction, but oh, well. Stella hurried across the gym, toward me, as I pulled my phone out of the pocket of my dress. She arrived next to me in time to hear my conversation with the 911 dispatcher. Her dark green eyes widened as she listened to me, and she darted glances toward the equipment room, as if a bogeyman might run out any minute.

I'd barely finished telling the dispatcher what had happened when Officer Awesome, Stella's boyfriend, ran through the door. He dashed over to us.

"You two all right?" he asked. His last name was actually Bossum, but I'd misunderstood him the night we met, and the nickname had stuck.

We nodded, even though I wasn't sure how all right I was. I took him over to the equipment room.

"She's in there," I said.

"Okay. Stay back. Stay over in the corner." He pointed in the general direction of Stella. Other officers were piling in, along with some EMTs.

I trotted back over to Stella's side.

"What happened?" she asked.

"She's in the closet, and she's dead." I took a shaky breath. At least I didn't blurt out the details. I didn't want to think about the details. "Did you know her?"

"She was my math teacher my senior year. It was her first year of teaching." Stella looked so shaken, I led her to a folding chair.

Melba had been the one who called and asked if I'd run the equipment swap. She'd been my champion with the board when a couple of board members didn't think I was the person for the job. Melba stuck up for me because the last person had quit promoting the swap and fewer people were participating.

"Was she a good teacher?" I asked.

Stella hesitated. "Yes. Everyone loved her. When

she retired from teaching and ran for the school board, there was a huge uproar."

"Why?"

"No one wanted her to leave the teaching field. There was a huge party at the town meeting hall. People cried. I think some even offered her money to stay on as a teacher. But she felt it was time for a new challenge. After five years on the board, she became superintendent." Stella swiped at a tear that rolled down her cheek.

"Did she have any issues while she was on the board or as superintendent?" I tried to think back if I'd heard anything about the school system over the past year. But my life had been so crazy, and since I didn't have any kids, I hadn't paid much attention. The only thing I could think of was the controversy over installing Astroturf on the football field, although most of the town had been all for it and had helped raise the money to get it installed.

Stella frowned. "She was pro-teacher, having been one herself. Sometimes the other board members didn't like that. Melba wasn't a big fan of the new football field."

"But didn't they use funds they raised?"

"Mostly, but she saw a bigger picture of what that money could be used for."

"Like what?"

"Art, music, drama. She wasn't anti-sports. She just thought other things were important, too."

Even I had gone to a few of the high school football games last fall. I could hear the beat of the drums in my apartment on lonely Friday nights. I'd walk over, buy a ticket and some hot chocolate, and join half the town in cheering the Ellington Eagles on. I thought back to the cold seeping through the hard metal bleachers, trying to remember if I'd seen Melba there. I wasn't sure. What I was sure of was that she had seemed pleasant enough and had gotten along well with the five-person school board.

"You hesitated when you said everyone loved her."

"I hated her class."

"Was she mean?" I asked.

"No. She was a doll. But algebra." Stella did a fake shiver.

It wasn't my favorite, either. "So as superintendent, she should have had a good understanding of what teachers needed."

"I think that's why she was hired," Stella said. "I'll check with my aunt Nancy. She might know more." Her aunt Nancy Elder was the town manager, with aspirations to a bigger political future. If anyone knew what was going on in this town, it was her.

Awesome walked toward us. I felt a weariness settle over me. Another statement to give.

Chapter 5

DiNapoli's Roast Beef and Pizza was packed when I walked in at one-thirty. I came not only for the wonderful food but also for the company of the DiNapolis during times of trouble. Rosalie and Angelo were surrogate parents, since my own were back in California, where I'd grown up. They'd been especially solicitous since CJ's departure, always sending me home with extra food or dropping some by unexpectedly. I'd lost almost ten pounds, and they were trying to make sure I ate. Little did they know that my freezer was stuffed and I'd taken to giving food to Stella or leaving some outside Ryne's door.

I waited in line, trying to decide what to order. A lot of people stared at me, which must mean they knew about Melba's death. On one hand, I was starving. On the other, every time I thought about Melba . . . I toyed with the idea that I should bolt.

"Sarah, what can I get you?" It was Rosalie. Just

hearing her voice made me feel better. Seeing the concern in her warm brown eyes almost brought me to tears.

Behind her I saw Angelo whirl around at the mention of my name. He had a ladle in his hand, and it was dripping with red sauce. "You go to the hospital and don't call us? You took a taxi home?"

Angelo was motioning with the ladle, and red sauce was flying. Gale, one of their employees, ducked, and sauce splattered onto the back of a guy chopping vegetables. He looked up in surprise. The kitchen had a low wall between it and the dining area. I was never sure if that was so Angelo could keep an eye on the crowd or if it was so they could watch him. People held up menus, trying to protect themselves. Another streak of sauce landed on the far wall, just missing a woman eating a slice of pizza. Her kids laughed as it rolled down the wall.

"I'm sorry, Angelo. I should have called." That seemed to satisfy him, and the sauce attacks ended.

"How did you know about the taxi?" I asked Rosalie. That they knew this was even beyond the normal level of gossip in Ellington. And since I'd had someone stalking me last winter, I was a little more paranoid than I used to be.

"Your taxi driver was Angelo's second cousin twice removed. He recognized your name on your credit card."

Yeesh, nothing slipped by the people in this town.

Rosalie leaned in. "How are you doing?"

I glanced at the line of people behind me. The place was way too busy for any kind of discussion, so I just shrugged.

"We have a special today, half a roast beef sandwich with a side salad. It's half off if you rode with Angelo's cousin in his taxi in the past two days."

I managed to smile at that. Rosalie was always thinking up some reason to give me a discount.

The guy behind me leaned around. "I rode with Angelo's cousin."

I heard a few other people chime in with a "Me too."

"Show me your receipts," Rosalie said with a sweet smile. "Not you," she said to me. "I know you were with him."

The people behind me grumbled good-naturedly. The guy right behind me said, "It was worth a try."

Stella showed up and joined me at my table. I picked at the Greek salad that came with my sandwich. I tried hiding some of the roast beef under the lettuce so it would look like I had eaten more than I had.

"Don't think you're fooling me by pushing your sandwich under your lettuce," she said. "But if you're not going to eat your croutons, I'll take them and the kalamata olives, too."

I scraped both onto her plate. "Any other news from your aunt about Melba?"

"Nothing. She's gone radio silent."

"But it's already all over town. Do you think something else happened?"

Stella shrugged. She looked over my shoulder toward the door, and her eyes widened. "Incoming," she said.

Before I had time to turn around, Pellner appeared by my side.

"Sarah, would you come down to the station with me?" he asked. His tone formal, his dimples deep.

"Of course." I scooted back my chair and stood. No need to make a spectacle of myself. Although this would be breaking news before we hit the door.

Pellner held the door open for me.

"Wait," Angelo yelled. He hurried toward us. "What's going on? Sarah, don't say anything without a lawyer."

"She's not in any trouble," Pellner told Angelo. "We just want to pick her brain on a couple of matters."

"I'm calling Vincenzo," Angelo said, wagging his finger at Pellner.

"You don't need Vincenzo," Pellner said when he sat me in the interrogation room at two-thirty. Vincenzo was Angelo's cousin and had reported ties to the Mob in the North End of Boston. He'd helped me out of more than one bad situation.

"Then why am I in here?" I gestured around the room, with its two-way mirror, recording equipment, and cameras.

"Because we are a little busy today. And the state police showed up and want to talk."

Only three towns in Massachusetts were big enough to have their own homicide divisions—Boston, Lowell, and Worchester. State troopers were in charge of investigations in all other municipalities, which meant I probably didn't know whoever wanted to talk to me. I thought about Angelo's "Never talk to the cops without a lawyer present" rule.

"In that case, I'm going to give Vincenzo a quick call."

Pellner frowned and left the room as I dialed. Fortunately, I was able to reach Vincenzo without any problem. He made me promise to clam up and call him back if I became concerned about the line of questioning. Angelo wouldn't be happy if he found out, but it would save us all time. I still had a garage sale to organize this afternoon.

Pellner came back with a round man with a round head and round eyes. Even his thin brown hair seemed to round his head. He wore a state trooper's uniform and introduced himself as Simon Ramirez as he settled on a wobbly chair across from me. Pellner stood by the door.

"Tell me about the attack on you last night," Ramirez said.

That surprised me. I'd been expecting to talk about Melba's death. "Why?" I asked.

"There've been two crimes very close together at the same place."

"I already told Pellner what happened. He must have shown you my statement."

"He did. But I'd like to hear it from you."

I shrugged and ran through the events of last night. Ramirez typed into a laptop while I talked. Repeating the story wasn't any easier than telling it the first time. It made me shudder, and I started to feel every sore muscle again.

"Are you okay?" he asked.

I nodded. What was I going to say? "No, I'm terrified"? He wanted the facts, not what I felt.

"Did you see your attacker?" he asked.

"No. The lights went out, and then I heard him. Or at least his footsteps."

"Why do you think it was a man?" He ran a chubby hand through his hair. A gold wedding band dug into his ring finger.

"Good question." I ran through the whole incident again in my mind. It was still way more vivid than I wanted it to be. "The footsteps I heard were heavy."

"That doesn't mean it wasn't a woman," Ramirez said.

Pellner just stood there, hands folded in front of him, listening.

"The person was really strong."

"Women can be strong."

I thought of Gennie "the Jawbreaker." Of course that was true.

"Think. Maybe there's something that didn't seem significant in the moment that will give us a clue as to who did this."

"And why," I added.

"It was a robbery, Sarah. Don't make it into something it's not," Pellner said.

Ramirez gave him a sharp glance.

"Right." I closed my eyes but snapped them back open, not liking the images I'd conjured up. "Aftershave. The person wore some kind of distinctive aftershave. It wasn't perfumy. It was masculine. Musky."

"Any chance you recognized the scent? Have a name for it?"

"No. Sorry."

"Let's move on, unless you can think of anything else that would be helpful."

We talked about the items that had been stolen from the gym. I gave Ramirez as thorough a description as I could of each item.

"And that's all that was stolen?"

"As far as I know."

"What's that mean?" he asked.

"It means there was so much sports equipment in the room that some of it could have been taken and I'd never know."

"You didn't have any kind of inventory list?"

I was not a slacker when it came to my business. "It wasn't necessary for this event." Yeesh, I had explained this to Pellner last night. "It was a swap. Nothing was being bought or sold except for the silent auction items."

He nodded but didn't seem happy. "Did you know Melba Harper?"

"Yes." I thought about Vincenzo. He'd tell me to just answer the question and not elaborate.

"How long have you known her?"

"We met last summer."

Ramirez tapped his fingers on the keyboard. "Where?"

"At an auction at a farm near Carlisle."

He nodded like he knew what kind of auctions I was talking about. And I was relieved not to have to explain that most auctions weren't filled with high-end antiques, gems, and paintings. My favorite auctions were the kind at someone's house or farm. That was where I'd found the best deals over the years. I thought about Vincenzo again. If I just kept answering the questions, I'd be here all day, and I had things to do.

"We were admiring the same desk before the auction started, and seemed to be drawn to the same pieces. We bid against each other more than once that day."

Ramirez leaned in. "So you had a rivalry."

I considered that. "Maybe a friendly one." I glanced at Pellner. His dimples deepened, like he didn't like me saying that. "Melba usually won, because I was on a tight budget."

"Did you resent that?" Ramirez asked.

"Heck no. After bumping into each other at several more auctions and a few garage sales, we went out for coffee. Of course, we ran into another problem, because she liked Starbucks and I love Dunkin's."

Both Ramirez and Pellner nodded. People were passionate here when it came to things like coffee or sports teams.

"We'd compromised on an independent place. We liked each other, but both of us were busy and never managed it again. We'd see each other at different events on and off."

"Did she ever say anything that made you think she had any enemies?" Ramirez asked.

I dug around in my memory. "No. We mostly talked about our shared interest in bargain hunting. She loved buying things for the schools. I loved buying things for my house, friends, or the occasional client."

Ramirez looked disappointed. "How did you end up being in charge of the swap?"

"She called me and asked me to stop by her office about a month ago." Her office had been decorated with the things I'd seen her bid on. The desk from last summer looked great, and I had told her so. "She asked me if I'd do it. I said yes and then attended a meeting of the school board."

Ramirez leaned forward. "And everyone was on board with you handling the swap?"

I smiled at his pun, but when he didn't smile back, I dropped it quickly. "Lance Long wasn't crazy about it originally but came around quickly. In fact, I need to get to their house soon. I'm doing a sale for them next week and have a lot of work to do."

"Did you hear why he didn't want you to do it?"

"Something about he thought the last person who'd done it was good enough. Nothing wrong with being loyal."

"Anyone else have a problem?"

"Anil Kapoor wasn't too happy, either, which was unusual, because from what I've heard, he usually did whatever Melba wanted him to."

"What was his objection to you?"

"He thought the swap was a waste of time and resources. It cost the district money to keep the school open, and he didn't think the auction would raise enough to make up for the cost. That kind of thing. None of it seemed personal."

"Can you think of anything else?"

"No. I'll call you if anything comes to me." I knew that was what he'd say next, and I thought I'd save him the trouble.

"What about the murder weapon? Have you seen any other antique ski poles like it before?"

"Sure."

Pellner grimaced. Maybe I should be more careful about what I was admitting to.

"Where?" Ramirez asked.

"There were some at the swap. My grandparents had them. I've seen them at flea markets." That surely was enough information.

"How many were at the swap?"

"I'm not sure. Since it was a swap—"

"You didn't keep an inventory." He frowned. "Can you make an estimate?"

I thought back. "Somewhere around a half dozen?"

"You don't sound too certain."

"That's because I'm not."

"Were any taken last night?"

"I have no way of knowing. I don't remember seeing them when I got back to the school, but other people were helping organize things, too."

"Can I have their names?"

I quickly listed everyone who had helped and gave numbers where I could.

"I'm going to go print your statement so you can sign it." Ramirez left the room, and Pellner followed. I drummed my fingers on the table, stretched, and blinked my eyes to stay awake while I waited. I could hear voices out in the hall but not what they were saying.

A few minutes later Pellner came back in with the printed-out report.

"Do you have any thoughts about who killed Melba?" I asked.

Pellner shook his head, not in an "I'm saying no" way, but more like in an "I can't believe you expect an answer to that" way.

"Please tell me that the person who attacked me wasn't the person who killed her. What was her time of death?" A little beat of panic fluttered through my stomach. I didn't want there to be a connection between me and Melba's death. I just wanted to go about my life, setting it in order, getting over CJ's abrupt departure.

Pellner opened his mouth, closed it, and then said, "I need you to sign this."

His nonanswer seemed like an answer to me. I was going to be dragged into this mess whether I wanted to be or not. If I didn't have to help set up the garage sale, I'd go straight back over to DiNapoli's and see what the local gossip was. I read the statement and signed it.

"If you have another minute or so, someone else wants to talk to you."

I glanced at my watch. I still had twenty minutes to get to my appointment. "Okay. Who is it?"

But the minute I said okay, Pellner hustled out and closed the door behind him. It made me wonder who wanted to see me and why. Maybe I should call Vincenzo. A few seconds later Seth Anderson, the district attorney for Middlesex County, stepped in and sat in the chair Pellner had just vacated. I dated Seth during the period after CJ's and my divorce and before we'd gotten back together. I hadn't seen him since before CJ left.

His deep brown eyes were hooded and dark circled. His face was shadowed with what looked to be a two-day growth of beard. But his shirt, expensive-looking silk tie, and tailored suit made him look like he'd just stepped off the front page of *GQ*. Which, given his status as Massachusetts's Most Eligible Bachelor, was entirely possible if not for his eyes, which looked so tired.

Seth's presence usually caused an immediate physical reaction in me. But not today. Too tired, too fresh off the hurt of CJ's absence, too worried about getting to my client.

"I heard what happened. I was here, anyway. Heard you were." He paused between each statement, like he was searching for the right thing to say.

"I am here." It came out more clipped than I meant it to. Seth had never done me any harm and had always respected my decisions. I put up a little wall in my brain to keep any other memories from seeping out.

He cleared his throat. "I wanted to keep things professional."

What things? I just nodded in response.

"Are you okay? Do you need anything?"

I looked into his eyes and managed a bit of a smile. "Thank you for asking. I'm tired but okay. I don't think what happened last night was personal. Wrong place, wrong time." I really wanted to believe that. "And I don't think what happened to Melba had anything to do with me, either."

Seth studied me and then nodded. "Let's hope so."

I scooted my chair back and stood. "I have someplace I need to be. And I'm sure you do, too."

Seth stepped in front of me, but only to open the door. His scent of citrus and soap washed over me. I steeled myself, apparently not as immune to Seth as I had hoped. But he'd said he wanted to keep things professional, so I would, too. My heart needed a rest.

"Good luck with the investigation," I said as I left the interrogation room.

I felt him watching me as I walked down the hall. I glanced back as I turned the corner. He wasn't even there. So much for my spidey sense.

Chapter 6

I pulled into Lance Long's driveway at three-fifteen and drove up the loop toward his sprawling brick house. The lawn was edged to perfection. Flowers bloomed enthusiastically, looking perky even in this heat. A Red Sox banner hung proudly by the door. I'd spent a good deal of time here pricing things that Kelly, Lance's wife, had put out in the garage, and I would continue to do that today. The garage door rolled up as I parked in a side spot. Kelly waved to me, her dark hair pulled back in a low bun, and her brown eyes sparkled in the sun. She wore a tennis outfit, and the skirt swished around her tan legs.

She'd found out about me when Lance complained to her that I'd signed on to organize the swap. Yeah, she'd told me that. Kelly wasn't one to hold back any thought that passed through her brain.

"I can't believe you came. Lance told me what happened to you." She paused. "And poor Melba."

"I'm fine." Horrified about Melba, but didn't want to talk about it.

"You can't be after what you went through."

"I'd rather stay busy. It beats sitting home, feeling sorry for myself."

"If you're sure?" She tilted her head.

I nodded.

Kelly beamed. "I have a fabulous idea."

Oh, no. I wasn't prepared for fabulous ideas today. "What?" I tried to inject some enthusiasm in my voice.

"A theme. Urban. Vintage. Chic." She held her hands up in the air, as if she was framing each word.

I realized I was supposed to be reacting with something other than weariness. "Great. What do you envision?"

"I grabbed a bunch of magazines and then studied Web sites on how to throw the best garage sale." When I didn't react, she added, "Oh, this is no reflection on you. I've heard you're fabulous." Fabulous, I'd learned over the past week, was Kelly's favorite word. "I wouldn't have hired you otherwise. But I just want to take it up a notch."

"Great." I smiled or bared my teeth, I wasn't sure which.

"I'm seeing a large tent, chandeliers, beautiful vintage dresses hanging. Oh, and rooms set up so there will be a kitchen area, a bedroom, a living room. Sparkly lights around the room. What do you think?"

"What is your goal for this garage sale?" I asked.

Kelly tilted her head again. She reminded me of

a Westie a friend of mine had growing up. "I don't understand."

"Usually, people throw a garage sale for one of three reasons. Either they want to make money, they want to get rid of stuff, or it's a combination of both." Usually, this was easy for me to figure out from the get-go, but that wasn't the case with Kelly.

"Oh. Oh." She squished her mouth to one side. "I want to get rid of stuff. But I also want it to look beautiful."

"And money?"

"Don't worry about that." She studied me for a moment. "If you don't want to do this . . "

"I'm happy to do whatever you want me to. I just want us to be clear on the end goal." I wasn't convinced that we were on the same page, and I could picture this ending badly. Although how much worse could it be than my first sale of the spring season, where someone had died?

"Excellent," she said.

"We'll need to track down a tent right away. It's outdoor wedding season, and one might be hard to come by. And get hold of an electrician for the lighting." I was really glad I'd had the foresight to charge Kelly by the hour.

She waved a hand in the air. "Don't you worry about that. I have a source or two."

"Okay." I added another "great" to try to reach her level of enthusiasm. "I'm worried you won't be able to recoup your costs if we do all that."

Kelly patted my cheek. "That's my problem. Or

Lance's." She trilled out a laugh. "What about refreshments?"

I knew my standards, Dunkin's coffee and donut holes, wouldn't work for Kelly. "I have some old washtubs I can fill with ice. We can stick in bottles of sparkling water and Italian soda."

"Perfect," Kelly said. "What about food?"

"With the heat, we don't want anything that will give people sticky fingers and hurt the merchandise." I tapped a finger against my cheek. "How about a pretzel bar? We'll set out an array of pretzels, with cute little paper bags. People can fill a bag and shake on toppings. Maybe even some bacon bits, jalapeños."

"That could get messy, too."

"We'll have it set up for as they leave. I'll work that part out."

Kelly clapped her hands. "I love it."

"Do you want to charge people for the refreshments?"

"No. Of course not."

"Okay," I said. "Anything else?" I hoped not although that wasn't very gracious of me.

"Not that I can think of right now."

"I'll just get to work, then."

"And I'll leave you to it." Kelly turned on her heel and strutted back into the house.

The first thing I did was write a list of the things we had just talked about. I'd have to run to the grocery store sometime this week to buy everything.

Amounts were always tricky, because you never knew how many people would show up. But better to buy too much. Kelly and Lance had a passel of teenagers at their house every time I'd been here, so I was sure the pretzels wouldn't go to waste.

After I finished jotting down notes I decided to price a selection of vintage kitchenware first. My grandmother had had a lot of these things when I was a little girl. Utensils with wooden handles painted in bright reds or pale greens. I'd always loved the old hand mixer that Grandma had let me beat eggs with. I quickly priced them and turned to a nut grinder with a glass bottom and a metal top with flowers painted on it. It worked by dropping a couple of nuts in and then turning the handle. I moved on to pricing metal canisters with the contents labeled in bright letters, a bunch of old picnic baskets, and sets of mixing bowls, from Fiestaware to Pyrex.

I'd never asked Kelly where she'd gotten all of this. But it was all highly collectible right now. The regular pricing stickers I usually used weren't what Kelly had wanted, so I'd ordered some online that looked like old-fashioned tags with preprinted prices in Courier type. I'd spent my evenings last week tying strings on the tags as I watched the Red Sox play. At least it had passed the time and kept me from thinking about CJ.

The rest of the day passed swiftly, and the heat kept my muscles from aching. By the time I was ready to leave at eight, I'd accomplished a lot.

Chapter 7

The world's longest text from Laura prevented me from going straight home and falling into bed. Brody had been released from the hospital. He had a concussion that required rest which they felt he could do in the car. So they had hopped in the car and taken off for Washington, hoping to get across country before the moving van with their stuff did. In the military, it was called a door-to-door move and was the most desirable outcome of any move. Otherwise, your household goods were put in storage, and it could be several weeks before they were moved from storage to your new home.

Brody had realized once they were several hours away that his coach had all his baseball equipment, including his favorite mitt. The coach was getting ready to move, too, so Laura wanted me to run by his house as soon as possible to get Brody's things. I sent a text saying I could go now, and Laura sent back his address. He lived in Concord.

I swung through Dunkin's and got the largest

iced coffee they had, hoping it would provide me with enough energy to drive over to Concord and back. According to my GPS, the coach's house was a scant six miles away. On a normal day, it would be nothing, but the shock of the attack, the hard physical labor this afternoon, and my lack of sleep were all taking a toll.

I sucked in a deep drink before turning right on Great Road and then left on Concord Road. It had cooled off enough to roll down the windows and enjoy a light breeze. I drove by Sleepy Hollow Cemetery, famous for its Authors Ridge. Then I passed the Colonial Inn, a haunted historic inn and restaurant. Couples sat at tables on the porch; bits of conversation and laughter wafted to me. It all looked so lovely that I blinked back unexpected tears. Good heavens, I was weepy today. But I decided to cut myself some slack. A lot had happened in the past twenty-four hours.

I took the rotary, turned right on Main Street, and followed it for about a half mile. After another left and right, I pulled into the coach's driveway. A SOLD sign sat atop a larger Realtor's sign that proclaimed her number one status in Concord. The house was a Victorian, complete with white gingerbread trim. I rang the bell, and a harried-looking woman, hair in a messy ponytail, yanked open the door. Packing boxes lined the hall behind her. A child cried from somewhere. I explained who I was, and she pointed to a large plastic garbage bag.

"Thanks for picking this up. We don't need one more thing to do right now," she said.

"I've moved a million times. I know what it's like."

"Military?" she asked.

"Once upon a time." I never knew quite how to explain my connection with the military. I hadn't served, in the eyes of some. But in a way I had, because I had followed CJ around, participated in lots of base activities, and hosted his troops at our home frequently. Military life was about relationships and helping others. It could be difficult, but for me the good had outweighed the difficult times.

"I hope this is our last move." She sighed. "We're off to the Pentagon. He's hoping for a star. I promised him twenty years of doing this. We're up to twenty-six." She shook her head. "I guess I'd miss it. Do you?"

"Sometimes. But I love it here."

"I did, but it's been a rough year. My husband is a baseball nut and loves coaching. There've just been too many injuries, long nights, travel with the team, on top of the long hours on Fitch. Plus, our son and daughter are on the team."

"Your daughter plays?"

"Did play. Catcher. The last concussion knocked her out for the season."

I watched enough baseball to know what a wild pitch could do to a player. "That's too bad," I said. "I hope you enjoy your Pentagon assignment."

"At least the winters won't be as long or as cold. I won't miss that. But I'll miss this house." She patted the door frame. "I needed a break from living on base."

Not everyone lived on base, and there wasn't enough housing for everyone on most bases even if they did want to. I had always loved living on base but had been forced to leave when CJ got in trouble. "It can be like living in a petri dish."

"Yep. Everyone always knows your business."

"Mom," a boy yelled. "I'm hungry."

"I'd better go. We're doing one of those 'clear out the frig and pantry' meals. I think it's pancakes and Shake 'n Bake."

"I'll just take that and get going," I said. I grabbed the lumpy bag and hefted it up. "Good luck with your move."

As I pulled into the drive, another text sent me over to DiNapoli's. The coffee had worked well enough that I still had a bit of energy. The attack had made me want to be around people instead of home alone. I cut across the lawn of the town common. The shadows were long. The clock on the Congregational church glowed in the last light of the day, and I counted as the bells chimed. Nine o'clock.

The sign on DiNapoli's was flipped to CLOSED, but I went in, anyway. Rosalie was scrubbing down the counter and Angelo, the grill.

"Can I help?" I asked.

But they both yelled no and pointed me toward a table that was set for three. The tables were plain and mismatched, as were the chairs. I noticed a quarter under the leg of the one they'd pointed me to. I'd keep an eye out for a replacement for them.

There was an uncorked bottle of Chianti and three glasses on the table, so I poured. A couple of minutes later they came over. Angelo carried a pan of lasagna, which he set in the center of the table. It smelled delicious, and I loved a good lasagna. Rosalie brought a salad and a basket of steaming garlic bread. After Rosalie dished everything out, I bit into the garlic bread. Just the right amount of crunch before I hit the buttery, garlicky goodness. I devoured the rest of the piece. Rosalie pushed the bread basket over to me with a concerned smile.

"I wanted my lasagna fresh in your memory before you set out to taste the others," Angelo said.

I realized that was a guise to find out something else, because concern troubled Rosalie's eyes. I took a bite of the lasagna. The noodles were cooked perfectly. The Italian sausage had just the right amount of spice. The sauce seemed to have a stronger basil flavor than I remembered from past lasagnas here although it wasn't always on the menu so it had been awhile. Should I mention it?

They both watched me intently.

"Be honest," Angelo said.

"There seems to be a bit more basil than usual," I said, hoping Angelo wouldn't be offended. He took pride in his cooking and the food he served.

"Ha!" Angelo said. He turned to Rosalie. "I told you she's perfect for this. Of course there's too much basil. I wanted to check your palate before you set off to taste my competitors' food."

"Sorry, Sarah. You really don't have to go through with this," Rosalie said. "Especially after last night and this morning."

I smiled. "Of course I will help. I'd do anything for you two."

Angelo busied himself with clearing the plates. "Let me go get the real lasagna." He came back with a deep pan of lasagna and served each of us a piece. Cheese dripped in long gooey strings. My stomach rumbled in anticipation.

"Are you okay?" Angelo asked me.

"Angelo, we agreed to let her eat first," Rosalie scolded.

I almost laughed. Angelo's name in Italian meant Messenger of God. It was a role Angelo fulfilled very well. If he saw an injustice, he wanted to make it right, kind of like an Italian superhero. But it often got him in trouble, and not just with Rosalie.

"I'm okay." I wanted to leave it at that. They knew me well enough by now that they wouldn't buy it if I tried to gloss over everything.

Rosalie reached over and patted my hand. "How fine can you be after being attacked last night and finding Melba today?"

"Attacked, questioned by the police, and don't get me started on CJ." Angelo was waving his hands around as he talked. At least he didn't have a ladle full of marinara sauce this time.

When CJ and I divorced over a year ago, Angelo and Rosalie had staunchly sided with me. As they had when we reunited, and again now. It made me smile to think of it. I took a bite of my lasagna, trying to give everyone a moment to relax.

"What's in this, Angelo? It tastes amazing."

"It's the recipe my mama taught me when I was a boy. It never changes."

"Angelo, don't lie. God will get you." Rosalie crossed herself. "He tried a new combination of spices."

"It's brilliant," I said.

"Of course it is." Angelo pointed his fork at me. "But don't try to change the subject."

It was almost impossible to pull a fast one on Angelo.

"With the swap meet and planning a garage sale, I really haven't had time to think about what happened." I put down my fork.

"See, Angelo. She's quit eating. I warned you."

"I'm just getting a sip of wine. I'm not done." I didn't want to be the cause of a fight. I took a sip of wine, then ate some more lasagna.

While we finished the meal, we talked about vacation plans (I had none), the weather (it was chilly one day, boiling the next), and the last books we'd read. I thought perhaps I was off the hook, until Angelo set a platter full of Rosalie's homemade Italian pastries down in front of us.

"Talk," he said.

I thought about stuffing a cannoli in my mouth, but that was delaying the inevitable. The DiNapolis listened closely while I filled them in on the attack and my trip to the hospital. I gave them facts, but not the emotions that went with them—uncertainty, terror, anger, and a lingering unease.

Rosalie sighed when I finished. "You haven't answered Angelo's original question. How are you?" She accentuated the word *you.*

I took a moment. "Anxious. Sore. I keep wondering if it was random, like Pellner thinks. It's what I want to believe. But if Pellner noticed my car, why didn't my attacker?"

"Maybe they had a timeline. Someplace they had to be," Angelo said.

The equipment had little value, but all the silent auction items could be resold. I made a mental note to do a search online when I got home. The police might have already done it, but I was better at decoding virtual garage sale language because I ran a virtual garage sale.

"Like a late-night appointment with Superintendent Harper? Have you heard anything about a time of death?" I asked. I assumed it had to have occurred after the police finished up at the school after I was attacked and before I had gone back in the morning. The rest of the time, too many people were around.

"One of the stylists from Giovani's salon came in for a dinner take-out order. Her sister-in-law is a dispatcher at the station. She said they're putting the time of death between one and five in the morning," Rosalie said.

It's what I had thought. But it meant I might have been sleeping out in the parking lot when the murder occurred. Had the murderer walked right by me? Seen me sleeping in my car? "How'd they come up with that?"

"The police left the gym around one. Then you and your friends were in the gym by five thirty," Rosalie said.

It confirmed my thoughts. I knew from my time with CJ that the police depended as much on the last contact between the victim and someone as they did the condition of the body. I tried to stifle a yawn. It was almost ten. Time for me to go and let the DiNapolis get home, too. I stood.

"Thank you for the dinner and company."

"You aren't leaving without some leftovers," Angelo said.

I couldn't say no, because it would offend them. I'd stick it in the fridge and dole it out tomorrow.

It was dark out when I finally waved good-bye. The warm and humid air pressed in on me. I stuck to the sidewalk, instead of cutting through the deep shadows of the town common. The Congregational church stood out, white against the night sky. Crickets chirped, bushes rustled, and I was jumpier than the frogs of Calaveras County. The walk was less than two blocks, but it felt like a hike up Kilimanjaro. I waited for the light to change as a few cars whizzed by on Great Road. Music blared; teens laughed. It accentuated my loneliness.

I trudged along, carrying the bag of food. My body had stiffened while I was sitting with the DiNapolis. The aches from the attack last night all made themselves known. And then I heard the footsteps behind me.

Chapter 8

I hurried up, and so did they. I broke into a run, and so did they. I ran up the sidewalk to the porch. The light was off. I yanked open the screen and ducked inside. I slammed the heavy wooden door. Fumbled for the lock. It squeaked and groaned with lack of use as it clicked into place. Through the door I heard the footsteps pounding closer. I held my breath, but they went on by. My heart pounded as I unlocked the door and peeked outside. It was just someone out for an evening run. I left the door unlocked and headed upstairs.

Back in my apartment, I stuffed the lasagna in the refrigerator. I took the box of pastries, headed back into the living room, and slumped onto the couch, still a bit shaken. I loved this little apartment, though. The ceiling slanted down on one side to meet a four-foot-high wall; a worn Oriental rug covered the wide-planked wood floors, which I'd painted white; and my grandmother's rocker sat next to the window that overlooked the town common.

I clicked on the TV and selected a cannoli. The Red Sox were winning. I was almost comatose as I finished the cannoli. Sleeping on the couch seemed like a better option than trying to move. A knock on the door jolted me upright.

I stumbled to the door and lifted the little piece of metal that allowed me to look through my newly installed peephole. Every time I used it, I thought of CJ, because he'd installed it his last day here. I hadn't even been home. Stella had seen him climbing the steps to my apartment, with a toolbox in hand, and had gone to see what he was up to. He'd been installing this, and I was still confused about it. Was he saying he loved me? If that was it, why'd he leave? Was it a way to keep me safe? Or was he trying to control me?

I peered out, and it chased all thoughts of CJ away. Ryne stood out there, tapping his fingers against his leg. What the heck did he want? I thought about backing away, but between the creaky floor and the TV, he had to know I was home.

I pulled the door open and stepped forward to keep him out in the hall. It was then I noticed the top of my dress was coated with a light dusting of powdered sugar from the cannoli. I thought about trying to brush it off, but the less attention paid, the better.

"What?" I asked, in no mood for social niceties or company.

"Someone came into my uncle's antique store today, around four, and tried to get an employee to buy what he called an old, valuable hockey stick."

I perked up.

"I think it might have been stolen from your silent auction." Even though Ryne was new to the area, he had already plugged into the local gossip and somehow knew about the theft or maybe he heard about it at the gym this morning.

I waved him in, he followed me to the couch, and we sat on opposite ends. The couch, a garage sale find, was stuffed with down and slipcovered in white. My mom had made the slipcovers for me. Ryne stared at the box filled with cannolis and Italian cookies.

"Help yourself," I said.

"So you're the one leaving all the food on my doorstep."

I hadn't wanted the food to go to waste, but I also hadn't been in the mood lately to knock on his door, which would have required a friendly little chat. I shrugged. "The DiNapolis are trying to fatten me up."

"You could use it."

I closed my eyes for a long moment. There had been a point in my life when I wished someone would say things like that to me, but now wasn't the time. "So why do you think the hockey stick was from the silent auction?"

"It was signed by a Bruins player."

"A signed one was stolen from the auction." I

clasped my hands together as excitement surged through me.

"The person who was trying to sell it didn't have any explanation for how he came to own it. When our employee questioned him, he didn't answer at first and then said a friend gave it to him."

"That's entirely possible."

"The kid left when my employee asked for ID."

"It does sound suspicious. I have pictures of the ones that were supposed to be in the auction. Do you think your employee would recognize it?"

Ryne nodded. I grabbed my phone, asked for Ryne's number, and sent him the photo.

"Did you get a look at the guy?" I asked.

"I was out of the store at the time. My employee just said he was an average-looking teen, sandy hair, nothing that made him stand out."

"It doesn't seem very smart to try to sell stolen goods in the next town over from where they were stolen."

"No one ever said thieves had to be smart."

Ryne had a point, although the burglary in some ways seemed thoughtfully planned out. If it wasn't for me being there, it would have gone unnoticed for many hours.

I stood. "I'm exhausted." I needed to process all that had been going on. "Did you tell the police?" I asked as I walked to the door and opened it.

Ryne followed me. "If I called the police every time someone came in with something I'd be on the phone all day. I wanted to chat with you first."

"Thank you," I said. "But maybe you should call them."

"Will do." He frowned down at me. "Take care of yourself."

"Thanks for de-escalating the bidding war today at the swap."

"Aye, and that was a dicey bit, wasn't it? Feared for me beautiful jawline for a moment." With that, he grinned and left.

I shook my head as I closed the door.

My plan to head straight to bed was diverted when I glanced down at my computer lying so innocently on the trunk I used as a coffee table. If the stolen goods were already out there, maybe someone was trying to sell them online. I settled back on the couch, opened my computer, and started searching. I didn't find anything on my virtual garage sale site, which was no surprise, but Ryne's comment about thieves not being smart rang through my head. I checked virtual garage sale sites in Concord, Lincoln, Bedford, and Lexington, the towns closest to us. I even checked the one for Fitch Air Force Base, which lay smack-dab in the middle of all those towns. Nothing.

I slowly broadened my search, yawning as I did so. I thought about making a pot of coffee but decided to press on. Three minutes later I struck gold with a page in Lowell, a town about thirty minutes north. A guy whose screen name was Sportzfan had lots of pictures of signed sports items. His profile picture was of a Red Sox cap, so I couldn't even tell if he had the sandy-colored hair that Ryne had described. He was selling everything from photos to baseball cards to items that looked awfully similar to the ones from the silent auction. My conundrum was that a lot of what had been taken, and what was listed on this site, wasn't that hard to find.

I picked three items that most closely matched my silent auction items. I wrote "Interested" under each item and followed it with a "Sending pm," a private message. I was using an account that wasn't connected to my business or personal page. My profile picture for this account was a dollar sign, and the user name was BargainHunter. In the message I told him which three items I wanted, and asked if we could meet in the morning, around seven-thirty, at a Dunkin's on Fifth Street in Lowell. It was virtual garage sale courtesy to go to the town of the seller if they didn't say they were willing to drive somewhere to meet. Meeting at seven-thirty should give me time to get to Lowell and then back to Kelly's to do some more work. She'd asked me to come by at nine.

I didn't like to go to a stranger's house, although I had plenty of friends who did this without ever encountering a problem. One friend had actually been invited into a house for a tour when she told the seller how lovely her home was. About halfway through the tour, on the third floor of the house, she realized how quiet it was and that no one knew where she was. Another friend went to pick something up. The woman had an illegal day care running in her basement and asked my friend to watch the kids while she got the item for sale. That was why I stuck to public places, if possible.

Ten minutes later Sportzfan wrote back, saying that he could meet me and that the Dunkin's I had suggested would work just fine.

I almost had the road to myself as I drove up Route 3 to Lowell. Lowell was an old mill town, like so many towns in Massachusetts. The Merrimack River flowed through it and had once powered the mills. It was home to the University of Massachusetts Lowell. And it was the place I'd first laid eyes on Seth Anderson, at a bar. I still blushed at the thought. At the time I hadn't known he was the newly appointed district attorney for Middlesex County. Normally, DAs were elected, but Seth ended up finishing his sick predecessor's term. Nor had I known that he was Massachusetts's Most Eligible Bachelor, now for three years running. And I'd never dreamed I'd hurt him, because one look at him and a girl would think, *He's a player.* But I'd manage to hurt him, anyway.

The GPS on my phone kept giving me directions that I knew were incorrect from previous trips up here, whether it had been to go to a garage sale or to see Seth when he used to live up here. I ignored it and went off memory. It hurt my bruised hand to grip the steering wheel too tightly. My head still ached, as did most of the rest of my body.

Fifteen minutes later I pulled into the empty

parking lot of the Dunkin' Donuts. Oh, no. There was a big OUT OF BUSINESS sign on the door. No wonder the GPS was telling me to go somewhere else. The building it adjoined was being torn down. No construction workers were around since it was Sunday, which made me a bit uncomfortable. But it was a bright, sunny day, and I'd seen a few cars go by on the street. It seemed safe enough to stay.

I backed my car into a space facing the street so I could speed off at a moment's notice if I felt uneasy. It didn't take long to realize it was a stupid move. A big black SUV pulled in front of my car, trapping me in the space. Since an incident a few weeks ago, I didn't like feeling trapped. I grabbed my phone and purse and then hopped out of the car. At least this way I could run, if my aching body would cooperate.

I started to walk around to the driver's side of the black SUV but stopped when the back passenger door opened. I blinked twice, startled by who'd popped out.

Chapter 9

"What the hell are you doing here?" Mike "the Big Cheese" Titone asked me. He sounded steamed, beyond steamed, more like furious. He had a wiry runner's body. There was no way I'd be able to outrun him, even on a day when my body didn't hurt.

But I was just as miffed. "Get out of here. I'm trying to buy something, and I don't want you scaring the guy off." Mike lived in the North End of Boston, the Italian section, where he owned a cheese shop, thus the nickname. Vincenzo had gotten him off a racketeering charge, and it was rumored that Mike was in the Mob. He had some connection to Seth that I didn't understand. In the past I wasn't even sure I wanted to know what was going on between them, but maybe it was time to find out. I put it on the to-do list running in my head.

"You're BargainHunter?" he asked.

My jaw dropped a bit. "Don't tell me you're Sportzfan."

Mike studied me for a minute, and I realized that there was a controlled fury in his icy blue eyes, which I'd never seen before. His hands were clenched in tight fists. Little fans of hot panic spread through me like the start of a wildfire. I took a step back but bumped into someone. Then I realized I was surrounded by four of his men, all big, brawny guys, who apparently moved like ninjas. Mike had helped me out of a jam once. I'd seen various versions of him, but until today none had made me this afraid.

"No. I'm not," he finally said.

"Then how did you know I was BargainHunter?"

"Because I saw BargainHunter was interested in some of the items I was. I thought I'd outbid you. Not that I knew you were behind BargainHunter then."

"So you were supposed to meet Sportzfan here, too?" I asked. I'd heard of people doing this. Telling two different customers they could have the item, and then, when they all showed up, the seller sold to the highest bidder. I didn't allow it on my virtual garage sale site. It was unethical, lousy, and another reason I always tried to meet in a public place.

"Yes. But Sportzfan is a double-crosser, among other things."

"What other things?" I didn't tell him I was looking for stolen goods. Which had been a stupid, stupid idea, born out of fear and exhaustion.

Mike stepped in close. I held my ground, but

more because I had nowhere to run than any kind of bravado. My knees were visibly shaking.

"Stay outta this."

"Out of what?"

"Sportzfan." Mike opened the door to my Suburban and more or less shoved me into the driver's seat.

"Ow," I said. He'd jarred my injuries.

"Sorry," Mike said.

For a second the Mike I'd come to know showed back up. The one who'd helped me.

"Go home." He turned away as I clenched the wheel like it was a lifesaver ring.

A car rumbled down the street. It slowed, but when Mike turned to look, it sped off. Mike jerked his head toward his SUV, and his men clambered back in. He followed and slammed his door without looking back. The SUV glided off.

My hand shook as I fumbled for my key and stuck it in the ignition. I fired up the Suburban and pulled forward far enough that I'd have an escape route no matter what. CJ had taught me to always have an escape route around me in the car. Not to pull up too close behind someone at a light or a stop sign. I should have followed it today. After a couple of deep breaths, I pulled out of the parking lot and drove to the Dunkin's my GPS was still spouting directions to, just to make it happy. I went in, ordered a large latte and a donut—make that two donuts, a coconut and a chocolate glazed.

I sat at a table and gobbled them down, grateful to be around people having a normal Sunday morning. Some looked like they were ready for church, others like they'd just finished a night of partying, and one family had a passel of kids and a crying baby. I wanted to hug them all. When my breathing was no longer coming out in short pants, I finished my coffee and drove back to Ellington.

Kelly sent me a text saying they'd decided to go to church and out to lunch. She asked me to come by at one instead. I was fine with that. My apartment needed cleaning, laundry needed to be caught up on, and I needed rest. But the first thing I did when I got home was grab my laptop. I wrote a scathing note to Sportzfan about not showing up and trying to sell to two people. Then I deleted the whole thing, because I needed to find him. Instead, I wrote a note apologizing for an apparent mix-up, said it was my bad, and asked if we could try again. After that I tried to decide which of the people on the thread was Mike. But we weren't the only two who'd responded "Interested" and "Sending PM." There was a whole string of us.

I started nodding off so I set my computer aside. I woke around noon, still on the couch, after a restless dream-filled sleep that reflected all my anxieties. I showered, trying to ignore the bruises splattered like abstract tattoos on my body. The laundry and cleaning would have to wait because I'd slept longer than I'd planned.

* * *

The afternoon at Kelly's house sped by. As I worked, the air became thicker and more oppressive. I stepped out of the garage a few times to watch clouds swirling and re-forming off to the west. I found a stack of pristine magazines from the fifties in a box. *Ladies' Home Journals*, *Better Homes and Gardens*, *McCall's*, complete with Betsy McCall paper dolls in them. I took a break and flipped through a few. Ads for cigarettes showed women in gowns, gloves, and pearls, looking elegant. Articles gave advice on how to be the perfect housewife and keep your man happy. I was exhausted just reading it. But I did love their Christmas issues, with illustrated stories and recipes for odd gelatin concoctions. These would go fast.

At four o'clock I knocked on the door to the house to let the Longs know I was leaving. Lance answered and stepped out into the garage.

"How's it going?" he asked.

"Good. This should be one spectacular sale."

"I was actually asking about you. Are you okay?"

Wow. Lance had been the board member to hold me at a distance since Melba first suggested I run the swap meet. "Yes. I'm fine." It was the answer people expected to hear.

He frowned. It made him look more like a boy than a businessman. As did his wardrobe of a pink polo shirt and plaid shorts. He could almost pass for one of his teenage boys today. Although, as always, he looked like a walking advertisement for Ralph Lauren. "Have you hired a lawyer?"

I leaned away from him. Did he think I killed Melba? "No."

"So you aren't planning to sue the school board?"

For a moment, I just stared at him, trying to determine what the heck he was talking about.

"You were attacked on school property during a board-sanctioned event. Although, I still wonder why you were there so late. These are litigious times. Are you going to sue us?"

"No. Of course not." I shook my head for emphasis. "I can't even imagine where you got an idea like that." Had I said something to someone? I didn't think so.

"I heard that Angelo was talking to you about hiring Vincenzo yesterday at DiNapoli's."

Small towns. This was the downside. "He was worried about me talking to the police without a lawyer present. No mention was made of suing anyone."

"You'd be willing to sign forms stating that you don't hold the board or the district responsible?"

"I'll sign whatever you want." Beyond having never thought of suing, I could imagine the effect on my business if I did sue. It would be all over town, and I'd be a persona non grata in minutes. Lance must be the member of the board who worried about all the legal aspects. Maybe he was a lawyer. I really didn't know.

"If you can wait here a minute, I'll go print the form out."

"Sure," I said.

He returned a couple of minutes later with a

simple one-page form that wasn't shrouded in legalese. I read it over and took the pen he held out.

"I'll have to get my lawyer to look over this before I sign."

Lance opened his mouth, but no words came out.

"I'm kidding," I said as I signed. Lance didn't look amused.

He took the form from me with a tight smile. "Thank you." He paused. "You're sure you're not heading to a lawyer next."

"I don't have time. I have to go to Concord to an antique store where a teenager tried to sell sports jerseys that sound similar to the ones stolen yesterday. I have to eat, do laundry, see Seth Anderson, and then I'm going to search for the stolen items on line. All of that will keep me way too busy to hire a lawyer to sue the school district."

"Okay, I'm sorry I brought it up. I hear you loud and clear. You aren't going to sue anyone," Lance said.

"Right." I walked to my Suburban, feeling a little like I'd been slimed. Fat raindrops started to fall as I climbed into my car.

I headed to Concord to Ryne's uncle's antique store, Seventh Time Around. It was four thirtyish, so maybe whoever had come to sell the athletic things yesterday would be back. Bolt after bolt of lightning flashed across the sky making me jump as I drove through the heavy rain. I turned onto Main Street in Concord, followed it, and took a left.

Ryne's uncle's antique store sat at the very end of the business district. Rent could not be cheap here. I'd been in a few times before Ryne had come to town. I'd always gotten the impression that the merchandise was dusty and overpriced. I pulled into a parking place two doors down, jumped out, and dashed through the rain into the store.

The lighting was dim—a few bare bulbs hung from strings. I turned a full circle, taking in the store. It was hard to tell if there was less dust or not.

"Of all the gin joints in all the towns—"

I about jumped out of my shorts at Ryne's voice and peered around for him.

"In all the world—"

"Yeah, I walked in here." I smiled. His goofy quoting of a line from *Casablanca* was a relief after the incessant lightning, Melba's death, the attack, and my weird interaction with Mike this morning.

He sat in a dimly lit corner, with a book across his lap. I headed back to him. Ryne was in a wingback chair, one long leg crossed over the other. A floor lamp with a frosted-glass lamp shade that looked to be from the thirties provided just enough light to read back here. *The Scarlet Letter*, by Nathaniel Hawthorne, lay open on his thigh, spine up.

"I'm reading through the local authors," Ryne said.

It made me realize I had no idea where he'd lived before he showed up six weeks ago. The Irish accent sounded real enough, but it was used only sporadically.

"There are plenty of good ones around here."

Ryne stood, and it forced me to look up at him. He had on a checkered button-down shirt, rolled up to the elbows, showing strong arms feathered with dark hair over pale Irish skin. A pair of tan slacks completed his look.

“What can I help you with? An eighteen hundreds sideboard? Or a painting of a relative so dour, the family couldn’t stomach having him on the wall?” He gestured to the dark oak sideboard, ornately carved and heavy looking. Above it hung a portrait of a balding man with eyes so cold, I almost shivered.

I walked back and forth in front of it. “Oh, yuck. His eyes are following me. No wonder the family got rid of him. Who could live with him glaring down at you all the time?” I ran a finger across the sideboard. No dust.

“I’ve been trying to teach the employees the importance of keeping the store clean. My uncle has cataracts thick as an Irish fog. Can’t see the dust. Won’t get the surgery. There’s no need, in his opinion.”

I withdrew my finger. “Sorry. Bad habit.”

“Am I right in assuming that you didn’t stop by to check out my reading habits and how much dust topped the furniture? Or that you didn’t come by because you craved some good company during a storm?” He looked toward the front of the store, where the rain pelted the windows and lightning continued to flash.

Ah, there was the Ryne who was so flip that he should have been a gymnast. But I would rise above this once. "I was hoping to talk to the employee you mentioned last night."

"Ah, well, in that case, you're in for a bit of a disappointment. He called in sick."

"Darn. Do you know when he'll be back?"

"Soon. I assume he has the Irish flu."

"There's a flu going around in the middle of the summer?" I took a step back from Ryne. The last thing I needed was to get sick. I almost had more work than I could manage over the next few weeks.

"Aye, and you catch it by going to Gillganins and drinking too much Irish whiskey. He should be fine and back in the store tomorrow."

"Well, then, I'll stop back tomorrow." I turned toward the door.

"Would you like a beer? You'll get soaked if you leave now." Thunder boomed. The lights dimmed for a moment.

I tried not to jump. I came from Pacific Grove, California, the next city over from Monterey. Thunderstorms there were rare. Give me an earthquake any day. Driving through this storm or sitting alone in my apartment, waiting for a tree to fall on it, held less appeal than hanging out with Ryne. "Okay. Thanks."

Ryne disappeared to the back of the store, and I wandered around. How odd that someone would bring sports equipment here, antique or not. It just didn't fit with the store. There was a jumble of furniture, lots of paintings, ornate glass windows, a stack of Trixie Belden books, and then I spotted a corner filled with sports things. I didn't remember ever seeing this section when I'd been in here before. Ryne's uncle had everything from trading cards to signed bats to framed posters. Did that mean whoever had stolen the stuff had some connection with this store?

Ryne came through a swinging door with a tray full of beer, glasses, and, oh, yum, a plate of nachos. That explained his lengthy absence after he said he was going to grab our beers.

Ryne set the tray down on a table near where he'd been reading. I walked over and sat on a small velvet-covered settee. Ryne pulled a bottle opener out of his pocket, popped the tops off two Sam Adams Summer Ales, and poured the perfect glass, with only a skim of foam at the top.

Ryne raised his glass. "Here's looking at you, kid. Eat up."

I dug into the nachos. Gooey cheese, just the right amount of jalapeños—so there was a little heat but no mouth afire—tomatoes, and black beans. The toppings to chips ratio was perfect.

"I didn't think you ever ate," Ryne said after I'd scarfed down several chips.

"Why would you think that?"

"Like I said last night, you keep leaving food outside my door." He tilted his head. "Heartbreak does that to a person."

I looked at Ryne good and hard. Maybe he'd left wherever not just to help his uncle but also to get over someone. The whole topic made my stomach roil, as I thought of CJ. I set down my plate.

"I'm eating just fine."

"I saw how you looked the day we first met, and I see how you look now, six weeks later. It brings out my nurturing side, and fortunately for you, I make amazing nachos."

I laughed. "You do. I should get going." It sounded like the worst of the storm was over.

"You don't need to bolt," Ryne said.

I stood. "Not bolting. Things to do. Thanks for the beer and the nachos." I hurried to the front door. "The nachos were amazing," I called back.

He held up *The Scarlet Letter*. "She had not known the weight until she felt the freedom! Chapter eighteen. 'A Flood of Sunshine.'"

I stared at him for a moment and then fled.

Chapter 10

I didn't make if far, because I bumped right into a teenage boy with an armful of stuff. After I made my apologies, I watched him walk into Ryne's uncle's shop. Were those football jerseys in his arms? Could this be the kid who'd tried to sell stuff yesterday? I did an about-face and hurried after him. Once in the store, I saw that Ryne was already talking to him. He didn't seem surprised to see me walk back in.

"Where'd you get all of this?" Ryne asked.

I made my way slowly toward them, looking at this, picking up that and setting it back down. I hoped I looked like a customer because I didn't want to spook the kid. I whipped out my phone and started snapping pictures of random things while the kid talked. What I really wanted was a photo of him.

"My uncle," he said in answer to Ryne's question.

It took him a while to come up with that, but he said it with so much confidence that I almost believed him. I turned and snapped a photo of him.

"What are ya doin'?" he asked.

"Just taking a photo of that Dresden girl," I said, pointing to a figurine near his left elbow. "Do you have any Red Sox jerseys? My husband is a big fan." My voice caught on the word *husband.* Ryne looked at me, and a line formed between his eyebrows. I shoved aside the pain thinking of CJ brought me. I knew we had a Red Sox jersey at the sale, one that went missing.

"Naw. I've got a Celtics jersey signed by Kevin Garnett."

Ryne started yammering on about provenance and proof of authentication, and the kid's eyes glazed over.

"My uncle sent me over. If that ain't good enough, I'll move on." He started gathering up the jerseys.

"How much for the Garnett jersey?" I asked him.

"Four hundred."

"That seems steep to me," I said.

He shrugged.

"I'll give you a hundred," I said.

"Sarah, you shouldn't," Ryne said.

"I have cash." I pulled a wad of ones out of my purse.

"Deal," the kid said.

He responded so quickly, too quickly. I forked over the hundred. "And I'd like to look through the rest of your stuff."

He stuffed the money in his pocket and handed over his jerseys. I went through them quickly. None of them seemed to be from my sale. "If you get any Red Sox stuff, especially anything signed, let me know." I wrote out my phone number on a piece of paper and handed it to him.

"I'll keep an eye out," he said.

"Ever try to sell anything online?" I asked him. I wondered if he'd had any dealings with Mike or if he knew of any other sites that might not be on my radar. Sites for moving stolen goods.

"Sometimes."

"Any site in particular? I really want the Sox jersey."

"Just do a search, lady."

"Have you had any dealings with Sportzfan? I've had good luck with him." I added the second bit because I thought I saw the slightest reaction to the name.

He shrugged. "I deal with lots of people." He turned and walked out.

I hustled out of the store to get away from Ryne's frown.

After I finished cleaning, doing the laundry, and having a dinner of DiNapoli's leftovers, I plopped down on my couch with my laptop. Still no word from Sportzfan, but he had posted more items for sale. Nothing matching the items missing from the auction, though. Because I wanted to contact him, I wrote "Interested" under a couple of items and sent him more private messages. I waited, hoping for a quick response, but nothing happened. I searched some other sites and checked back. I had a private message. I eagerly opened it.

All it said was, **I told you to stay out of this. M.**

Mike Titone. I shook a fist at the computer, then leaped off the couch to pace my small apartment. I stopped in front of the window and looked out over the dark town common. The church stood watch over the common, a candle in each window of the four stories. Through the wavy glass, they looked a little creepy. Creepy like Mike had become. How the heck was I going to get him to leave me alone? Just a few short weeks ago, I'd sought his help in desperation. Man, had things changed.

Hot puffs of humid air came in through the screen. But I was already steamed without nature's help. I looked at the time on my phone: nine. I snatched up my car keys, hustled down the stairs, and banged out the screen door. By the time I was in my car and had it running, I knew what my next move would be. The visit to Seth I'd been putting off all day. He and Mike had something going on that I'd never understood. Maybe it was time to. If nothing else, maybe Seth would tell Mike to leave me alone.

As I walked up the drive to Seth's Cape Cod–style house in Bedford, I heard loud techno music pounding. It seemed so un-Seth-like. His screen door was closed, but his front door stood open. I looked down his hall but couldn't see anyone, so I rang the bell and pounded on the door. He didn't respond.

"Seth," I yelled. There was no way he could hear me over the music. A screech sounded above the music. What the heck was that? Wisps of smoke drifted along the ceiling toward me. The smoke detector. I dug in my purse for my phone as I upped the pounding on the door. I dialed 911, pulled on the screen door, and yanked it open.

"Seth," I shouted, even though it was futile over the noise of the music and smoke detector. I told the dispatcher there was a fire and gave him the address as I ran down the hall toward the kitchen. Maybe this was just a cooking disaster. Or maybe he was grilling outside and the smoke had come in the back screen door. But it didn't smell like meat cooking; it smelled like chemicals.

The smoke thickened, and I dropped to my knees, still yelling. The dispatcher shouted at me to get out. My eyes watered as I stuffed my cell phone in my pocket. I saw flames in a pan in the kitchen. A dishtowel ignited. I spun around to head out. Seth lay on the floor in the dining room. I shouted his name again, but he didn't move. I grabbed his right arm as flames licked up the wall behind the stove.

I coughed and tugged. He slid a few inches toward me on the wood floor. A streak of blood trailed behind him. I wiped my eyes and spotted a wound on his left shoulder. Blood was flowing out of it. Waiting for help wasn't possible. I had to get him out.

Chapter 11

I stood and pulled harder. Choking. Gasping. A sharp pain stabbed through my injured hand. I tried to ignore it. Seth moved a few more inches. Sweat beaded on my forehead. The smoke was too much, so I dropped back to my knees and hooked my arm under his uninjured shoulder. I dragged Seth behind me as I crawled. He didn't make a sound, which scared me even more. This had to be hurting him.

Once I got him off the rug under the dining room table, the rug I'd picked out for him, and on the wooden floor, he slid more easily. I made it to the door, pushed the screen open with my rear end, and managed to get Seth halfway out the door. But without the wood floor to slide him along, I couldn't get him to budge. I yelled out, "Fire. Help."

A man ran up from somewhere. Between us, we managed to get Seth out on the front lawn. Blood spurted from the wound on Seth's shoulder. This was no accident. I collapsed next to him, gasping in the fresh night air. I closed my eyes and listened as sirens screamed toward us. What the hell had just happened?

I turned to look at Seth. He was so pale in the dark, with his white shirt splotched with blood. The man who'd helped me get Seth out of the house knelt beside him. He pressed a T-shirt on Seth's wound. The one he'd been wearing. His hairy chest shone in the moonlight. He was bald and had a slight paunch but muscular tattooed arms. I tried to choke out a thank-you but alternated between coughing and gasping.

"Can you hold this for a minute?" he asked. He sweated profusely.

I nodded, which was easier than talking, pushed myself up, and took over. Seth's dark lashes lay on pale skin. His breath was rapid and shallow.

"Come on, Seth. Massachusetts can't do without its most eligible bachelor." I remembered his words about wanting to keep things professional. "The county needs you as the district attorney. You're good at it." More sirens. They didn't sound too far from here. My arms felt weak and shaky as I pressed down on the now bloody T-shirt. My hand throbbed. I looked around. Where the heck had the other guy gone? I could use some help. I tried to draw in a few deep breaths but ended up coughing.

The EMTs and firemen arrived. Minutes later I sat in the back of an ambulance, with an oxygen mask over my face. Another ambulance sped off, with Seth in the back. Bedford fire and police rushed around. I'd refused to go to the hospital. This time no one was around to make me. A police officer from Bedford waited impatiently beside me for the oxygen mask to come off so I could answer his questions, until someone called to him and he walked away. The man who'd help me pull Seth out of the house hadn't reappeared. It made me suspicious.

I sucked in breath after breath of the oxygen. The EMT finally took the oxygen mask off. She looked up my nose. "Not bad."

"What are you checking for?" I asked.

"The amount of soot in your nose. It indicates how bad the smoke inhalation is. You seem to be breathing okay, and you aren't hoarse. Color's good. But you really should go to the hospital or see your doctor."

I thanked her, but I'd had enough of hospitals the other night. "Do you have any news on the man the other ambulance took?"

"I couldn't say anything if I did know. A friend of yours?"

I nodded. Was he?

She looked around. No one was close by. "They took him to Lahey. They'll take good care of him there."

"Thank you," I said.

She motioned at the police officer who'd been waiting to talk to me. He hurried over, held out his hand, and helped me step down out of the ambulance. "I need to ask you some questions," the officer said.

"After I make a phone call." My tone was firm. I managed to drag my phone out of my pocket. I Googled a family friend of Seth's, Nichole More. Nichole was a defense attorney, a longtime family friend, and Seth's mother's choice for his wife. At one time I'd been in the picture, not that any of them had liked the idea. That was in the past, and I didn't know what that meant for Nichole's future. Seth hadn't been interested, but things could have changed. I wasn't anxious to call her, but someone needed to let Seth's family know what was going on. Nichole was the only person I could think of. Her office number popped up. She worked for a law firm, and I hoped she'd answer on a Sunday night.

When she picked up, I quickly explained what had happened. Nichole's tone went from icy cold to the nearest thing to frantic she'd ever expressed in front of me.

"You're sure he's at Lahey?" she asked.

"That's what the EMT told me."

"How badly is he injured?" Her voice cracked.

"I'm not sure. He wasn't conscious." I didn't want to scare her more than necessary. My hand trembled as I remembered the image of the blood. The smoke. Who would go after Seth?

"Can you call his parents or give me their number so I can call them?" I asked.

"I'll do it. It would be better coming from me."

"I agree." I looked at the police officer, who frowned at me. "I have to go."

"Thank you," Nichole said before I disconnected.

One of the firefighters came over and joined the

police officer. Both of them wrote down my name and address in notebooks.

"Can you tell me what happened in there?" the firefighter asked as she flipped to another page of her notebook.

"I'd like to hear, too," the Bedford officer said. His tone was serious, and it seemed like he wanted to tell the fireman to butt out.

I quickly explained what had happened.

"You're saying it didn't look like a cooking accident, then?" the firefighter asked.

"I didn't smell any food burning. Just a chemical smell." I thought back. "I didn't see much, because there was a lot of smoke. Flames in a pan. I was trying to get Seth out of the house."

The firefighter asked a few more questions before she headed to the house.

"You didn't see anyone on the street or in the house?" the cop asked.

"Just the man who helped me pull Seth out onto the lawn."

"What man?"

I described him and again looked around for him. "He took off his T-shirt and held it against Seth's wound. Then right before the ambulance showed up, he asked me to hold it for a minute. That's the last I saw of him." Saying it out loud made it sound stranger and even more suspicious. I'd been grateful to him before, but now I was worried. Why had he left?

"You didn't see which way he went?"

"I was concentrating on keeping pressure on

Seth's wound. He could have gone anywhere. Maybe he's a neighbor."

The officer nodded. "Did you see anyone else?"

"No. It's a quiet street. I would have noticed if someone was around." I would have, wouldn't I? Maybe I hadn't been paying close attention, with all the things on my mind. "I think I would have noticed," I said, amending my answer. "In the house, I was focused on getting Seth out."

"Why'd you go in if the house was on fire?"

"Something just felt wrong to me . . . the loud music, the door being open. I couldn't not go in."

"Wait a minute. Aren't you that woman from Ellington I keep reading about in the paper who keeps saving people?"

"A series of coincidences."

"And your husband's the chief of police over there."

"He was the chief of police." I wasn't going to go into the details of my personal life with this guy.

"Seems to me like you could have come over here, stabbed Mr. Anderson, and staged the fire."

"Are you crazy?" I felt weary. I needed to sit, but there wasn't anywhere to take a seat, unless it was in the cop's car. "Then why would I call nine-one-one or bother to get Seth out?"

The cop studied me. "Just wanted to see how you'd react to that. Stranger things have happened."

I saw a dark SUV drive by. It looked like the kind Mike and his men drove. But lots of people drove dark SUVs, and I didn't know one from another. The cop turned to see what I was looking at.

"Someone you know?" he asked.

"I don't think so. Anything else? I'm exhausted, and I smell like I rolled around in ashes."

"Yeah. Don't leave town."

"I'm going to Ellington, and my husband's been in the cop business a long time. I know you can't tell me that."

"Gotta try. Works more often than not." He turned, walked to his car, and took off.

A couple of firefighters were rolling up hoses. Police, crime-scene techs, and the arson squad all roamed around. A few neighbors stood around, but I didn't see the man who'd helped me anywhere. I dragged myself to my Suburban and hoisted myself in. As I started the car, a TV station van pulled up. An attack on the DA would be big news. I didn't want to be part of it, so I drove off.

I thought about going to the hospital to check on Seth, but it really didn't work with his "Let's keep things professional" philosophy. Besides, since I wasn't a relative, they probably wouldn't give me any information, anyway. I certainly didn't have the energy to pretend to be his sister or cousin. Hopefully, tomorrow I'd be able to find out something at DiNapoli's. Even though Seth lived in Bedford, he was well known in Ellington, too.

I hurried past Stella's apartment, not wanting to talk. I bounded (okay, walked slowly) up the stairs. Just as I stepped on the landing, Ryne came out of his apartment. He had on jeans and a T-shirt and smelled so clean, it almost cleared the last of the smoke smell out of my nose.

He frowned when he saw me. "Have you been to a cookout?"

"Something like that," I said. I walked by him and unlocked my door. I glanced over my shoulder when I didn't hear him go down the steps.

"Are you okay?" he asked.

I was so sick of people asking me that. "Just peachy." I shoved my door open but felt guilty for being so short with Ryne. "Thanks again for the nachos today."

He nodded and left. I was grateful to be alone.

Chapter 12

I showered, trying to scrub all the smoke smell off of me, then I threw on shorts and a sleeveless shirt. It was eleven by the time I called Lahey, but as suspected, they wouldn't give me any information about Seth. For a few seconds, I debated calling Nichole. I gave in and dialed her number. All it did was ring. I grabbed a Sam Adams Summer Ale from the refrigerator. It was hot in the apartment, so I opened all the windows, hoping for a breeze. I flipped the TV on and settled in to watch the Red Sox play the Toronto Blue Jays.

Their promising spring season had melted into a promising early summer. This had fans nervous that some disaster would soon befall the team and that a shot at the play-offs and the World Series would fade into nothing. But as far as I could tell, Red Sox fans were always nervous about how the season was going to go. The only day they weren't nervous was the day the team actually won the World Series. But by the next day, they were back to worrying about spring training—it was an endless cycle.

Not too long ago I would have been watching a romantic movie or action show. But now watching love stories made me too sad and I'd had more than enough real action in my own life. That pretty much left me with sports. The Jays' pitcher threw a wild pitch. It hit the Red Sox player in the head. He tossed off his helmet and started his trot to first base. Seeing the helmet lying there reminded me I still had Brody's sports equipment in the back of the Suburban. If I didn't get it out soon, the Suburban would probably smell to high heaven. Just as I forced myself up off the couch, there was a knock on my door. I debated answering it, because I was in no mood to entertain anyone. Another knock sounded so determined, I got up to answer the door.

I peeked through the peephole and was surprised to see Anil Kapoor, one of the school board members, standing out there. He was looking over his shoulder and fidgeting. Then he turned and looked at the peephole so fiercely, I jumped back. What the heck was he doing here?

I opened the door. Anil brushed by me and walked into my apartment.

"Can I help you?" I asked. Anil was already slumped on the couch. His skin, normally the color of sand from the Sahara, had a gray tinge to it.

"Someone's setting me up," he said.

I pulled my grandmother's rocking chair over closer to the couch and settled on it. "What are you talking about?"

"The police have interviewed me three times about my relationship with Melba."

"What kind of relationship?" *Wow.* Wouldn't that be something if he and Melba had had something going on? They'd seemed close during my interactions with the board and from what I'd read in the newspaper. Anil had always sided with Melba on any issues or votes.

"Our *professional* relationship. I'm a happily married man." His normally calm voice lilted heavily with his native accent.

Anil jumped up and started pacing across my living room. It didn't take long. After a couple of laps, he returned to the couch. "They seem to think I have something to do with her murder."

Great. Just what I needed. "I can recommend Vincenzo DiNapoli if you need an attorney." It seemed odd that he'd drop by my house for advice on legal help.

"I don't need an attorney. Yet," he muttered. "I need you to help me."

Another person asking me for help? This was getting weirder by the minute. I was fine with Angelo asking me to check out his competitors for the bake-off, but I didn't know Anil that well. "What could I possibly do to help you?"

"Find out who did it."

I shook my head. "That's best left to the police."

"You're good at figuring things out. Please say you'll help me."

"I'm not the person for the job."

"Think of it as a search at a garage sale. You're looking for something, and you go from sale to sale to find it."

"That's finding an inanimate object, not a murderer."

"But you've solved others."

"Dumb luck." *Jeez.* How long was it going to take to get him to accept that?

"That's not true. It's persistence, a dogged determination to get to the truth."

What it had actually been was a need to save someone I loved. "It wasn't like I'd wanted to be involved. Circumstances drew me into it."

"Can't I be a circumstance?" His dark eyes were long lashed and intent. He leaned forward, arms on his knees.

I held in a sigh. "You need a professional. A PI or legal help." I was starting to sweat, and it wasn't from the heat. This would be the perfect time for someone to stop by or call. But no such luck.

"At the very least, will you just hear me out?"

Listening didn't cost anything, and it might make him realize what a poor substitute for a professional investigator I was. Or maybe it would dawn on him that the police were asking routine questions and it wasn't that they suspected him. "Okay. What's the first thing they asked you?"

"Where was I late Friday night and early Saturday morning."

That sounded routine. "And you said?"

Anil shifted on the couch. "At home."

"And were you?"

He nodded.

But I didn't believe him. "The whole time?"

He started to nod, but it changed to a shrug.

"If you want me to help you, you have to tell me the truth." I looked him right in the eye doing my best impression of a police officer. "But I'm not going to lie to the police unless you give me a very, very good reason."

He stared down at the floor like a petulant little boy. "I wasn't there the whole time. My wife doesn't even know. She's a very sound sleeper."

I knew a little something about sound sleepers. I'd always told CJ he could sleep through an earthquake. "I think we should end our conversation here and you should call a lawyer. I would have to testify about anything you say to me."

Anil opened his hands wide. "But I'm innocent."

"Even if you are, anything you tell me can be twisted in court by the right attorney." I thought about Seth, who'd be in charge of prosecuting the case. If he was well enough. When he was well enough.

"Melba called me at one-thirty in the morning and asked me to meet her at the school. That it was important. I went, but she never showed up."

A call in the middle of the night? Oh, boy. "Can you prove any of that?"

"Only that she called. There's a record of that. But not that I didn't go into the school. I don't think the police believed me when I told them that."

I'd already been attacked and taken to the hospital by then. "Was that unusual for her?" Random nocturnal calls sounded really unusual to me.

He shrugged. "She's called at odd times before. It's like her brain doesn't shut off."

"Do lots of people in town know she does this?"

"Anyone who's served on the board does. I'm not the only one she called at odd hours."

"Everyone's okay with that?"

"Not everyone. But Melba was a good superintendent, so we put up with a few quirks to keep her. She'd had more than one offer from bigger school districts that could pay her more."

"Who wasn't okay with it?"

"Betty Jenkins. They had it out about the late and early calls. Betty's husband is a physician, so they have enough late-night calls. Plus, she used to be a nurse and worked shifts. Melba left her alone. Mac Danucci grumbled about having his market to run, but he'd show up when called."

"Any chance Melba was under duress when she called you that night?"

Anil closed his eyes and sat quietly for a minute. He opened his eyes. "If she was, I didn't notice. I was sound asleep when she called. I'm not sure I was thinking that clearly."

Three things raced through my mind. Melba really had called him. The killer had tried to lure Anil to the school. Or Anil was the killer and was trying to cover his tracks. Only the first one gave me any ease of mind. "Were you working on something with Melba that might have caused a problem for anyone?"

Anil sat for a few moments. "Only the budget. It's always contentious, but this year was no different than any other."

I pondered that pause before he answered. Was he hiding something or trying to think of a possibility that would result in Melba's death?

"Everything here sounds routine. Tell the police the truth."

"That's not it. There's more."

I gestured for him to go on.

"Someone made it look like I was selling the stolen goods online."

"What?" If the items were being sold online, why hadn't I seen them?

"I don't even know how to buy or sell anything online."

"Then how do you even know about this?" I asked.

"Someone sent me a message saying they were interested in what I was selling." He clasped his hands together. "That's the only reason I knew. I looked to see what it was and realized it was the items stolen from the silent auction."

"Can you show it to me?"

"I deleted it all. Someone created a fake account to make me look bad."

Deleting it might look worse. "You should have told the police."

"But it makes me look guilty."

"So does deleting all of it. They probably could have traced the origins." I stood. I was tired and didn't have anything to offer to Anil. "I don't know how I can help you."

"Please, you have to."

I was too tired to argue. "I'll do what I can. Don't get your hopes up." I ushered him to the door. "But be careful. Don't agree to meet anyone in the middle of the night anyplace."

His face paled. "You think I could be in danger?" His voice squeaked on the last word.

I shrugged. "I'm not sure. Just watch your back."

He glanced over his shoulder like he expected Charles Manson to be standing there. "Okay."

My phone rang as I locked the door. Nichole. "Hello."

"Seth's in surgery, but the doctor is confident he'll come out of this with no long-term damage." Her voice was brisk, like making the call took everything she had.

I slumped onto the couch, legs shaky with relief. "Thank you for calling me. I was worried."

"Do you have something to take down a number? It's so you can call the hospital for a recorded message of updates."

And that way we wouldn't have to talk, a win for both of us. I grabbed a pen and an old envelope. "Go ahead."

Nichole recited a number and pass code. I read it back to her.

"Yes. Well . . ." She paused. "Thank you. And Seth's parents asked me to thank you also. Who knows how long it would have been before we found out without your call."

I started to say, "You're welcome," but the phone connection broke before I could finish. I guessed Nichole and I weren't going to become best buddies now.

I poured out my now tepid beer and turned off the TV. It seemed unlikely that the Red Sox would blow a ten-point lead. I'd promised to help at the thrift shop on Fitch tomorrow. Hopefully, despite all that had happened today, I'd be able to sleep. I went through my "wash my face, brush my teeth" routine and climbed into bed. I could hear Ryne moving around his bedroom. It always made me feel awkward to know he was on the other side of the thin wall.

It made me wonder again what he'd heard before CJ left. I remembered the night I told CJ that I wanted to live in Ellington. That I didn't want to move to Florida. CJ had reminded me that I'd promised I wouldn't let him die a lonely old man. That I was the only person he wanted to be with. I'd asked him to stay, to make a life with me here. Instead, he'd walked out.

Chapter 13

Monday morning at nine I arrived at the visitors' center at Fitch Air Force Base. My friend Eleanor Wood had sponsored me on since Laura had moved. Getting on a military base without a dependent's ID was a bit of a hassle. Someone had to sponsor you one which meant they had to go to the visitors' center and fill out a form or have their spouse fill it out from an official government e-mail address. I stood in line waiting for my turn to fill out paperwork, show identification, a driver's license, and proof of car insurance. Sometimes I knew the troops working because they had worked for CJ, but I didn't recognize any of them this morning.

After I got my pass I drove down Travis Road, which cut from one side of the base to the other. The base was situated on low rolling hills and lended some New England charm to the utilitarian government buildings. I passed the parade field, gas station, shoppette (similar to a 7-Eleven), and outdoor rec, where you could rent everything from tents to skis. The thrift shop was just up the hill on the right. It was going to be strange to be there without Laura, because we'd worked here together for the past couple of years. But that was the military life for you. People came and went.

I pulled into the parking lot behind the shop and parked. Was that why I wasn't taking CJ's departure to Florida harder? I was used to people cycling in and out of my life? Did I hold out some thought that he'd cycle back in? Or maybe the time we'd spent apart during our separation and divorce had prepared me for life without him.

I felt tears welling up. Tears I thought I'd finished crying. So much for thinking I was taking things well. I gripped the steering wheel. I'd made my decision when CJ drew a line in the sand in May. I was staying here. On my own, to figure out my life without a man. It was time. CJ and I had been together since I was in my late teens. Life was different without him, but it wasn't awful. I got out of my Suburban and slammed the door a little harder than necessary.

The thrift shop was quiet, as it tended to be in the summer, with so many families moving and others on vacations. Eleanor greeted me with a big smile.

"Thanks for not quitting because Laura's gone."

"I would miss volunteering here. What do you need me to do?"

"The storage shed is crammed full. Would you

mind helping me drag some of the bags from it to the back room and doing some sorting?"

"Sure." People who donated things to the thrift shop often stuffed them in bags or boxes. If the thrift shop was closed, they could stick them in the storage shed behind the building.

Eleanor and I spent the next fifteen minutes hauling stuff inside.

"Are you off for the summer?" I asked. Eleanor was the school nurse at Ellington High School.

"I am."

"That's got be a tough job," I said.

"It can be. But most of the time, I like it. Some days it seems like the hardest part is sorting out who is really sick and who is faking it." She flipped open a box we had carried in. It was full of toys, all of them clean. "It seems like every year there's some illness kids latch onto, and day after day one kid after another comes in with the same complaint."

I started pulling the toys out of the box. A pink princess castle, a bright yellow dump truck, and some dolls. "Kind of a mass hysteria thing?"

"That or they see one kid get out of school, so everyone else tries to use it as an excuse. Last year everyone had migraines, this year it was concussions, and two years ago it was the flu. I actually caught a kid holding a thermometer to a lightbulb."

I laughed at her expression. We heard someone come in the front, so Eleanor went to work the register and I continued to sort. Since it was mindless work—keep, toss, recycle—I thought about

Anil showing up. I had read the newspaper this morning, but there was no progress on Melba's murder. At least nothing that the police were willing to share. There was an article about Seth, the fire at his house, and that he was in stable condition at the hospital. I was grateful that it didn't mention me. But I knew there had to be a lot more going on in both investigations. An attack on a district attorney would get high priority. Was it personal or work related?

I found a stack of sports jerseys, which made me think more about Anil. I still didn't see any way I could help. It also made me think of Mike and his telling me to stay out of it. Why should I? I'd been attacked over what? A few autographed sports items? What I did was none of his business, unless his business was buying stolen sporting goods. When I got home, I was going to bid on some more sports stuff and see what happened.

Two hours later I walked out into an aggressive June heat. It was unusually warm after an unusually mild winter. I unlocked the Suburban, hopped in, gagged, and leaped back out. *Yuck. Brody's clothes.* They'd smelled a little off when I got in the car, but I'd driven through Dunkin's, and the aroma of the coffee had fought off the smell of Brody's uniform. I opened all the doors, rolled down the windows, held my nose, and stood outside hoping some of the smell would dissipate before I drove home.

Thirty minutes later at eleven-thirty I dragged

the garbage bag full of clothes up to my apartment and dumped everything out in a corner, making sure it all landed on the wood floor and not on my ancient Oriental rug. The cleats still had grass and dirt in them. I quickly tossed the washables—uniform top, pants, a lightweight jacket—in one pile. I put the cleats, scarred bat, bright blue dented helmet, and grass-stained baseball in another. I stuffed the washables back in the bag and carried them to the washing machine and dryer in the basement.

Back in my apartment the smell lingered. So I scrubbed the cleats, bat, helmet, and ball with some warm, soapy water. That helped a little bit. I put a towel down in a corner of the living room and set everything on it to dry. I sat on the couch with a glass of iced tea and ticked off the things I needed to do. The most fun item was meeting Carol for dinner at Tony's in Billerica. Tony was one of Angelo's competitors. Angelo didn't think Tony was much of a threat, because according to Angelo, Tony used fake cheese and inferior ground meat. It didn't sound too appealing, but I'd promised. Harder to deal with was keeping my promise to Anil to look into Melba's death and trying to suss out what Mike was up to.

It was one of my worst faults that when someone told me not to do something, it made me do the exact opposite. It was why I'd met CJ. My mom had told me to stay away from the military guys attending the Defense Language Institute in Monterey. But I had gone out of my way to meet one. I shook off those thoughts. Finding out what Mike was up to and trying to track down the things stolen from the swap meet seemed a lot easier than trying to help Anil, so I pulled out my computer. Maybe somehow it was all connected, anyway.

First, I went to the site where I'd contacted Sportzfan. I wanted to try again to track down Mike's online name. If I could do that, I could see what he was trying to buy and see if he was also selling things. But to my astonishment, there was no trace of Sportzfan on the site anymore. I tapped my finger against the side of my laptop. *What the heck?*

I did a general search for Sportzfan and found one guy in Chelsea with the name Sportzfan1. His profile picture was of him sitting in an apartment decorated with sports memorabilia from all the professional teams in Boston. He wore a Patriots jersey and a Red Sox cap. This Sportzfan didn't seem to be on any buy-sell sites, but I decided to contact him, anyway. I made up another account. This time I called myself BostonFan928. Who knew there would already be so many people using BostonFan as their name? I shot off a message saying I was a buyer of sports memorabilia and did he have anything to sell? I sent him a list of a few of the stolen items and threw in a couple of things I could see in his profile picture so it wouldn't look so obvious what I was after.

While I waited to hear back, I started searching for the items that had been stolen. I found a few similar things and sent messages to a few of the sellers. My computer binged. Sportzfan1 said he was selling what I was buying. We arranged to be at a Dunks, as he called it, in Lynn in two hours. This time I verified that the Dunkin' Donuts was actually still in business. First by looking at their Web site and then by calling. I finished Brody's wash, carried everything back up to the apartment, and headed to Lynn.

I arrived at the Dunkin's in Lynn at one-fifteen. The place was packed even this late in the day. I ordered a cup of coffee and a coconut donut. Then I returned to my car to wait. I'd parked strategically so I could see the entrance and would be able to spot Sportzfan1 when he showed up. Part of me wondered if this was really Mike or one of his cronies. After I finished my donut, I saw a beat-up truck with a Red Sox license-plate holder, a Patriots flag, a Bruins bumper sticker, and a Celtics logo on the back window pull in.

A guy who looked like the guy in the profile picture climbed out and hitched up his jeans. He looked around, so I got out, too.

"Sportzfan-one?" I asked.

"BostonFan-nine-two-eight?" He looked me over and smiled.

"Yes."

"Let me show you what I have." He popped open the tail of his truck and opened a plastic container in the bed of the truck. I looked through his jerseys and a couple of framed photos. None of it was similar to the things stolen from the swap. Disappointment whirled through me.

"Sorry," I said to him. "It's not exactly what I'm looking for."

He ran his eyes over me. "I might have something else you're interested in." He gyrated his hips and grinned.

I backed away from him. "Get lost." I turned and ran into the Dunkin's.

One of the employees hustled over. "I saw that creep out in the parking lot. Are you okay?"

I opened my mouth. No words came out. The employee, a young Latina woman, patted my shoulder. We both looked out the window. The truck peeled out of the parking lot with a squeal of tires.

"Would you like a donut? On the house," the woman said.

"Sure." I wasn't going to pass up a free donut.

Chapter 14

Back in my car I checked my messages. Someone else had some jerseys to sell. I wrote back, saying I was in Lynn. I finished my second donut and drank the last of my coffee. I felt a little hyped up on caffeine and sugar. The person asked me to meet them by King's Beach, which was a short drive from where I was.

I drove over and found a parking place on Lynn Shore Drive, near Red Rock Park. Heat shimmered in waves on the hood of the Suburban when I climbed out. The beach was crowded with people sunning. Some were brave enough to dart in and out of the still cold water. That was beaches in New England for you—burning hot sand, frigid water, not unlike my hometown, Pacific Grove.

I passed plenty of people as I walked along, so I wasn't afraid. But as I got nearer the meeting point, I saw a familiar person climb out of a dark SUV, with two brawny guys on either side. Mike Titone again. I darted behind a parked truck to take a minute to decide what to do. Confronting him was my only answer, but I decided to walk behind the line of cars and show myself at the very last minute. If he spotted me coming, he might take off.

I duckwalked down the street, keeping as close to the cars as I could. I didn't want to get run over. A couple of cars honked, and one group of guys yelled out. Not a good way to go unnoticed. I peeked over the top of one car. Mike's men seemed more interested in the women on the beach, a diverse group, than in who might be approaching them. I got to a pickup truck, stood, straightened my clothing, and walked over. I tapped Mike on the shoulder. He spun around and frowned.

"What the hell!" he said. The two men on either side of him jumped. It turned out it was his brothers. I hadn't seen them since February, when Mike had lived next door to me briefly. We took a few minutes for hugs and catching up before Mike and I faced off again. This time, instead of looking furious, he looked resigned.

"I should have known better than to tell you to stay out of this."

"Why is that?" I asked, hoping for answers. I noticed that people who were out on a stroll or heading to the beach made sure to give us a wide berth.

"What's your sudden interest in sports gear?" Mike asked, instead of answering my question.

Time to improvise. "I'm just looking for a birthday gift for CJ."

"Nice try, but CJ left you."

Damn. How did he know that? He took a step closer to me. *Don't back down,* I told myself. Standing firm when I wanted to take two giant steps back wasn't easy. His brothers stood on either side of him. The three of them looked like a wall of muscle.

"Get in the car," Mike told them.

A group of young men tossing a football to each other ran by as Mike's brothers moved toward the SUV. As they passed, the breeze picked up. A whiff of musky aftershave floated by me, the kind that my attacker had worn. As soon as his brothers got in the SUV, the smell was gone. I might not have moved, but it felt like all the blood in me had drained out. I swayed a little. Mike's hand shot out, and he steadied me before I jerked away. Was the smell from his brothers or the guys with the football? I decided it had to be the latter, or else I would have noticed the smell when I hugged them.

"Don't bother telling me to stay out of it again. I'm going to find out who stole the stuff from the swap in Ellington." I jabbed a finger in his chest and heard before I saw one of his brothers get back out of the SUV. "I'm going to find out who killed Melba." Jab. "And who attacked Seth. Because an SUV that looked a lot like yours drove down Seth's street that night." Jab. "And who attacked me." Jab. Jab. Another car door slammed, but I didn't break eye contact with Mike.

He looked away, but I got the feeling he was trying to hide a grin, which made me even madder.

When he looked back down at me, any trace of humor was gone. "Like I said before, stay out of it." He whirled around and started to climb into his car. Mike paused for a second but then pulled his leg into the SUV and slammed the door. I stood there until they pulled out. Then my shoulders slumped and I dropped on the nearest bench. What had I been thinking to threaten Mike? I stared out at the ocean for a while, listening to the waves pound the shore. My phone binged, letting me know a text message had come in. From Mike. I'll help you.

I hadn't responded to Mike's text when I let myself back into my apartment. Why did he want to help me all of a sudden? I'd spent the entire drive home going over our conversation, trying to understand what I'd said or done for him to change his mind. I spotted the envelope with the number for the hospital and decided to check to see how Seth was doing. It was a very generic message, but it said Seth was in stable condition which is what the newspaper said this morning. I took my laptop over to my grandmother's rocking chair and sat down. I looked for Sportzfan1, but all traces of him were gone. I wasn't surprised. I Googled other Sportzfan combinations but didn't find anything.

I did some new posts on various sites that were ISO, or in search of listings. I'd try again to find the missing auction items. It was the only way I could help Anil at this point.

* * *

I arrived at Carol's house at six-thirty to pick her up for our dinner at Tony's. Her twin boys and her daughter attacked me when I arrived, giving me their strongest bear hugs, each one trying to outdo the other. I laughed until I was gasping for breath and tears were in my eyes.

"Where's Uncle Chuck?" they asked, almost in unison. They called us aunt and uncle, even though we weren't really related. I hadn't been here since CJ left.

"Kids," Carol's husband Brad said, coming down the hall.

I hadn't seen him, either. "It's okay." I turned to the kids. "He moved to Florida. It's a beautiful place with lovely white sand beaches. I bet he'd love it if you went to visit him."

"Can we go, Dad?" Now the kids hopped up and down around Brad.

He gave me a look like "Thanks a lot." "Maybe sometime."

"Does he live by Disney World? Can we go see Mickey Mouse, too?"

"Maybe Aunt Sarah wants to take you there," he said.

Carol saved me by yelling from the back of the house, "Pizza's ready."

The kids all flew down the hall toward the kitchen, leaving Brad and me alone.

"How are you?" Brad asked.

I'd been asked that so many times lately, my automatic response had become "Great," so I just went with it. Brad opened his mouth to say something more, but Carol saved me again by walking down the hall.

I always joked that she looked like a Barbie, tall, thin, and built. Carol had on jeans, boots, and a sweater because she was always cold, even in the summer. She kissed Brad on the cheek. "We're out of here."

Fifteen minutes later we were seated in a wooden booth at Tony's Pizzeria in Billerica, the town just to the north of Ellington. We both had glasses of Chianti and menus. While Tony's looked a little nicer than DiNapoli's, Angelo always disparaged Tony's food. I guessed we'd find out if that was accurate or not.

"Why did you want to come here?" Carol asked. "I thought you were totally loyal to DiNapoli's."

I remembered Angelo had asked me not to tell anyone what I was up to. I hated keeping secrets from Carol, but I would this time. "Everyone needs a change of pace."

"What are you going to have?"

I pretended to study the menu. "I think I'll try the lasagna."

"No pizza?"

"Not tonight. What are you going to have?"

"The spaghetti and meatballs sounds good."

Our waitress came by, and we added salads and garlic bread to our orders.

"I know you told Brad you're great, but how are

you really? You just got attacked three nights ago," Carol said after the waitress left.

"I'm fine. Keeping busy."

"Doing what?"

"I have several garage sales to get ready for this week."

"I saw in the paper that Seth Anderson was stabbed and his house set on fire. Have you talked to him?"

"No . . ."

"But?"

"I'm the one who pulled him out of his house."

"What?"

I filled Carol in on what had happened that night. "That's all I know, except that he's still in the hospital recovering."

"The paper said the fire was contained to the kitchen. I guess he has you to thank for that, along with being alive."

"He doesn't have to thank me. It's just lucky I stopped by."

"Why did you stop by? You aren't interested in him again, are you?"

While Carol had supported me after CJ and I broke up the first time, she'd never really been happy that I'd dated Seth. She probably still hoped that CJ and I would somehow end up back together. "I'm not interested in anyone. I need to take care of myself."

Fortunately, the waitress came by with our salads and the basket of bread just then. After she left, we both stared down at our plates. The salad was awash in some kind of Italian dressing. The lettuce was brown on the edges. There was a limp piece of onion and a tomato so pale, it was almost white. I flipped the napkin off the bread and chose a piece. It was soggy. I took a bite and knew this was some kind of fake garlic-flavored butter. One bite was plenty. If this was any indication of how the lasagna was going to be, Angelo had nothing to worry about.

"How are things at Paint and Wine?"

Carol's face lit up. "I love the paint camps I started this summer. I'm doing them in the morning, which was usually a slow time for me. It's so exciting to see how happy kids are to create art. You should come by some morning."

"I'll do that."

We both pushed our food around and talked. Carol didn't even try the bread when she saw that I had set mine down after one bite. Our main courses came. Carol's had watery-looking sauce and four giant meatballs. It didn't look too bad.

"Careful. The plates are hot," the waitress said as she slid my lasagna in front of me.

The noodles looked like they were topped with the same sauce Carol had. The edges of the noodles were burnt. Some congealed white cheese covered part of the top. I poked it with my fork, and it didn't move. I dug in and took a bite. The noodles were soggy in the middle and had a watery taste. I cut around the burnt edges because they were too tough to bite into. Instead of ricotta, the dish was stuffed with cottage cheese or at least a cottage cheese–like substance. The sauce had very little flavor, and I suspected it came from a jar. While this didn't bode well for Carol and me, Angelo would be ecstatic.

I looked over at Carol. She was chewing a bite of meatball, and chewing and chewing and chewing. "I'm sorry," I said softly. "This is a disaster."

Carol nodded. "How do you think they stay open? Maybe their pizza is good?"

I shrugged. "At least it's cheap. And the waitstaff is friendly."

We both finished our Chiantis.

The waitress came back and looked at our almost untouched plates. "Not hungry?"

"We filled up on salad and bread," I said. We all looked at our full salad plates and the bread basket.

The waitress leaned in. "Lucina's has an excellent lasagna." She winked.

Lucina's was one of the restaurants on my list. "I'll take mine to go."

The waitress looked surprised. "Whatever floats your boat, honey."

"Really?" Carol asked after telling the waitress she was fine. "I'm not taking mine, and Brad will eat almost anything."

"Maybe it will taste better warmed up."

Carol snorted. "In your dreams."

My phone buzzed. I had a text from a woman responding to my ISO post. She wanted to meet in Bedford. So I suggested Bedford Farms Ice Cream. I was still hungry, and there'd be lots of people around on a nice summer night. She agreed and told me to watch for her curly red hair.

"What's going on?" Carol asked.

"I have to meet someone at Bedford Farms."

"Why?"

"To look at some stuff they're selling."

"What stuff?" Carol asked.

The waitress came back by with my boxed lasagna and our check. I paid and left a good tip. It wasn't her fault the food was awful.

"Some sports stuff." I stood up and started walking to the car.

"Sarah Winston, are you telling me that you're trying to find out what happened to the stolen things from the swap?"

I wasn't telling her that, but she had realized it on her own. I sighed as we climbed into the Suburban. "Yes."

I listened to her rant about me being attacked and Melba murdered. "Do you want to come with me?" I asked as I started the car.

"Of course I do." She grinned.

Chapter 15

At eight-thirty we drove around the Bedford Farms' parking lot, looking for a place to park. Finally, someone pulled out, and I slipped the Suburban into the space. Driving a big vehicle had taught me how to finesse my way into a spot of almost any size. We got in line and looked around for a woman with red, curly hair but didn't see anyone. If Mike Titone showed up instead of a woman, I might just shoot him. If I had a gun. When it was our turn, I ordered my usual kiddie cup of Almond Joy, and Carol ordered the chunky chocolate pudding.

We found an empty bench to sit on and dug into the ice cream. While they called this the kiddie size, it was a scoop bigger than a softball. I kept looking for dark SUVs, but so far I hadn't spotted one. Then I spotted a young woman standing beside a beat-up multicolored two-door sedan parked on the other side of the lot.

I nudged Carol. "I think that's her." I pointed with my spoon. I scooped my last bite of ice cream in as my phone buzzed. It was a text saying, **I'm here.** "I'll go over. You wait here and keep an eye out." Carol had kids. I needed to make sure she was safe. Brad would kill me if I got her in any kind of trouble.

"For what? What am I keeping an eye out for?"

"Trouble," I said before I walked over to the woman.

After brief introductions, the woman popped open her trunk. It was stuffed full of every kind of sports jersey imaginable and for every team, not just the Boston area ones. I looked at several different jerseys. They were all signed in black Sharpie. That in itself wasn't so unusual, but the handwriting was the same on all of them, even though it was supposedly different athletes who had signed them.

I gave the woman a good hard look. "I don't know what kind of scam you think you are running, but these are obviously fake signatures."

"No they're not. Each one is authentic. My boyfriend told me."

I proceeded to show her how all of the signatures were alike. "You need to stop this. Next time you might run into someone who isn't as forgiving as I am. Or you might sell one to a cop and end up in jail. Ditch the merchandise and find a new boyfriend."

The woman slammed the lid of the trunk closed and flipped me off as I hurried back over to Carol.

"That seemed to go well," Carol said with a smirk on her face.

I shrugged, and we left.

* * *

Thirty minutes later, after I had dropped Carol off, I turned down the alley behind DiNapoli's, where Angelo had asked me to park. He didn't want anyone to see me bringing in the leftovers. I saw the curtains twitch at a house across the alley as I grabbed the bag from Tony's and slipped out of the car. Herb Fitch lived over there and, as a retired cop, still kept an eye on things. I waved in that direction as I closed and locked the Suburban. I knocked on the back door. Angelo opened it, looked left and right, and yanked me in before slamming the door behind me.

"What was that for?" I asked.

"I'm not gonna trust anyone until this contest is over. Did you see anyone lurking in the alley?"

I was starting to get a little worried about Angelo. "No. I saw Herb's curtains twitch. He'd know if anyone was back there."

Angelo nodded. "Let me make sure the coast is clear. Rosalie was just shooing the last customers out." He walked down the hall, looking right and left, before motioning me forward.

I placed the bag, which had Tony's Pizzeria scrawled on it in a large fancy font, on a table in the dining area. Angelo frowned. I waved to Rosalie who was scrubbing a counter in the kitchen. Angelo and I both glanced at the large front window. I hurriedly took the box out of the bag and wadded the bag into a fist-sized ball. Angelo took it from me and tossed it toward the kitchen. I flipped open the lid on the box, and Angelo jumped back.

"What is that?" he asked, pointing at the lasagna in horror. Rosalie hustled over to look and grimaced.

"It's the lasagna I ordered," I said.

They both picked up forks and poked it gingerly, like it was going to leap out and bite them.

"Did you try it?" Rosalie asked.

"Yes. You've got nothing to worry about other than food poisoning."

Angelo stabbed one of the noodles and lifted it. It hung like a sad fish that had lost the battle with a fisherman. "How can something be burnt and limp at the same time?"

"You've gone above and beyond with this one, Sarah," Rosalie said.

"Let me fix you some real food," Angelo said.

"No thanks. I had ice cream at Bedford Farms." And I still had a freezer full of meals at home.

The door rattled and slammed open. A big man came in. He had a shocking head of dark hair, which was standing up all over the place. His thick mustache twitched above a mouth twisted into a snarl. He looked somewhat familiar to me, but I couldn't place him. Rosalie stepped in front of the food and threw a napkin over it.

"What da you think you're doin', sending her over to my restaurant?" He pointed a finger toward me.

Angelo puffed up. "No idea what you're talking about, Tony."

Tony? Of Tony's in Billerica? How the heck would

he know who I was or why I was in the restaurant? Now I knew why he looked familiar. I'd just seen a caricature of him on the cover of his menu and on the take-out bag. What I had thought was a caricature, anyway. It seemed fairly accurate now that I saw him in person.

He pointed a shaking finger at me. "I saw her at my restaurant. It took me a while to put it all together. I recognized her from the newspaper, knew she was friends with you. I told my staff to let me know if anything suspicious happened leading up to the contest." His glare swept over the three of us. "And she was suspicious. If she's trying to sabotage my lasagna, there will be trouble."

"I'm not sabotaging anything," I said. "A friend asked me to meet her for dinner. I took some of it home. Isn't that allowed in your restaurant?"

Tony looked confused. "Of course it is. But I'm warning the other chefs that you're up to something." He walked out and slammed the door after him.

We all stared after him.

"Don't worry about him," Angelo said. "He's all air."

"And bad food," I added.

I walked into my living room ten minutes later and shrieked. Mike Titone sat on my couch, a foot up on my trunk, flipping through a copy of my *Vintage Finds* magazine. A glass of red wine sat next to his elbow, on the end table. He looked like he belonged there. He didn't. I heard feet pounding up the steps.

"Welcome home," Mike said, tossing the magazine back onto my trunk.

There was a knock on my door. Someone to my rescue.

"Get rid of whoever it is," Mike said.

I walked away and answered the door, and Stella stood there, looking anxious. "Are you okay? I thought I heard you scream."

"I had an unexpected guest who surprised me. Come on in and say hi." Mike Titone could not tell me what to do in my own apartment.

Stella followed me into the living room. An irritated look flicked across Mike's face before he smiled. He stood and gave Stella a kiss on both cheeks. Her face reddened.

"Stella, I never thanked you properly for letting me stay here last winter."

Good grief. The man was smooth.

"I brought you both gift baskets to thank you for putting up with me."

"Yeah? Where are they?" I asked, looking around.

"On your kitchen table. I hope you don't mind. Your door was unlocked, and I was concerned when no one answered my knock."

Unlocked, my ass. I remembered locking it when I left.

"That was so thoughtful of you, Mike." Stella actually fluttered her eyelashes at him.

I wanted to smack her for buying what he was selling. She was a terrible judge of men, except for Awesome. He seemed okay. Mike went into the kitchen and brought out two giant cellophane-wrapped baskets filled with cheese, crackers, and wine.

"You didn't have to do this," Stella said, accepting hers.

When I didn't reach for mine, Mike set it on the trunk. "What's in it?" I asked. "Arsenic? Bombs? Booby traps?"

"Sarah," Stella said. "That's not very gracious of you."

Mike threw his head back and laughed. Stella joined him.

"You are so witty, Sarah," Mike said. He grabbed Stella's elbow and started steering her to the door. "I really appreciate you helping me out, Stella. It's not something everyone would do." Seconds later Stella was out in the hall and Mike was closing the door behind her. I could hear her singing some aria as she went down the steps. *Traitor.*

"What are you really doing here?" I asked.

Mike put his hand over his heart. "I'm hurt you don't believe I'm here to thank you both."

"You can knock off the charm now. It's just us."

Mike relaxed on the couch again and took a sip of his wine. "You didn't answer my text."

Chapter 16

"Take a hint. I don't want your help. I don't need your help. And your 'help,'" I said, complete with air quotes, "comes at too high of a price." Mike had helped me once before but had made me promise not to tell anyone. Actually, it was more of a threat than a promise. But I'd held to it, even though it had cost me greatly in the end. Even as I said it, another part of me was yelling, *Yes, yes, you do need his help.* I tried to ignore that thought.

But I couldn't. "What are you planning to help me with?" *Ugh.* Curiosity and the cat and all that. I was playing with fire and would probably get burned.

"What do you need help with?" Mike said as he leaned forward.

I ticked the things off on my fingers. "Who attacked me, who stole from the equipment swap, and who killed Melba." The lasagna situation I could handle on my own.

Mike started to say something, but I held up my hand and cut him off. "And what's going on between you and Seth Anderson? Don't say nothing, because it's something, and if I start poking around, it's going to get messy and come out."

Mike leaned back in surprise. Apparently, he was the one used to giving orders instead of getting them. A bemused expression crossed his face. Then it dawned on me. I'd just threatened Mike Titone. Again. I must have a death wish, but I couldn't, wouldn't back down now. He made a funny sound. Then he laughed, loudly.

"I've got to hand it to you. You have balls." He swiped at his eyes. He'd laughed so hard, tears had formed. "It's been a long time since anyone spoke to me like that. Except my mom. She'd love you."

Mike stood up. He got close, leaned down, and spoke low. "Stay out of my business with Seth."

He left, and I just stared after him.

I quivered with disgust. Mike was a clever one. He'd told me he'd help, I'd told him what I needed help with, and now he knew it wasn't anything of concern to him. Except for Seth. What the heck did they have going on? I'd seen them playing poker together last winter, so maybe they were involved in some high-stakes gambling ring. What else was the Mob known for? Racketeering, drugs, prostitution. It was impossible to imagine Seth doing any of those things. Maybe he owed Mike something, like

I did, and had no way to extricate himself. Maybe that's why he'd ended up in the hospital.

I called the hospital again, since Seth was on my mind, and got another generic update. Seth was doing better or at least not any worse. I looked around for something to do rather than just sitting here worrying. Brody's stuff. I crawled into the attic space off my living room, found a box, and dragged it out into the living room. I started packing Brody's now dry things in it. The helmet and bat were hard to get in. I sealed the box and made a label for it. After sticking the box in a corner, I got ready for bed. What a freaking day.

I spent most of Tuesday running errands including mailing Brody's box, talking with a couple of new clients, and buying all the fixings for the pretzel bar. I spoke with Kelly to confirm she'd found a tent and had an electrician to set up the lighting. Things were looking good for her sale. If only chasing down who attacked me and helping Anil were half as easy. Maybe I needed a fresh start instead of continuing to obsess about the items stolen from the gym. I started by brushing up on Melba's background. I read her bio on the Ellington school district Web site and her obituary. Both were very impersonal. She'd dedicated her life to educating children. She had no living relatives. There was nothing about hobbies, although I knew she liked auctions and garage sales.

I Googled her and found out that in the past six

months she'd been almost militant about wanting to increase the number of students in each classroom. Fewer teachers meant more funds for other programs. That seemed to have caused some ripples of discontent among the school board and the teachers, who had always supported her. Was a teacher mad enough about more kids in their classes that they killed Melba? Fortunately, Stella and I were going out to dinner, so I'd quiz her about all of that then.

Stella and I drove to Lexington for dinner. It was only five, but we had decided to eat early because I planned to attend the visitation for Melba in Ellington tonight. The air was warm, but not frying. I wore what was fast becoming my summer uniform, a sundress. I'd gone to a great garage sale in Lincoln, Massachusetts, a few weeks ago. A woman had been selling a ton of dresses in my size because they didn't suit her anymore. Fine with me. It was hard to beat a buck a dress for name brands like Talbots.

Instead of heading straight to Villa Bella to eat we strolled along Massachusetts Avenue, stopping at the statue of a minuteman on the Lexington Battle Green. A man dressed in colonial clothes was telling a group of tourists about what had happened here.

"We learned all of this in high school," Stella said. "But it's fascinating. Let's listen."

"British regulars fired on seventy-seven minutemen the morning of April nineteenth, seventeen seventy-five. Eight minutemen were killed, and ten were wounded," the man said before Stella pulled me away.

"After that skirmish the regulars went on to Concord, where the minutemen fired back," I told Stella.

"Yeah, yeah. I've heard it all a million times."

I guessed she didn't love the history of the area quite as much as I did. Maybe that was the difference between growing up here and landing here.

We peered into shop windows. There were a couple of antique stores I'd visited before, but their wares were way beyond my income. Still, it was fun to look.

It was five-thirty when we arrived at the restaurant, so we were seated right away. Villa Bella looked like a traditional Italian restaurant, with checkered tablecloths and candles stuck in Chianti bottles. It might have been romantic if I were here with someone other than Stella. I took a seat so I faced the front of the restaurant instead of the kitchen. I thought my odds of discovery would be lessened that way.

I, of course, ordered the lasagna, along with an appetizer of stuffed mushrooms, a salad, and garlic bread.

"You must be hungry tonight," Stella said. "That's a good thing. I've been worried about you."

Too many people were worrying about me. "No need. I'm fine." I didn't want to tell her the truth. I'd eat everything else so it wouldn't look odd when I took one bite of the lasagna, and then asked for the rest to be boxed up.

"Wasn't that sweet of Mike to give us the baskets as a thank-you last night?" Stella said.

"Yeah, he's just a wonderful man. What did Awesome think about Mike giving you the basket?"

Stella turned a light red. "I dismantled the whole thing before he came over. Why create conflict when there isn't any need? Besides we've been dating only a couple of months."

"Why borrow trouble and all that?" My tone might have been light, but there was some worry behind it. I didn't want Mike causing problems for Stella and Awesome.

"Exactly."

"Do you want to go straight to Melba's visitation after we leave here?" I asked.

"I forgot to tell you, I can't. I'm teaching a private lesson at seven. They switched nights. I'm sorry to bail on you."

"It's okay." Doing things alone was good for me.

The waitress brought the stuffed mushrooms, bread, and salads.

We dug into the mushrooms, which were stuffed with bread crumbs, Parmesan cheese, garlic, and a little basil.

"Mmm," I said. "These are heaven." If the lasagna was half as good, Angelo was going to have some stiff competition. I sighed. I really hoped he'd win.

"I forgot to tell you. My aunt Nancy wants you to stop by her office."

"She does?" *Oh, boy.* We'd met recently to discuss New England's Largest Yard Sale, which I was hired to run again in the fall. What else could be on her mind?

Stella nodded. "We had a family dinner last night, and she mentioned it."

"Did Awesome go?" I asked.

"No. He had to work, or so he said. Frankly, I think he's scared of my aunts and mom, since they found out he's a Yankees fan."

"I can see being scared of them. Poor Awesome."

The waitress came with our entrées. Lasagna for me, of course, and baked ziti for Stella. My lasagna looked exactly like what one would expect, nothing fancy or special. At least it looked much better than Tony's. I kept eating my salad and the bread, and I finished off the mushrooms. I cleansed my palate with a glass of water.

"Aren't you going to eat that?" Stella asked, pointing her fork at my lasagna.

"I'm stuffed. But I'll take a bite." I dug my fork in but couldn't get a bite to come free without using my knife. I smiled. *Yay*. I held it up and looked at it, trying to decide if they used real cheese.

"What's going on?" Stella was watching me stare at my bite.

"Just admiring the artistry of the layers." I stuffed the bite in my mouth before I said anything else. It was good, solid food, but not fantastic or award winning, in my opinion. Although, with judges, you never knew who would like what. That was why there were rows of pasta sauces at the grocery store, something for every taste. I ate a couple more bites for show and then asked to have the rest of it boxed.

I dropped Stella and the lasagna at home. I'd have to take the lasagna to the DiNapolis later, because next on my list was going to the visitation for Melba. I wanted to pay my respects, but I also wanted to talk to all the school board members. Maybe I'd find out something that would help Anil, or maybe he'd feel like he no longer needed my help, which would be even better. I planned to use my nose to sniff out anyone who wore the same aftershave as my attacker had. Although for all I knew everyone and their second cousin wore the stuff.

Chapter 17

The funeral home was packed. The line to pay respects twisted and turned like a line at an amusement park. Lots of students—past and present, judging by the age range—plus parents waited to pay their respects. Town officials milled about up near the coffin. Closed, thank heavens. I shuddered a little as I thought about the last time I'd seen Melba. While people seemed sad, no one seemed distraught. The five school board members stood on either side of the coffin. Lance and Anil stood to the right and the three others on the left.

As I got closer, I realized Anil was sweating profusely. He kept taking a white handkerchief out of his suit coat pocket and dabbing his face. Granted it was warm with all the people, and he was wearing a suit, but Lance stood next to him, as cool looking as could be. Anil leaned in when I shook his hand.

"Have you found anything out for me?" he asked in a low voice.

"No." I took a deep sniff. Anil certainly didn't

smell of the scent I was searching for. If anyone could actually smell like fear, Anil did.

"I thought you were going to help." He fussed with his tie. His white shirt was partially untucked, his hair messy, and his eyes a little wild.

"I'll do what I can. I've been trying to track the stolen items. Have you heard more from the police?"

"Nothing."

"That's good news."

Anil shook his head. "I've heard from multiple people that the police are asking questions about me." His voice squeaked on the word *me*. He grabbed my wrist, but I yanked it free.

"Don't touch me."

"I'm sorry." He patted his forehead with his handkerchief again. "I can't lose my security clearance. Or my job. My family . . ." Anil's voice broke. "I'm feeling desperate."

I realized I didn't know exactly what Anil did outside the board. But if he had a clearance, he worked either for the government or a defense contractor. "I understand. But if you start acting irrationally, it will make things worse."

Fortunately, the person talking to Lance moved on, so I could, too.

Lance clasped my hands in his. They were cool and dry. Everything, from the lapels of his hand-stitched suit coat to his hair, was in place. Such a contrast to Anil. "Thank you for doing such a wonderful job leading up to our garage sale." He said it in a loud voice and smiled at me. "Kelly is thrilled with how things are coming along."

I wasn't sure how thrilled she would be when she saw how little money she was going to make. Thank heavens I'd charged a flat fee for a lot of the setup. I got as close as I could to Lance and tried to breathe deeply without being obvious. But Lance stood too close to the blanket of roses on the coffin. That was all I could smell.

"The *Ellington Citizen* is doing a feature story on the sale, thanks to you." He smiled again and then turned to the person behind me.

"Really?" That would be good for business. "Thanks for letting me know."

Since the line moved along I did too. Next was Betty Jenkins, who was my very first paying customer when I set up my garage sale business last spring. We chatted for a moment about her family.

"Who arranged all this?" I asked. "I understand that Melba didn't have any living relatives."

"We did—the school board. I didn't want to be up here but was overruled."

Someone cleared their throat behind me, so I said my good-byes to Betty. That left the last two board members, both men. They both wore suits and were the middle point, dress wise, between Anil and Lance. I stepped in as the first one, Mac Danucci, reached out to shake hands. He looked startled and stepped back, but not before I almost sneezed at the overpowering scent of cigars. He had always reminded me of the worst stereotype of a used car salesman.

I turned to Rex Sullivan, who stepped closer to

me, which made me want to step back, but instead I inhaled. I realized he reeked of bourbon. After murmuring my condolences, I mingled a bit in the room where cookies and coffee were being served. My nose was on overdrive as I moved about the room. I finally caught a whiff of the aftershave and tried to figure out where and who it was coming from. I moved from position to position but didn't have any luck. What did it prove, anyway? Every department store probably sold the stuff, so anyone with enough money could buy it. I needed to think of another tactic.

As I crossed the parking lot to my Suburban, I heard a commotion behind me. I turned in time to see Anil being handcuffed and stuffed into the back of an Ellington police car.

I caught the DiNapolis just as they were locking up. "Come in, Sarah," Rosalie said as she gestured to me.

I handed the bag from Villa Bella over to Angelo. He opened the box carefully, set the lasagna on a plate, and looked at it from all angles before carrying it over to a table.

"It looks good," Rosalie said.

Angelo frowned and nodded. He went to the kitchen and got three forks.

"You're going to need some knives, too," I said.

"Really?" he asked. But he grabbed some knives and brought them over.

We all took a bite.

"Hmmm," Angelo said. "Let me heat it up, and we'll give it another try." He wrapped the lasagna in tinfoil and stuck it in the oven. DiNapoli's didn't have a microwave. "Let's have a glass of wine while we wait." He opened a bottle of Chianti with a flourish, poured three glasses, and we settled at the table.

"I went to Melba's visitation."

"We planned to but were so busy, we couldn't get out of here," Rosalie said.

"The police handcuffed Anil Kapoor and stuck him in the back of the police car as I left."

"They think Anil killed Melba? Does that mean he attacked you?" Angelo asked.

"I don't know. I hope not. He came over to my house the other night and asked me to help him. He said he was being set up."

"Did he say how?" Angelo asked.

"Melba asked him to meet her at the school the night of her murder. He went, but no one was there."

The oven dinged. Angelo brought the lasagna over to the table. We all dug in again. Angelo lifted a forkful to his nose and breathed in like he was smelling a fine wine. We all ate a few bites, chewing slowly, considering.

"It's good," I said. "But not as good as yours. It doesn't taste award winning to me."

Rosalie nodded.

Angelo took another bite. "A little too much fennel in the sausage and oregano in the sauce. It's not as good as mine." Then he smiled and topped off our glasses of wine.

"Did you know Melba well?" I asked them.

"Our son had her for math, and he wasn't good at math. She took a lot of extra time with him, and he got it," Angelo said.

"She was a very private person. Wonderful with the kids, but hard to get to know." Rosalie swirled her Chianti thoughtfully.

"What?" I asked.

"I always wondered if she had some kind of secret life." Rosalie smiled. "But that's probably me just imagining things."

A secret life. The thought wouldn't let go as I walked home. I stopped in front of Stella's door and listened but didn't hear anyone singing. I hoped that meant her private lesson was over. I knocked on thc door.

"Want to go on an adventure?" I asked when she answered. Her tuxedo cat, Tux, came out and rubbed against my ankle. I bent down and scratched his ears until he purred. "Who's a handsome boy?" I asked.

Stella pursed her lips. "Last time I went on an adventure with you, I almost got arrested."

"True, but you also met Awesome."

"Let me get my purse. Come on, Tux." Tux followed Stella back into her apartment. Minutes later she came back out and locked her door.

When we climbed into my Suburban, Stella twisted toward me. "Where are we going?"

I backed out of my parking space and drove along the edge of the town common. "I thought we'd drive by Melba's house."

"That's it? That's the big adventure?"

I glanced at her, surprised. "Why? What did you have in mind?"

"I don't know. I've just been feeling restless lately." Stella sighed. "Don't mind me. I'm fine."

"I looked up Melba's address. It's over close to the base and Gillganins. Want to go have a drink afterward?" Stella liked to drag me with her to karaoke nights there. My voice was okay, but no match for Stella's operatic one. "Maybe Ellington is too little for you," I said. "That could be making you feel restless."

"No. I like it here. Especially since I started dating Awesome." Stella shifted in the seat. "Can you keep a secret?"

"Of course I can." I glanced over at her but then looked back at the road, which was narrow and lined with a granite curb. Granite curbs and tires weren't a good mix.

"I tried out for a part in a production of *The Phantom of the Opera.*"

"That's fantastic."

"I'm scared I won't get. I'm scared I will get it." Stella closed her eyes for a minute. "What if I get it and I freeze or I'm horrible? I haven't been onstage for a long time."

"But you've been singing at faculty events at Berklee. You're always brilliant."

"I know. But this is a step back to an old life that I loved and hated."

"Whatever happens, you'll be fine. I'd love to see you in action."

Stella smiled at me nervously. "Thank you."

I turned down South Street and then onto the street Melba had lived on. Most of the houses were one-story ramblers. Some of them were duplexes. I slowed as we looked for her street number in the dark. We pulled up in front of the house. I wasn't sure what I expected to see. Maybe something that would indicate what Melba's secret life was about. If she even had one.

"Look. Her front door is open," I said.

"That seems odd."

I saw a bit of light bouncing around inside. "Is that a flashlight beam in the house?"

"It is." Stella flung her car door open and leaped out.

"Wait. Get back."

But Stella kept heading for the door. I grabbed my cell phone and laid on the horn as I dialed 911. I didn't want Stella to walk into a dangerous situation. I slid out of the car and ran after her as I talked to the dispatcher. I grabbed Stella's arm. A door slammed at the back of the house. A person wearing all black rounded the side of the house and dashed down the driveway. Something silver was tucked under his left arm. His right arm pumped furiously.

"He took something from the house." Stella started in his direction.

I'd noticed that, too. "It looked like a laptop. Get in the car," I yelled. "We'll have better luck following that way."

We bolted back to the car. An engine started up down the block and a small yellow pickup truck squealed away from the curb. As I started the Suburban, I heard the dispatcher yelling not to follow anyone. I zoomed down the street, anyway. We saw the truck two-wheel it around the corner. I tossed my phone to Stella.

"Tell the dispatcher where we are," I said as I took the corner, too. The truck had jetted down several blocks. I didn't want to drive too fast, because we were still in a residential neighborhood.

"Step on it," Stella shouted. "He's getting away."

It suddenly felt like I was in some kind of action movie, with bad guys and car chases and corny lines. I went as fast as I dared.

"He's turning left," Stella yelled. I was not sure if it was for my benefit or the dispatcher's.

I took the turn and accelerated. This road was less populated. We flew by the hockey rink as Stella gave the dispatcher the play-by-play. I heard a siren not too far from us. We were close to the Fitch Air Force Base FamCamp. A place where military people could stay in tents or RVs. Only military people were supposed to use it, but there weren't any gates or guards, although the grounds were patrolled by base security and they did random ID checks.

I topped a hill and couldn't see where he'd gone. "Do you see him, Stella?"

We both peered into the dark as I crawled forward. There were some long driveways on either side of the road and lots of trees. We got to a stop sign where the guy could turn right back toward the center of Ellington or go straight onto the FamCamp.

"There," Stella yelled. "I see taillights."

He *had* driven onto the FamCamp. Just as I pulled in, a police car caught up to us. I pulled over so they could go on. Stella hung up.

"The dispatcher said to leave it to the police," Stella said.

"Should we?" I asked.

Stella shook her head no. Instead of staying put, I followed the police car. A few minutes later we caught up. The little yellow pickup was stopped in the middle of the road. The driver's side door was open. Another cop car pulled up behind us. I rolled down my window as the officer walked up.

"Stay put until I can question you," she said. As I nodded my agreement, she approached the truck. She talked into her shoulder mike and then hustled down a path in the woods.

Thirty minutes later another police car pulled up. I saw Awesome climb out and walk over to my window.

"Go home," he said. "The guy's on the run. You

two don't have an ounce of sense between you." Then he jogged away toward the abandoned pickup.

Stella and I remained silent on the drive home. I felt the sting of Awesome's words about us not having any sense. It wasn't true.

Stella sighed.

"Awesome was just worried about us." I said as I turned onto Oak Street. "He didn't really mean we don't have any sense."

"It sounded like he meant it to me," she said.

I pulled into the parking area next to the house and parked. "Give him a chance to apologize," I said as we walked toward the house.

Stella stopped on the sidewalk and pointed at my living room window. "It looks like you've got company. Did you leave your door unlocked again?"

I looked up. A silhouette of someone sitting in my grandmother's rocker could be seen through the gauzy white curtains I'd hung for the summer. "I locked the flipping door. Mike Titone seems to have a way with locks." I obviously needed to spend the money to get a new one that was more challenging to get through.

Stella went with me to my apartment. I tried the knob, and it was locked. *Yeesh.* After unlocking the door and stepping into the hall, I yelled to Mike, "Quit breaking into my apartment."

I turned the corner into the living room, powered by a righteous indignation. I halted three steps in and clapped my hands to my mouth. Stella barreled into my back, making me stumble forward. She screamed behind me. It wasn't Mike. It wasn't anyone. A mannequin sat in my grandmother's rocking chair, with a vintage ski pole plunged through its chest.

Chapter 18

Ryne ran in, wearing what looked like a hastily pulled on pair of jeans. The top button wasn't even closed. "What of all that is holy was that noise?"

"Stella screamed," I said.

He looked at the mannequin sitting in the chair. "Is that your idea of art?"

"It's my idea of a threat." I inched closer. The mannequin was pure white, with no defined eyes, nose, or lips. Someone had arranged its arms so they were holding the arms of the oak rocker. Its feet rested on the floor. It looked like something out of a nightmare. The gauzy curtains blew gently in and out in the breeze. The scent of night-blooming jasmine came in, too. All of it added to the dreamlike quality of the scene. For once I wished it was Mike sitting in the chair.

"Don't touch anything," Stella said. "I called the police."

Ryne looked from Stella to me. "That's terrible. Who would do something like that?"

The police hadn't released anything about the murder weapon. No one knew about the ski pole except for me, a handful of officials, and—I hugged myself—the killer. My mind raced. Whose toes had I stepped on? No one that I could think of, although I had been pursuing the stolen items with almost relentless abandon. Was this a "back off" message or something worse? "You might want to put some clothes on before the police get here," I said to Ryne. I wanted to think about anything but that creepy mannequin.

He looked down and reddened. Stella looked over and smiled appreciatively at Ryne's bare feet, bare chest, and tousled hair. "Do you want to wait in my apartment?" he asked.

"Good idea," Stella said. "We didn't even look to see if anyone was in here."

We all whipped around and looked behind us like we expected the bogeyman to be standing there. No one was.

"I'm going to look around. There's three of us here." I ducked my head into the kitchen. It was mannequin free. In my bathroom I yanked back the shower curtain. Empty. Likewise, there wasn't anyone or anything unusual in my bedroom closet or my bedroom, and yes, I looked under the bed, too. All clear.

Pellner and another officer arrived. Ryne left to

get dressed after explaining who he was and why he was there.

"Oh, that's just creepy," the officer with Pellner said as he whipped out his phone and snapped a couple of photos.

Way to make me feel better.

Even Pellner looked like he was weirded out by the mannequin. His dimples were as deep as I'd seen them, and it looked like he was repressing a shudder.

Before Pellner had a chance to ask, I filled him in on my past several hours. Dinner with Stella—Pellner looked at her, and she nodded—a stop at the visitation, and then DiNapoli's.

"I came home and asked Stella if she wanted to go for a drive." I didn't think mentioning that I had called it an adventure would make Pellner happy.

"A drive that just happened to take you two by Melba Harper's house. And then chasing after someone like you're Charlie's Angels minus one," Pellner said.

The other officer guffawed at that, but Pellner shot him a look.

"Did you find the guy we were following?" I asked.

"No. You two yahoos probably scared him straight, though," Pellner said.

Getting told you didn't have an ounce of sense and then being called a yahoo wasn't really much of an ego booster. "Can't you track him down through his truck?"

"Nope," Pellner said.

"Stolen?" I asked.

"How'd you know?" the other officer asked me.

I managed not to say aha out loud.

Pellner slashed a hand across his neck to stop the officer from saying anything else. "She didn't. She's just nosing around."

"Do you know what he took from Melba's house?" I asked.

"None of your business," the other officer said.

Pellner nodded his agreement.

Footsteps pounded up the steps, and Awesome came in. Ryne slipped in behind him. His feet were still bare, but at least he'd pulled a black T-shirt on. He'd probably chosen the black because it brought out the green in his eyes. Not that it needed bringing out. His hair had been combed. Ryne carried a tray with a pot of coffee and mugs. He poured and passed out mugs. I took a big swig of mine.

"Thank you for this." I held up my mug.

Ryne nodded in response.

I kept my hands clasped around the mug because they felt cold, even though the apartment was warm.

Awesome looked a little green when he saw the mannequin. That surprised me because he'd been a homicide detective with the NYPD before he came here. He must have seen much worse. Everyone's reaction to the mannequin was almost scarier than the mannequin itself. Oh, who was I kidding? The thing was terrifying. And when I thought about how I could have been home when it was delivered . . .

Awesome looked at Pellner. "Do you mind if I ask them a few questions?"

"Be my guest," Pellner said. He turned to the other officer. "You can take off. I'll take care of this." He gestured toward the mannequin.

"Fine by me," the guy said. He hustled out the door without looking back.

"I have some follow-up questions about the incident at Ms. Harper's house," Awesome said.

I nodded, but Stella ignored him. Still stung by his earlier comments, apparently. He gave her a perplexed look. Men could be so freaking clueless.

"Can you describe the person you saw?" he asked.

"He was dressed in dark clothes, but that's all I saw. It was dark, and he ran by quickly. Right, Stella?" I looked over at her. "Oh, and he was carrying something silver. Probably a laptop."

She nodded her agreement.

"How do you know it was a guy?" Awesome asked. "If you didn't get a good look at him?"

"I guess I just assumed it was." It was like I always assumed a bad driver was a man and CJ had always assumed it was a woman.

"So you don't know for sure?" Awesome asked.

"No," I snapped. Apparently, I wasn't quite over his earlier comment, either.

Awesome looked over at Stella, but she ignored him. "Stella, anything to add?"

"Well, since I don't have an ounce of common sense, I don't think I can be of any help."

Pellner raised his eyebrows and looked over at

me. I shrugged. Pellner had dated Stella in high school, so he had probably seen this kind of attitude before.

"Look, I'm sorry. I shouldn't have said that. But Melba Harper was murdered, and someone was searching her house. If you saw anything that can help, please tell me."

Stella sighed, and the atmosphere in the room thawed a bit. "I really don't have anything helpful to add. Like Sarah said, it was dark and the person ran fast." She accented the word *person* a little more than necessary.

"Okay, then," Awesome said. He looked like he wanted to say more but then seemed to remember he had an audience.

I guessed there would be some major groveling going on later tonight.

"Doesn't this let Anil off the hook?" I asked. "He was in police custody when Melba's house was broken into and this happened."

"The incident at Melba's house could just be an opportunist. He might have known the visitation was going on so a lot of people would be preoccupied with that. Isn't that why you two were going by?" Awesome asked.

I glanced at Stella. She shot dagger looks at Awesome. He certainly wasn't doing a good job of worming his way back into Stella's good graces. I thought about telling him that we were out for a drive because it was hot in here and that we planned to go to Bedford Farms. But that sounded flimsy even to me, since it was in the other direction.

"I asked Stella to go with me. I was just curious about where Melba lived and what her life was like." I snapped my mouth shut before I added that Anil had begged me to look into it for him. That wouldn't help his cause any.

We heard a noise at the door. It was the crime-scene people.

One of them took a look at the mannequin and said, "We're going to need a bigger evidence bag."

It made us all laugh and broke the tension in the room. After they took pictures, they pulled the ski pole out of the mannequin's chest.

"Is this yours?" one of them asked me.

"No. I don't ski," I said. My parents skied, but I'd never enjoyed it.

"Could it have come from the swap?" Pellner asked.

"It could have," I answered. "But lots of people ski around here, so it could have come from anywhere. It's a vintage pole. Leather handle, bamboo shaft, and a leather and bamboo basket." The basket was the round part at the bottom of the pole that kept the pole from going too far down in the snow. Ski poles today had ergonomically designed handholds, and the shafts were constructed of aluminum or carbon fiber.

"Vintage poles are popular for decorating cabins and ski lodges. My grandparents had similar ones in their attic." It dawned on me that this pole might be the partner to the ski pole that had been stuck in Melba's chest. I squeezed my eyes shut and tried to picture it. But the horror of seeing Melba dead had driven anything more than the vaguest impression of what the ski pole looked like out of my head. "How'd they get the pole through the mannequin's plastic?" I asked.

One of the crime-scene people examined the hole in the mannequin. "It looks like someone took an ice pick or something else sharp to get through it."

"Ice pick?" I asked, my voice quivering, as I imagined someone taking an ice pick to a mannequin. It seemed like they'd have to be very angry to do that.

The crime-scene people left with the mannequin and ski pole. Ryne put the empty coffeepot and mugs back on his tray and took off, too.

"How do you think they got in?" Pellner asked.

"I don't have any idea. I know I locked the door," I said.

"Sarah had to unlock it when we got back," Stella added.

"You don't have a key hidden anyplace?"

"No. I know better than to do that," I said.

Stella made a funny little noise.

"What?" Pellner asked her.

"I used to take care of the cat for the people who lived here before Sarah. They left a key on the ledge of the door frame." Stella glanced at me. "Maybe it's still there."

We all went out in the hall. Awesome felt the top of the door frame and pulled down a key.

"Oh, no. Sarah, I'm so sorry," Stella said.

"It's okay." At least one mystery was solved. I took the key into the apartment, and everyone else followed me back in.

Pellner looked around the living room. "I've got everything I need for now," he said. "Are you going to be okay, Sarah? Maybe you should spend the night somewhere else."

"I'll be fine."

Pellner nodded at Awesome and Stella and left.

"Why don't you come sleep on my couch?" Stella said.

"I'm not going to let someone scare me out of my home." I gave her a quick hug. Awesome stood awkwardly after Stella walked out without even glancing at him.

"For goodness' sakes, go after her. You don't have an ounce of common sense."

"You're right. I don't," he said as he hustled out the door. He called out to Stella as he trotted down the stairs.

I locked the door after him and heard him call out to Stella again. I carried one of my kitchen chairs to the door and wedged it under the knob. I doubted it would actually keep anyone out, but at least the noise of it falling over should alert me to trouble. After I washed my face, I lay down on the bed, fully clothed. I stared up at the ceiling, wondering if I'd ever manage to sleep again. The curtains in my bedroom blew in on a gust of wind, like they were reaching out and trying to grab me. Normally, I liked to watch them billowing, but this wasn't a normal night.

I grabbed my phone off the nightstand and called the hospital. The recorded message said that Seth had been released. That, at least, was good news.

Chapter 19

The Wednesday morning paper had a head shot of Anil, with an article about his arrest for the murder of Melba Harper. The more chilling photo was one of him staring almost adoringly at Melba at a school board meeting. I stared at that photo for a long time, trying to decide if I believed Anil's story that they were just good friends or if, as the article insinuated, there was something more going on.

Anil was in jail when the mannequin was placed in my apartment, so maybe the police really did have the wrong guy in custody. Or somehow something I'd done in the past couple of days had sent Melba's killer after me. Because it had to be her murderer—the police still hadn't mentioned the murder weapon and it hadn't been talked about around town, as far as I knew. The mannequin was sending a message. One that had me wondering if I should get out of town for a few days. Maine was nice this time of year. Of course, I couldn't do that until my lasagna tasting was done for Angelo and my garage sales were done for my clients. Leaving wasn't an option.

That reminded me that I needed to line up someone to go eat dinner with me tonight. I couldn't ask Carol or Stella again. They'd think I was nuts. Obviously, the DiNapolis were out. I could call someone on base, but why look farther than right next door? Besides, I had the perfect excuse.

I knocked on Ryne's door. He answered, fully dressed, and it looked like he was ready to leave for work. He looked down at me with his big green eyes.

"Can I help you?"

I wondered if he regretted moving in here. Things had been a little nuts in the past few weeks. "I wanted to thank you for helping out last night. Any chance you're free for dinner?"

"Since I just moved here and know only three people, my uncle, you, and Stella, I am free for dinner. What did you have in mind?"

"There's a great Italian restaurant in West Concord. Belliginos. Meet me there at seven?"

"Cheating on the DiNapolis?"

That's what Carol had said too. *What's with everyone?* I guessed I'd left enough food at his door for him to know how often I ate there. "Broadening my horizons."

"You think going to a different *Italian* restaurant is broadening your horizons? What about Indian food or Chinese or Mexican?"

"I've just been craving lasagna lately. Do you want to go or not?" I asked.

"Sure. Beats another can of soup here."

* * *

I finished reading the newspaper as I sipped a cup of coffee. There was a short paragraph about Seth being released and a quote from him thanking his well-wishers and saying he was eager to get back to work. I decided to call Nichole to see how he was really doing.

"He's staying with his folks in Beacon Hill while he recovers and the damage to that dreadful little house of his in Bedford can be repaired," Nichole said after we'd exchanged greetings.

Beacon Hill was a beautiful neighborhood of old brownstone homes in Boston. Seth would have plenty of people to take care of him there. I resented her calling his house dreadful, because it was amazing, even before I'd helped decorate. And it was a heck of a lot closer to where he worked than Beacon Hill. I managed to keep all those thoughts to myself and thanked her for telling me.

"He plans to start working from home tomorrow and hopefully will be back in the office by the end of the week."

I was surprised Nichole was being so, for her, chatty. Maybe it was to make sure I understood that she was in the loop and I wasn't. "Does Seth have any idea who did this to him?" I might as well try to take advantage of her willingness to talk.

"Humph."

Really? Who actually humphs at someone? I managed to keep myself quiet.

"He doesn't. He was attacked from behind and

passed out when he was stabbed. I'll be going over old cases with him to see if it's revenge for putting someone away. And obviously, his office and the police will be doing the same."

"Of course. I hope they catch whoever did this soon."

"Oh, we will," Nichole said before hanging up.

I finished the rest of my coffee before my thoughts turned to who I'd upset in the past couple of days. I moved restlessly around the apartment, which was warming quickly. I was guessing the person Stella and I followed last night wouldn't be too happy with me. But it didn't seem possible that he would have gotten a clear glance at me at Melba's house or when we followed him.

There was the woman with the fake stuff at Bedford Farms Ice Cream the other night, but unless she followed me home, she'd have no idea how to find me. That left all the other people I'd come across in my search for the stolen items. And Mike. We'd gone from a somewhat friendly relationship to an adversarial one in a very short time. The mannequin did seem like something he'd do to scare someone. Not me, I hoped. We were friends, sort of. He said he'd help me, but not how. Still . . . I couldn't rule him out.

Maybe I'd been too obvious in my sniffing of the school board members at Melba's viewing. It was possible that had set someone off. And really three of them had had smells that masked their smell—roses, bourbon, and cigar smoke. Maybe someone had seen me sniffing them and didn't like it. But that left a whole roomful of people and no way for me to know who it could have been. For now I'd concentrate on the school board members. Even though I didn't think there was a snowball's chance it was Betty Jenkins, I'd look into her life just in case. But how was I going to manage all of that? Maybe Nancy Elder would help, and Stella had said she wanted to see me, anyway.

After taking a quick shower and throwing on a pink polka dot sundress, I hustled up the stairs of city hall to Nancy Elder's office at nine. She would be on top of what the school board was doing. Plus she'd lived in Ellington all her life and she was politically savvy.

Nancy's office was empty, but the door was open and the lights were on, so she hadn't gone far. Calling the room plain, utilitarian, or small was overstating the facts. Nancy had done her best to give it some warmth by bringing in a rug with thick swirls of bright reds. It didn't help. An ugly pipe angled across one corner of the room but had been painted the same shade of off green as the wall to try to disguise it. The joints in the pipe had rusted, and a large damp spot had spread across the ceiling, where the pipe disappeared. No one could accuse the town of wasting funds here. And I suspected Nancy kept the office like this so the good people of Ellington would know that.

"Can I help you?"

I turned to see Nancy striding down the hall

toward me. Her chin-length hair bobbed around her head. In a past life she must have been a drill sergeant. She had the voice and commanding presence.

"Oh, it's you, Sarah. Good. Come in," she said when she reached me.

She had stacks of paperwork on her desk. Behind her was her wall of fame. Photos of her with John Kerry, Patrick Duval, and Tom Menino when they were respectively a senator, a governor, and a Boston mayor. There was a picture of her throwing out the first pitch at a Red Sox game, and there were plaques from various organizations.

Nancy sat in the chair behind her desk. "Have a seat."

"Stella said you wanted to see me. Is it about New England's Largest Yard Sale this fall?"

Nancy leaned forward and placed her arms on her desk. "Let's cut the BS. We both know why you're here. You want information about Melba."

I sat back, stunned. "You asked me to come. I thought—"

Nancy waved a hand to cut me off. "This looks bad for our town, so what's your plan?"

I opened my mouth and tried to speak, but nothing came out. I was used to people telling me to butt out, not asking me what I planned to do. This had been a very strange week. "My plan? The police made an arrest."

"It's ridiculous to think Anil would kill someone," Nancy said. "I want you to get this matter cleared up as soon as possible."

"Me? Isn't this better suited for the police?" I'd just told Anil the same thing the other night.

"Well, as you know, we are down one chief. It's a small department, and resources are strained. Plus, people seem to trust you. To tell you things." She picked up a pen and tapped it on a pad of paper. "I don't trust that state trooper to get to the bottom of this. He doesn't know this town or how to handle its people."

"I've already been threatened." Maybe that would get Nancy to back down.

"You mean the mannequin last night?"

I nodded.

"You are made of stronger stuff than that, aren't you? Were you really planning to let that stop you?"

When put that way, no, I guessed I wasn't.

"I'm assuming you want to continue to be in charge of our fall event—New England's Largest Yard Sale."

I nodded again. "Are you saying if I don't find out who did this, I can't run the sale?" It had been a large chunk of my income last year. I needed that money.

"I'm not saying anything. But I'd like this cleared up within a week."

I was astounded. First, that Nancy thought I was the key to solving this mystery. Second, that I wasn't going to get to do the sale if I didn't solve it. And third, that she'd given me a week to do so.

"I have a meeting in thirty minutes. Let's not waste time." Nancy glanced at her watch as she spoke.

"Okay then." Finally, I could form words again.

"Was there any unusual strife among the school board members?"

"Since the people of Ellington voted down the bond issue and the one-cent sales tax last fall, there have been some heated arguments about the budget."

"Is that anything new? Aren't there always money issues with a school system?"

"Yes, but the arguments were getting uglier. Anil wanted to drop arts programs and sports. He's very academically oriented with his kids and does a lot of tutoring. Melba was vehemently against that. She believed those who didn't excel academically still could find a place to shine through the arts or sports. Lance sided with her."

"Did that surprise you?" I asked.

Nancy folded her hands on her desk. "Not particularly. He played football and basketball at Ellington. All his kids have been on various sports teams."

"What about Betty Jenkins?"

"The woman has a spine of steel and lots of opinions."

That surprised me. She always seemed so pleasant to me. "So where did she stand?"

"She was going along with Melba's idea to increase classroom size, cut vacation days, and scale back their health insurance by getting rid of dental and eye care."

"What? I thought I'd always heard that Melba was a big supporter of teachers."

"She was, but she'd rather cut teachers' benefits

and perks than programs. Of course, the teachers weren't happy to hear that."

Ugh. Adding every teacher in Ellington to the list of suspects was mind boggling.

"However, she was hoping to work something out with the teachers and reintroduce the bond and sales tax next year. When everyone realized what a drastic impact not having either would have."

Okay, so maybe take the teachers off the suspect list. "What about the other two men on the board?"

"Rex Sullivan and Mac Danucci?"

I nodded.

"Both businessmen who were more middle of the road. They thought a five percent cut across the budget would be best. That way everyone and everything suffered equally."

Time to change tactics. "Do you know why her house was broken into?"

"You didn't hear this from me," Nancy said.

"I could probably find out whatever you're going to say at DiNapoli's."

Nancy shook her head. "Not this time. It's a well-guarded secret." She got up, looked out in the hall, and closed the door before retaking her seat. "Someone was in the middle of a search in Melba's home office when you and Stella arrived."

That wasn't too surprising. It seemed like anyone would surmise that from what had happened. I waited for a moment to see if Nancy would join the chorus of "What were you thinking by going there?" but she didn't. "Maybe they were just looking for valuables," I said. "It could be someone who knew the house was empty and decided to take advantage of that." That's what Awesome had said last night.

Nancy shook her head no again. It sent her hair swinging around violently. "There was an iPad sitting out in her living room, although a laptop was missing from her desk. They could tell because the cord was still there. Some files were scattered around on the floor. The person was definitely searching for something."

"Any ideas what?"

"No. That's one of the things I need you to work on." Nancy's phone rang, and she made a shooing motion at me. "Time for us both to get to work."

Chapter 20

Betty Jenkins lived in a rambling yellow farmhouse off Great Road, on the Bedford-Ellington line. It looked like each generation had added on another section to the house, making it longer and putting their stamp on the property. Since part of her property was in each school district, she'd long ago decided to send her kids to Ellington schools.

Betty opened the door after I knocked. "I was expecting you." Betty was the complete opposite of her house, neat and small. She looked like the kind of woman who should be out biking or hitting a tennis ball.

I raised my eyebrows. "Really?" I followed Betty through the foyer to a low-ceilinged living room.

"I just happened to call Nancy about something, and she said you were probably going to stop by sometime. Do you want some coffee?" She tucked a piece of short blond hair behind her ear.

"Coffee would be great, if it's no trouble."

"None at all. I'll be back in a minute."

Even though I'd done a huge garage sale for Betty last spring, every corner was still crammed full of furniture. A person wouldn't want to walk through this room in the dark. There was also a locked gun case full of old muskets that her husband used in local reenactments as a member of the Bedford militia.

Betty came back with two steaming mugs of coffee. "I guess you're here to talk about Melba?"

I nodded as I sipped my coffee. I set it down on a coaster with a photo of the old Bedford Flag on it. We sat in two wingback chairs that faced the fireplace, which was filled with candles and fresh flowers, mostly daisies and pink roses.

"Did Melba have any enemies that you know of?" It sounded like such a cliché, a line straight out of a bad movie.

Betty's eyebrows popped up in surprise. She drank some of her coffee in what seemed like a delaying action. "Not that I know of."

"Anyone who held a grudge on the board?"

Betty sat her coffee cup down. "Maybe Ma[illegible]."

"Why?"

"His oldest brother was the superintendent before Melba. He always blamed Melba for getting him fired."

"How could that be?" I asked.

"The man was a drunk. I guess he made a pass at Melba at some school event, and she reported him. Once that came out, lots of other stuff did, too, so it wasn't really Melba's fault." Betty crossed her ankles. "When she got the job after him, there was a lot of talk about whether he ever really made a pass or not."

I sipped on my coffee. That seemed like a possible motive for murder.

"However, even with that, we all worked well together. Sure, we had disagreements, but we usually pulled together as a team in the end. We all want what's best for the students attending our schools."

That sounded like an idealistic version of what most school boards were like. "You said *usually*. Anything recent?"

"We were working on the budget and hadn't figured out the best way to handle it."

The budget kept coming up. "What happens without her?"

"Work will continue, and someone will be named interim superintendent."

"Any idea who that will be?"

"One of the people from her office."

We heard a knock on the door. Betty answered it, and I could hear her talking to a man. She walked back in the living room with Pellner and Ramirez, the state trooper. Neither of them looked happy to see me. I stood and greeted them.

"Just let me know if you decide to do another garage sale, Betty," I said. "I'm booked for the next several weeks." I hoped she'd realize I didn't want the men to know what I was up to.

"Okay. I'll be in touch," Betty said. She grinned at me as I left.

* * *

Sullivan Luxury Car Sales was on the east edge of Ellington, right on Great Road. I decided this would be as good a place to talk to Rex Sullivan as any. The floor of the dealership was filled with beautiful cars, shiny, expensive, and way out of my reach. Sun flooded the space through large floor-to-ceiling windows. Lights beamed down on the red, silver, and black cars. Was that a DeLorean? I was no expert in cars, but I had seen all the *Back to the Future* movies. No one seemed to be around, not customers, not staff.

I noticed a case filled with trophies and, next to it, a wall lined with photos. There were pictures of Rex with kids in every sport imaginable: gymnastics, hockey, baseball, tae kwon do, and anything in between. They all stood in uniforms emblazoned with the Sullivan Luxury Car Sales logo. It was even stamped on all the equipment.

"Help you?"

I jumped a bit. A florid-faced man with greasy black hair stood behind me. He held a ham and cheese on rye and took a big bite.

"I'm looking for Rex."

He held up a finger, indicating I should wait. He chewed and swallowed, Adam's apple bobbing. "Yeah. Rex is out. I'm Tim Greer." He transferred his sandwich to his left hand, wiped his right one on his pants leg, and stuck his hand out to shake.

Ugh. I gave him a limp shake, trying not to touch more of his hand than necessary, and introduced myself.

"I have just the thing for you." He guided me

over to a sleek, low-slung red Porsche. It was sexy as hell and so far out of my price range, I wouldn't even dream about a car like this. But seconds later I was sitting in it, running my fingers over the leather-covered steering wheel.

"It suits you. Let's take her out," the man said as he stuffed the last of his sandwich in his mouth.

"I can't. . . ." But the guy waved a hand around, produced a key, found a temporary tag, which he attached, and minutes later I was driving down Great Road, feeling like a rock star. *Holy crap.* Now I knew what all the fuss was about.

"Let's take Route Three up toward Lowell so you can see what she can do."

The Porsche hugged the twisty, narrow roads leading to Route 3. When I goosed the gas to merge onto the three, we shot forward onto the open road. There wasn't much traffic this time of day.

As much as I'd like to escape and enjoy the ride I'd showed up at Sullivan's for information. Maybe Tim had some. I thought about all the trophies and team photos at the dealership. "Does Rex have kids of his own?" Maybe that was why he helped out so many teams.

"Three, all grown and gone. Lots of grandkids."

"They didn't stay in the area?"

"Naw. One's on the North Shore, two in Boston."

To me, someone who had lived the Air Force life and currently lived three thousand miles from her hometown, all those places were in the area. New Englanders had a different definition of *area.*

"Did any of them have Melba Harper? They must be devastated."

"Yeah, the youngest boy, and *devastated* isn't the word I'd use."

"Why not?"

"They blame her for him not getting into Harvard. She wouldn't give him an A his junior year."

"But they still worked together on the board."

"Rex hoped to oust her. That's the only reason he's there."

That was news to me. He'd always been civil and pleasant to Melba when I attended meetings. I wondered if the police knew about this. "Does he even have the credentials to be a superintendent?" As far as I knew, selling cars didn't qualify someone for the position.

"You bet he does. Years ago, he was the principal at the elementary school in Ellington. Has every higher education degree you can imagine."

"Why'd he quit?"

"I guess he didn't think it was lucrative enough."

"It doesn't seem like the superintendent position would pay that well."

"He's in a different place now."

"He must love kids, with all the sports teams he sponsors," I said.

"Yeah, the guy's a nut about them. And it's a tax write-off."

It might be a tax write-off, but that wouldn't begin to cover the expense of all that equipment. I passed a car like it was standing still. Then I noticed I was doing ninety and eased off the gas. My passenger didn't seem perturbed that I was going so fast.

Tim grinned. "Can't even tell how fast you're going in a machine like this one."

I sighed. "You can't."

"You think he's crazy about kids' sports, you should see his office. He loves pro sports even more." He leaned back against the headrest. "He has a signed Brady jersey framed and hanging right behind his desk. I'll show it to you when we get back. Turn around at Lowell." He closed his eyes and within seconds was snoring.

I perked up. Rex would have known about the auction items at the swap because he got all the emails where I updated the board on how things were going. All too soon we were back at the dealership. I had to give a snoring Tim a nudge when I pulled back into the lot. I tossed him the key as we reentered the dealership. "I hope you know I can't afford a car like that."

"Yeah, but it got me out of here for a while. Things have been slow lately."

I looked around. A couple of people sat in their offices, working, but there still didn't seem to be any customers.

"C'mon. I'll show you Rex's office."

We walked into a large office in the center of the dealership. A glass-topped desk sat on stainless legs and was obviously custom made. It was more art than work space. The walls were lined with autographed pictures of local sports stars. Rex was in many of them.

"His home is filled with even more stuff."

I nodded. "Do you know when Rex will be back?"

"Not today. He's going to be at the bowling alley tonight. You could catch him there."

"Thanks. And thanks for letting me drive the Porsche."

"Well, if you ever decide on a life of crime and can afford it, look me up."

I drove off in the Suburban, which felt like a clunker after the Porsche. I patted its dashboard. "I still love you." A life of crime was the only way I could ever afford a luxury car. And I'd seen enough crime to know that no car was worth it. At least to me. That got me thinking about Rex's very empty dealership and his passion for sports. So maybe he only needed to sell a couple of really expensive cars a month to make ends meet. That seemed unlikely when I thought about the cost of operating a place like that.

Was Rex a desperate man who stole the things from the gym, and did Melba discover this, and so he killed her? Maybe it wasn't even financial issues but a bitter grudge he had hung on to for years after she didn't give his son the grade he wanted. People had killed for a lot less than that.

Back at my apartment I opened my refrigerator to make myself something for lunch. There was some leftover pasta, but somehow it didn't sound too appealing, especially when I was going out for lasagna again tonight. Instead, I made a Fluffernutter sandwich: white bread, peanut butter, and Marshmallow Fluff. It was the state sandwich of Massachusetts, completely unhealthy, but the salty-sweet combo was hard to beat.

While I ate, I searched for articles online about the school board. Just because Anil had said he was being set up didn't mean he was. Maybe his motive would turn up here. The police had to have some reason to have arrested him besides "The evidence pointed us to Anil," the reason cited in the paper.

It didn't take too long to find it. An altercation had occurred during a vote at a board meeting recently. Anil had gotten so upset with Melba that Rex Sullivan physically restrained him. The article didn't say what the altercation had been about. However, once the meeting was over, another argument had started in the parking lot. Someone had called the police, and although Anil hadn't been arrested, he'd apparently been issued a stiff warning to stay away from Melba. That was a very different story from what Anil had told me. But that didn't mean he killed her. I needed more information. Maybe a visit to Mac Danucci was next.

Chapter 21

Mac ran a small market near the town center. I had been in it only once before and had been amazed it managed to stay open with a Whole Foods and a Stop & Shop nearby. Nothing had changed since the last time I was in. It was small, dark, and dingy. Maybe the dark was a good thing, because the dingy might have been worse in the bright light of day. It stayed open until three in the morning, so maybe that was why he stayed in business.

A teenage girl sat on a high stool at a register. As soon as she finished up with her customer, telling him, "Thanks, doll," and giving him a saucy wink, she turned to me. "What can I do for you, sweetie?"

I wasn't one who liked to be called affectionate names by strangers, but it was so heartfelt from this girl that I didn't snap my usual "Nothing, honey" back at her. Instead I smiled. There was something infectious about her. "I'm looking for Mac."

"Food inspector?"

"No."

"Loan collector?"

"No."

"Bounty hunter?"

"Uh, no."

"Police? FBI? CIA?"

"No to all three." I started laughing. She had to be joking, or at least I hoped she was.

"In that case, I'm sure he'd be happy to see you." She pointed toward the back of the store. "Down the produce aisle, take a left at the bathroom, and pound on the door with the sign that says LEAVE ME ALONE. Mac's in there. If he's not out back, smoking a cigar."

I walked down the produce aisle. If Whole Foods produce looked like a beautiful still-life painting, this aisle looked like a Jackson Pollock painting, only less appealing. A teenage boy was restocking oranges by tipping the box upside down. Some of the oranges bounced onto the floor. He picked them up and tossed them back on the pile. He looked at me as I passed. His eyes looked older than he did. One of those ancient soul types. I gave him a wave, but he just turned back to the next box of oranges.

I found the grimy door. Not only did the sign say LEAVE ME ALONE, but it also had a skull and crossbones on it. I knocked loudly, anyway, and heard a muffled "Come in."

I intended to leave the door open—after all, there was a chance that Mac was a killer—but the door swung closed automatically, and with a loud click. I looked in horror at Mac. He sat behind a metal desk, in a bloodstained apron. Then I remembered he was a butcher. I hoped he butchered only already dead meat and not people.

"What can I do you for?" Mac chuckled and locked his hands over his belly. I'd heard him use that phrase and laugh every time I'd ever seen him, except for at the funeral. The smell of cigar smoke was powerful in here, even though I could hear the hum of an exhaust fan.

I attempted a small laugh in return, but I sounded more like a mewling cat. "I heard something interesting and wanted your take on it." At least for once I'd planned out a spiel before I arrived.

"Shoot." Mac had a thick head of dark hair that always reminded me of an old shag rug, because it went every which way.

"I heard that Rex Sullivan was trying to oust Melba as superintendent."

"You did now, did you?" He scratched a spot on his apron right above his belly as he leaned back in his swivel chair.

I nodded, because I couldn't think of anything else to say. He'd been a lot more talkative in my imagination when I planned what I'd say to him.

"Yeah, he probably did want to," Mac finally said.

"Because of the—"

"Old affair." He finished the sentence for me.

What? "What affair?"

"Rex and Melba. You mean it's not all over town

yet?" Mac's chair creaked as he shifted in it. "It ended Rex's marriage."

Was this the secret life that Rosalie had alluded to? Melba was a notorious marriage wrecker? That wouldn't be a secret very long in a town like this. I tried to reframe my thoughts to put the Melba I knew with this picture. She had been a bit plump, had worn a tight bun, and had had a teacher's "I'm not putting up with any nonsense" attitude.

"You look surprised. So was I when Rex told me over a bottle of bourbon one night. Rex paid his wife off so it wouldn't get out and damage his reputation." Mac plucked a cigar out of a humidor on the left corner of his desk. The humidor was the only nice thing in the office. The walls were dingy. A bulletin board hung behind him covered with OSHA signs. instructions about employees washing their hands, and not smoking.

He put the cigar under his nose and inhaled. "Ummm. His wife died a couple of years later, so the story stayed undercover, so to speak. But Rex resented Melba for it. Blamed the affair all on her." He grabbed a lighter off his desk and stood up. "Rex probably won't be too happy that I told you that. But since the police know it, it's bound to get out sooner or later."

"How long ago was the affair?" What if Rex had slept with Melba to try to get his kid the grade he needed so he could get into Harvard?

"Years. But Rex didn't forget or forgive the trouble she caused."

It takes two to tango. I bit back my thought, because I needed more information. "Do you like Rex?"

"As well as I like anyone. He's a good businessman but can be a stingy bas—jerk."

"What about the other board members?"

"We are a darn good team. Made good things happen for the school district."

Mac was a regular Pollyanna. "Why would Anil murder Melba?"

"Beats me. The guy was all about tutoring teens and trying to get more money for the math and science departments. You just never know what'll make a guy snap."

I hoped that last statement wasn't drawn from personal experience. "What happened the night Anil and Melba got in a fight and the police were called?"

"I wasn't at the meeting that night, and no one's talking."

I sat in a booth at Belliginos just after seven o'clock, waiting for Ryne. A glass of Chianti and my phone were my only companions. I did a quick search for Sportzfan and various combinations of Sportzfan and numbers but came up empty. Then I did a quick search on Seth. A bunch of articles came up. Most of them were speculative, with no real answers about what had happened. My name came up in a couple. I hadn't been answering phone numbers I didn't recognize since that night.

A few reporters had left messages over and over, but I had ignored them.

Ryne slid into the booth, across from me. Just as he did, the restaurant lowered the lights. Jeez, I hoped he didn't think this was a date. However, from his slight frown, maybe he was thinking the exact same thing. That made me relax a little.

"So what's good here?" Ryne asked after the waiter brought us menus and Ryne a glass of Chianti.

"I've heard the lasagna is wonderful." I almost choked on my words. I didn't want lasagna. I was sick of it.

"The pizzas look good. Want to split one?"

Yes, yes, I did. I loved pizza, it was a food group to me, and I hadn't had one in at least a week. I realized I was nodding and stopped myself. "No. Thanks. I have my heart set on the lasagna." Maybe Ryne would like his pizza with too much meat or anchovies, so it wouldn't be so tempting.

Ryne had his head cocked to one side. God, he looked like a freaking Disney prince. All he needed was a steed and a cape to fling around. Maybe it was the lighting.

"What?" he asked.

"You're just too good looking. It's obnoxious." Chianti did that to me sometimes, made me say things I normally wouldn't.

"I apologize. I'll work on that." He said it with a jaunty grin that in no way was an apology.

"You must have women throwing themselves at you all the time. It's probably exhausting."

"I'm sure you've heard them beating on my door at all hours of the night. I may have to move."

I laughed.

A woman with gleaming long red hair approached us. She turned her back to me but slid something onto the table before sauntering off with a sultry backward glance.

Before Ryne reached for the piece of paper, I snatched it off the table. It was a business card with a number handwritten on the back and a note that said, *Call me.* Ryne just watched me, shaking his head.

"I swear this doesn't happen . . . often," he said.

"Yeah, right."

"Are you going to let me see it?"

"She's a massage therapist. I thought she looked like a professional, didn't you?" I flipped the card over to him.

"I have been a bit achy lately," Ryne said, rolling his shoulders.

"Me too. Ever since Friday night in the gym. Maybe I should call her. I bet she'd love that."

Ryne smiled.

The waiter distracted us by showing up and taking our orders. Lasagna for me, of course, and a *pizza bianca* with artichokes, peppers, onions, and kalamata olives for Ryne. I almost drooled just listening to his order. Even the waiter seemed a bit mesmerized by Ryne's deep green eyes and cleft chin. The guy ought to grow a beard to cover that thing up.

"How's your uncle doing?" I asked.

"Fair to middlin'. Won't listen to his doctor or me."

"Has anyone been back to try to sell you autographed sports items?"

"Is that the reason you asked me out for dinner? To grill me?"

"I wanted to thank you for your help last night with the mannequin situation."

"Situation? That's what you're calling it? It seemed like a threat to me."

"You have a lot of experience with threats?"

Ryne shrugged, which surprised me. Maybe his ailing uncle wasn't his only reason for moving here. "Do you have any news from the police about the mannequin?"

"No. But I haven't followed up." I repressed a shiver.

"It was a disturbing sight."

I nodded. *Chilling, frightening, warped.*

"I didn't answer your question, but it's no. No one's been by trying to sell us anything autographed or owned by a famous sports icon."

The waiter came by and set a stand for the pizza in the middle of the table. Seconds later he came back with the pizza, which smelled fantastic. "I'll be right back with your lasagna," he said with a wink. Apparently, he was an equal opportunity flirt.

He came back, carrying a plate with a piece of lasagna so beautiful, it looked like a sculpture with a little cheese oozing out, a dab of rich red sauce dripping down, and layers of noodles. Just as he lowered it toward me, another waiter ran up and whispered frantically in his ear. He looked at me, then up across the booths. I saw a man in a white chef coat, with his arms folded. I recognized him from the picture on the Belliginos' Web site. It was the owner/chef, and he was glaring in my direction. Tony from Billerica must have warned him I'd be around. I gripped the side of the plate of lasagna, which the waiter still held suspended over the table.

The waiter tried to pull the plate toward him. "I'm so sorry. There's a hair in it. Not up to our standards at all. I'll get you something else. How about a nice chicken marsala?"

"I don't see a hair. It's fine. I'm not a fan of marsala." I loved chicken marsala, but I wasn't going home without this piece of lasagna. Angelo was counting on me. I pulled the plate toward me in a bizarre game of tug-of-war. The plate was hot, but I wasn't about to let go. "I don't see a hair. Do you see one, Ryne?"

Ryne looked mystified. "Not really, but if our waiter says there's one, maybe there is."

The waiter rewarded him with a smile.

"You can share my pizza, Sarah," Ryne said.

"I want the lasagna. If there's a hair, it's probably mine."

"We can't be sure," the waiter said, glancing back and forth between the owner and me. "We can't risk it."

"How long will it take to get another one?" I didn't want to be here all night.

"We're out," the waiter said.

"This is an Italian restaurant. How can you be out of lasagna?"

The waiter looked panicked for a moment. "The, uh, supplier didn't bring any more lasagna noodles. We won't have them until tomorrow." He shrugged like he was trying to apologize as we both still gripped opposite sides of the plate.

I felt sorry for him but gave the plate a final tug, anyway. The waiter let go, and the lasagna went flying. Most of it landed on the table with a splat. Part of it landed next to me on the seat of the booth. I covertly covered the portion on the booth with my napkin. I looked up at the waiter with what I hoped was an innocent expression. "I'm sorry. I don't know what got into me."

"I'll clean the table up," the waiter said. "Would you like to order something else?"

I smiled. "It's okay. I'll just share the pizza."

Now Ryne looked surprised. He'd remained amazingly calm once again. It must be his superpower.

The waiter quickly cleaned off the table and brought me a plate. Ryne started to serve me a piece of pizza, but I covered my plate with my hand.

"I seem to have lost my appetite. It's my stomach. I'm really sorry." I used my napkin to pick up as much of the spilled lasagna as I could off the bench of the booth. I stuffed the whole thing in my purse, threw money on the table to cover dinner, and left.

Chapter 22

Fifteen minutes later at eight-fifteen I was knocking on the back door of DiNapoli's. Since they were still open, I couldn't very well hand them a napkin full of lasagna in front of a bunch of people. Angelo opened the door and motioned me in. Rosalie joined us. We huddled back by the bathrooms.

"I'm sorry I don't have very much," I said, keeping my voice low. I dug the napkin out of my purse and handed it over as I told them what happened. They both stared at me with their mouths open.

Angelo burst out laughing. He bent over and rested his hands on his thighs. When he stood back up, he had tears in his eyes from laughing so hard. He gasped in some air. "I'd have liked to have seen that," he managed to get out before another gale of laughter burst from him.

Rosalie was shaking her head. "No more, Angelo. You can't ask Sarah to do this."

"There's only one more restaurant," I said. "Tony

and the other restaurateurs are not going to scare me off. I'll figure out something. Maybe next time I'll wear a disguise."

Angelo carefully peeled back the layers of the napkin. We all stared down at the pitiful-looking mash of noodles, cheese, and sauce. Rosalie made a snorting noise; then she started laughing.

"I've never seen a lasagna look so awful in my entire life." She wiped at her eyes as she continued to laugh.

"It looked pretty when they brought it to the table. Like art," I said.

Angelo sniffed it. "Smells good. There's enough here to get an idea of what it tastes like." He frowned. "I've seen his Web site, with his fancy pictures of food, his lasagna included. But fancy looks don't mean it tastes good." When Angelo was upset like now, a long-gone Italian accent returned.

Rosalie swiped her pinkie through the sauce and tasted it. "It's good, Angelo."

Angelo frowned at her.

Rosalie patted his arm. "Yours is better, though. We need to get back to work." Rosalie grabbed my face and kissed both my cheeks. "You don't have to do this anymore."

But, oh, I did.

I'd changed out of my dress into a pair of shorts and a T-shirt before I went over to the Ellington Bowlarama to find Rex Sullivan at nine. I spotted him over on the candlepin bowling side of the building. The bowling alley had both the better-known tenpin games and candlepin, which was popular in New England but hardly anyplace else. I hadn't even heard of it until CJ and I moved here. I pushed thoughts of CJ to one side as I headed over to Rex.

I'd taken two steps when the lights went off, a siren wailed, strobe lights started flashing, and laser lights shot around. *Ugh.* Cosmic bowling night. Kids loved it. CJ and I had brought Carol's kids one night so she and Brad could go out on a date without paying for a babysitter. I'd vowed never to go again, yet here I was.

I walked a few more steps. The lights made me feel drunk, and I smacked right into someone. I apologized before moving on more cautiously. It was easy to spot Rex's team because they all had loud Hawaiian-print shirts with the Sullivan Luxury Car Sales logo on them. Rex was standing at the top of a lane, ball in hand, when I arrived. Candlepin balls were smaller than tenpin balls and didn't have any holes to put your fingers in. They also weighed a lot less, at just over two pounds.

Rex unleashed the ball down the lane. It flew along. Strength and speed were even more important in candlepin than in tenpin. The ball crashed into the pins. He knocked six of the ten pins over. Four fell out of the way, and two lay in front of the remaining pins. Unlike in tenpin, nothing picked up the pins that remained standing or swept away the ones that had fallen over.

Loud rock music blared as the strobe lights went off and disco lights came on. Rex would have three tries before it was the next person's turn. I waited to approach him until he had finished and high-fived his teammates. He took a swig from a glass that looked like it held bourbon. As he swallowed, he spotted me and waved me over.

"I heard you were at the dealership today." He almost had to yell in my ear for me to hear him. I inhaled again, hoping and worrying that he'd smell like the aftershave of the person who had attacked me. But again, all I smelled was bourbon. So far, of all the school board members, he seemed to have the most reason to want Melba out of the picture. "Let's go to the bar so we can talk."

I nodded.

Rex clasped one of his teammates on the shoulder, bent down, and spoke in his ear. The teammate glanced at me before nodding. I followed Rex to the bar and was relieved when the door closed behind us and the music became a dull background thumping. The lighting was dim in here, but at least none of it was flashing. We settled at a table after Rex ordered another bourbon, a double, and I ordered a gin and tonic.

"I heard you did a test-drive today." Rex swirled the bourbon in his glass, then glanced up at me.

Rex was a handsome man. His azure eyes were intense; his mouth was full and sensual. His silver-streaked black hair looked a little too perfect. I could see how a woman could fall for him. But I also noticed that age had left his face a little saggy and his eyes a bit bloodshot.

I smiled. "I did. It's an amazing car." I didn't want to get Tim, the salesman who took me, in trouble, so I felt like I had to choose my words carefully. Besides, I wasn't here to talk about cars. "I put it on my wish list." Unless a genie came along, that was where the car would always remain. I needed to get back on topic before he was called back to bowl. There were so many things I couldn't ask Rex: Did you have an affair with Melba? Did she keep your son from getting into Harvard? Were you trying to oust Melba?

I decided to play dumb. Men often expected blondes to be dumb, anyway, and lots of people didn't think running garage sales could even be a job. "Why do you think Anil did it?" I twirled a piece of my hair as I asked.

Rex tossed back the rest of his bourbon and twirled a finger at the bartender, indicating he wanted another. "To silence her."

I jerked my head up. "About what?"

"No idea. But why else would he do it?"

"Were they having an affair?" I really wanted to see Rex's reaction to that statement.

"With Melba?" He threw back his head and laughed.

Did that mean everything Mac had told me was a lie? Because this didn't seem like the reaction of a man who'd had an affair with Melba.

"I heard they were close."

"Not that kind of close, as far as I knew. Anil was a lot of things, but he seemed devoted to his wife and family." Rex didn't look at me when he said it. Guilt that he hadn't been?

"I heard that Anil got into some kind of argument with Melba and was almost arrested. What was that about?" I asked.

"Mac always calls it the night that Anil went nuts. Usually, Anil is cooler than a spring day. Nothing ruffles him. We were all shaken to see Anil had a violent streak."

"Violent? Did he hurt anyone?"

"Naw. I held him back. Not that I really think he intended to hit Melba."

"What happened that night to make him act that way?"

"It's just board business. People want different things and have different ways of trying to get them." He shook his head. "No one suspected it would end the way it did with Melba dead."

The more people refused to say what caused the altercation, the more curious I became. I didn't know about it when I talked to Betty or Nancy. Maybe one of them would give me more information. The bartender arrived with two more drinks. I hadn't touched my first one yet. Rex's eyes got misty, and he raised his glass. So I grabbed mine and raised it, too.

"Here's to Melba. A wise woman and good friend," he said.

We clinked our glasses.

"You knew her a long time?"

"Since high school."

"What was she like?"

"Not that different than she was as an adult. Studious, smart, loved kids."

"She didn't ever get married or have her own children?"

"No. She was focused, determined to go to Harvard, and she got in. Graduated with honors. Never heard her mention wanting to have a family."

Did something flicker in his eyes when he said "Harvard," or was it just the aftereffects of the strobe lights from earlier?

I couldn't figure Rex out. His side of the story seemed so different than Mac's. He certainly didn't seem to want any harm to come to her. The door to the bar opened. One of Rex's teammates stuck his head in.

"Rex, come on. We need you."

Rex stood and threw some money down on the table. "Stay and enjoy your drinks."

I took a sip of my gin and tonic as I watched Rex walk out. Strut was more like it. He walked with the confidence of a man who knew what he wanted and had it. He certainly supported the town. But did he resent that when he needed the town's support or at least Melba's, he didn't get it?

The night air was still warm when I walked out of the bowling alley a few minutes later. Cars glinted in the moonlight. All the cars except mine, because it wasn't where I'd left it. I walked around the parking lot, stunned. I thought I'd parked it by an old oak tree, but now a little blue Smart car sat in that space. I turned a full circle. The Suburban was big and easy to spot. It simply wasn't there. Someone had stolen my car.

Chapter 23

Fifteen minutes later I stood beside Pellner on the sidewalk outside of the bowling alley.

"How long were you in the bowling alley?" he asked.

"An hour, tops." I drummed my fisted hand against my thigh.

"You're sure you didn't leave the keys in it?"

What difference would that make anyway? You weren't allowed to take someone else's car even if the keys were in it. A fact the police had made painfully clear to me last winter in a snowstorm. But rather than be snarky, I dug through my purse, pulled my keys out, and dangled them in front of Pellner. "They're right here."

"Did you have a key hidden in the car someplace?"

Last night Pellner had asked me almost the exact same question about my apartment. "No. CJ would have blown a gasket if I'd done that. I know better." Even though CJ was no longer around, his influence certainly was. You didn't get over twenty years of marriage in six weeks.

"And you're sure you drove over here?"

"Oh, for goodness' sakes. Of course I drove over here. I'm not some loony tune wandering around town."

"You didn't loan it to someone?"

"No. Pellner, someone took it." My voice had grown increasingly loud.

"Do you have an extra set of keys at home?"

"Yes. Of course," I said.

Pellner and I stared at each other. Someone had been in my apartment last night. I hadn't noticed anything was missing, but I kept an extra set of keys in a junk drawer in the kitchen. I could have easily not noticed they were gone. A small crowd had gathered around us. Apparently, a stolen car was more exciting than cosmic bowling.

Rex Sullivan pushed through the crowd. "I heard someone stole your car."

Pellner and I both nodded.

"How are you going to get home?" Rex asked.

I looked at Pellner. "Will you give me a ride?"

Before he could answer, Rex spoke up. "How about I give you a ride back to my house? I have a loaner there that I let my customers use." He winked. "I've got plenty of cars."

I looked at Pellner, then back at Rex, astounded by his generosity. "Thank you."

"You can just keep it until you work out a new car

or they find yours," Rex said. "I'll go in and grab my gear while you finish up."

"I'm going to go in and see if they have any security cameras that cover the parking lot," Pellner said.

"I'll wait out here." The last thing I wanted to do was go back in the noisy bowling alley.

"You can take off whenever Rex is ready. I'll let you know what, if anything, I find."

"Thank you." I wondered what kind of car Rex drove. I'd seen lots of Mercedes, Lexus, and Jaguars sitting on his lot when I stopped by. A little thrill ran through me. It would be fun to drive a luxury car, even if it was only for a few days.

"Ready to go?" Rex asked when he came back out. He pointed down the lot toward a red BMW. What a beauty. We climbed in. The seat seemed to hug me. He shifted into reverse, backed out of the space, and shifted into drive. Soon we were sailing down Great Road.

Ten minutes later Rex pulled up in front of a newish-looking McMansion. It sprawled across a massive lawn like a fortress. But no lights shined in the windows, and it looked a little sad. There was a low-slung yellow sports car in the drive. I felt a little nervous as I walked toward it. What if I damaged it? But Rex walked right on by and stopped at an old pickup truck. It might have been green at one time, but now it was more rust than anything.

He patted the backend. "Hop in."

What the heck? My dream of driving a sports car

poofed away. Why was he loaning this when he had access to all those amazing cars? *Be grateful.* I went around to the driver's side and tried to open the door.

"Throw some muscle into it," Rex hollered over the top of the truck. "It's a little cranky sometimes."

I finally managed to wrench the door open, promising myself I'd conceal my disappointment.

"Watch out for the spring in the middle of the seat."

It was a bench seat that might have been leather at some point. A spring had burst through the very center of the seat.

"This was my dad's," Rex said. "I got it when he passed a year ago. It's better than anything I've got on the lot. Just got a new engine in it. The bodywork is next." Rex handed me the keys.

"Thanks so much," I said. "I'll get it back to you as soon as I can."

"No rush." As he walked up to his front door, security lights popped on. He waved while I stood looking at my new ride. In some ways this pickup truck might be more precious to him than the fancy cars on his lot. Rex's actions seemed to be so opposite of what Mac had told me about him.

"I'll take good care of you," I told the pickup as I climbed in.

It was hot in my apartment, but at least it was mannequin- and Mike Titone-free. Pellner had sent me a text saying that the bowling alley didn't have security cameras pointed at the parking lot. He'd let the surrounding communities know my car had been stolen. What the text didn't say, but I knew, was that it could be in pieces in a chop shop by now. There'd been some problems in Ellington with stolen cars last winter.

Something thumped against my door. I went over and cautiously peered out the peephole. The peephole was getting more use than I'd ever imagined it would. Stella stood there, hands full of scotch and wine, using her hip to knock again. I unlocked the door.

She held up the bottles. "Awesome called me and told me about your car. Which works better?"

I wasn't a big fan of scotch, but the burn it gave was tempting. "I'll take the wine. Come in."

I grabbed glasses, and we sat on opposite ends of my couch. I poured wine for me and scotch for Stella. I handed Stella her glass and noticed her deep green eyes looked serious. They reminded me of olives, while Rync's green eyes reminded me of emeralds.

"It's been a rough few days, on top of CJ leaving. Attacked, you found Melba, stuff stolen from the swap, saved Seth, the mannequin, and now your car's been stolen," Stella said.

"You forgot that we tried to follow a suspect." She didn't know about my encounters with Mike.

"How are you going to get around?"

"Rex Sullivan loaned me his old truck."

Her eyes widened. "He did? Oh. Well, uh, Rex can be very generous."

"But?"

"It's usually when he wants something."

"What could he possibly want from me?"

"I don't know. What do you think he'd want from you?" She waggled her eyebrows. "Maybe he sees you as a lonely divorcée."

"Oh, ugh. No." I shuddered. "I can think of something more important that he'd want from me."

Stella perked up. "What?"

"For me to believe him. That he's a good guy who didn't have anything to do with Melba's death."

"Do you?"

"I'm not sure, but I can't be bought."

"Or at least it's going to take more than a rusty old truck, right?"

I laughed. "Absolutely."

Stella took a slug of her scotch. "What's going on with you and lasagna?"

Uh-oh. "I have no idea what you are talking about."

"Yeah, right. I've been talking to people. First, you take Carol for lasagna. Then me, and tonight Ryne. Only, you didn't get any with Ryne, fought the waiter for a piece, and then left." She bolted up and whirled toward me. "The lasagna bake-off. Angelo put you up to something."

Unfortunately, Stella was good at observing and putting things together. "He might have asked me to check out the competition. You can't tell anyone."

Stella grinned. “I’m in. Where are you going next?”

“It’s a new place in Bedford. Lucina’s. But I think Tony—the guy from Billerica—warned all the other entrants in the bake-off that I was checking out the competition. He threatened to, and the incident last night at Belliginos was crazy.” I tapped my fingers against my leg. “I’m going to have to go incognito. Tony must have passed around my picture with his warning.”

Stella grinned a very wicked grin.

“What?”

“Just let me take care of our disguises. Berklee has an amazing costume department.”

“You’re going with me?”

“Did you really think I’d let you go alone?”

“Awesome wouldn’t like it if something goes horribly awry.”

“We date. He doesn’t run my life.”

“You’re sure?”

“Absolutely.”

After Stella left, I did another search for Sportzfan. Nothing. I followed that up with a search for the stolen items. There were a couple of possibilities, so I sent messages and made arrangements to meet a couple of people in the morning. Another knock on my door interrupted my search.

A glance through the peephole told me it was Ryne who stood out in the hall. I rested my head on the door for a minute. I felt bad that I'd made an excuse and left him at the restaurant, so I opened the door.

"How are you feeling?" Ryne walked in with a bag from Belliginos in his hand.

"Better. Sorry about disappearing."

"I brought you lasagna."

I didn't know whether to hug him or throw up. "Thank you. I thought they were out."

"I was able to get some after you left." He studied my face. "You know you're a little strange."

"Yeah. It's a lot of work, but I manage." Ryne handed me the bag. I noticed some red hairs on his dark shirt. "Looks like the lasagna isn't the only thing that reappeared after I left."

Ryne looked as his shirt and shrugged. "She isn't good at taking no for an answer."

"Oh, poor you."

Ryne spread his hands out. "It's a curse."

"Again, poor you."

"But she did order the lasagna for me. Otherwise, I wouldn't have any for you."

"Well, I guess I owe her, then."

"I'll take care of it for you."

I laughed and pushed him out the door. Everything had caught up with me, and I need to sleep. "Good night."

I put the lasagna in the refrigerator to take to DiNapoli's tomorrow. Ryne was turning out to be a good neighbor and friend. But that was all he'd ever be. I climbed on top of my bed. I didn't even bother to fold down my blue-and-white comforter.

Too hot to crawl under the covers and too tired to undress.

I could hear Ryne's voice through the wall and wondered if he was on the phone or if he'd brought the redhead home with him. Sometimes alone could be very lonely. I thought about CJ. I'd moved so many times for him, but he wasn't willing to stay in one place for me. I realized CJ didn't love me enough anymore. I'd made all those changes for him and loved doing it. He couldn't or wouldn't support me in the same way when I needed him to. But in this moment I wasn't angry or resentful. Maybe I'd finally moved on.

Chapter 24

Thursday morning a call from Pellner woke me up at eight. "Your car's been found."

"That's great news." I'd been worrying about having to replace it. "Is it in one piece?" I listened for an answer. "Pellner?" I looked at my phone to see if the call had been disconnected. It hadn't.

"It is."

"So what's going on?"

"Maybe you should come take a look."

Oh, boy. That didn't sound good. "Okay. Where are you?"

"The conservancy land down by the Concord River."

Ten minutes later I was driving Rex's truck across town. One of the perks of sleeping in your clothes was that it didn't take long to get ready to go somewhere. The sky was a cloudless blue; the humidity was heavy in the air, even this early in the day. I discovered the truck didn't have air-conditioning, so I had the windows rolled down. I turned down the road to the conservancy land and could see my Suburban and a couple of police cars in the distance. I bumped onto the gravel road leading to where they were.

Maybe the car was stuck and I was going to have to pay to have it towed. Although paying a tow truck would cost a lot less than buying a new car. Pellner had been so weird on the phone. Scenarios started going through my head. Oh, no. I slammed on the brakes. Dust from the road swirled up around me, and I coughed. I pictured the interior all slashed up. I could handle that. But why wouldn't Pellner just say that? I tried to push aside the thought that kept rearing up. The one saying there must be someone dead in the car. I let off the brake and crept forward, wanting and not wanting to know. But there didn't seem to be any crime-scene people out here, so I sped up a little.

Pellner walked out onto the road to meet me when I stopped. I slid out of the truck.

"What the heck are you driving?" Pellner asked.

"A loaner from Rex."

"All the luxury cars and that's the loaner you get?"

"Beggars can't be choosers. And it runs just fine." I sounded a little defensive. After all, it was Rex's favorite truck.

"It doesn't look very safe." He frowned. "But it has a current inspection sticker."

"What's going on?" I asked, pointing at my Suburban, which did look stuck in the swampy land.

Pellner gestured for me to follow him.

"Please tell me there's no dead body in it."

"No one that's never been alive is dead."

I trotted after him, mystified. The driver's side door was open, so I looked in. A mannequin leaned again the front passenger door, with a ski pole through its chest. Fury gripped me with a choke hold. I wanted to grab that thing, toss it on the ground, and stomp on it. Then take the pole and beat the person who was doing this. I must have taken a step forward, because Pellner grabbed my arm and held me back.

"Who's doing this? Why? What have I possibly done to someone to make them do this to me?"

"That's what I was going to ask you. Who've you pissed off lately?"

I'd talked to Nancy, Betty, Mac, and Rex yesterday. Oh, and Tim, who'd let me take the Porsche out. That covered it. No it didn't. I'd also talked to Mike, the lady with the fake signed jerseys, and the Longs when I'd been at their house working on the garage sale. And of course I'd been in a couple of Italian restaurants. Stella and Ryne. I'd talked to them, too.

"Yeah, that's what I thought. It's a long list," Pellner said when I didn't answer his question.

"Maybe it's a mistake. It's not the only white Suburban in town. Maybe you have a serial mannequin killer in town."

"Don't you think it's kind of a big coincidence that they left one in your apartment and one in your car? Face it. This is personal. So why don't you just spill what you've been up to."

I threw my hands up in the air. "Nothing important."

A sleek silver car came jouncing down the road. "Who'd you call?" Pellner and I said to each other almost in unison.

"No one," I said.

"It's not the crime-scene techs," Pellner said.

"Crime scene? It's not a dead person. Can't we just forget this and let me get my car back?"

"It's an attack on you. Chuck would never forgive me if I didn't follow up."

Chuck was what the police personnel had called CJ. "What does CJ have to do with this?"

Pellner hooked a thumb through his belt. "Plus, the car was stolen. They need to dust for fingerprints."

The car stopped a few feet away from us. Pellner and I watched as Seth eased himself out of the front passenger seat. He wore a white long-sleeved button-down shirt and dark pants. His left arm was immobilized in a sling, probably so his shoulder could heal. Nichole climbed out of the driver's seat. She didn't look happy, but then neither did Seth.

I tried to remember if I'd brushed my teeth or hair before I'd left the house. He walked over to us.

"I was at the office, catching up, and heard they found your car." His face was paler and thinner. But is was good to see him moving around even though it looked like it took a lot of effort.

Seth moved toward the Suburban, with Pellner

by his side. Nichole stayed put, and so did I. They talked in low voices. When Seth looked into the car and saw the mannequin, he balled his right hand into a fist. After a couple of minutes, he turned around and walked back over to me.

"A word?" he asked me.

I nodded.

He pointed over to a tree down the road a little bit. An iron bench with a curlicue back sat under it. Neither of us spoke until we were seated on the bench. It was slightly cooler here, but sweat beaded on Seth's forehead. I waited to hear what he had to say. Cicadas buzzed, adding a low background noise.

"First, I want to thank you for pulling me out of my house during the fire."

"You're welcome. How are you feeling?" That sounded professional. I gave myself a mental pat on the back.

"Better. Each day."

"And how about your house?" I really didn't want to talk about the mannequin.

"It's almost ready for me to move back into."

"That was fast," I said.

"The damage was contained to the kitchen."

I looked toward the silver car, where Nichole was tapping furiously into her phone. "Are you going to move back?"

"Of course. Staying at my parents' is temporary. The commute is a killer." He winced a little at the word *killer*.

"Why did someone try to kill you?"

Seth looked startled. His answer was a head shake.

"Do you remember anything that happened? Who attacked you?" I looked at my Suburban. "Does this have anything to do with Mike Titone? I know you have some connection to him. What is it?"

Seth's jaw set. He didn't look like he wanted to answer any of my questions. He stood. "Thanks again. And for getting hold of Nichole that night so my family knew what had happened before it hit the news." He turned and walked away from me.

Nichole hurried around and opened the car door for him. Wasn't that sweet? I waited until Nichole had backed the car around before I headed back to Rex's truck. I climbed in and slammed the door a little harder than I should have.

"Sorry," I told the truck.

Pellner came up to the window.

"Please call me when I can get my car back," I said.

I thought back over my conversation with Seth as I drove off. What had I said that made him leave so quickly? It must have been my question about Mike. Maybe Mike had ordered a hit on Seth. One that had failed. But in the past it had almost seemed like they were friends. I didn't even have an idea on how to dig any further. Something else had been bothering me about that day. The timing of the fire and my arrival. I worried that something I'd done had brought this on Seth. But I had no idea what that possibly could have been. It wasn't until I was almost home that I realized that the first thing Seth had wanted to say was thank you. I wondered what the second thing was and why the mention of

Mike Titone was so upsetting that he left without saying it.

I showered, blew my hair dry, and put some makeup on when I got home at ten. I threw on a yellow sundress with a full skirt and walked over to see Carol at Paint and Wine. She'd asked me to stop by and see her new classes, and I hadn't made it yet. Her summer camp class was wrapping up as I got there. Fifteen elementary-aged kids all had painted pictures of koala bears, and everyone wanted me to see theirs.

Carol's hair was pulled back in a low ponytail. Her jeans and stylish top were paint free, which seemed incredible to me. How did she manage that while working with all these kids? A little boy grabbed my hand and tugged me over to his painting. After I complimented his painting, I went from one to the other. The kids had varying degrees of talent, but each painting looked like a koala bear. Even more important, the kids all looked happy. Parents started coming in and picking up their jabbering kids. It was such a happy sight after the past few days.

Betty Jenkins from the school board walked in.

"Betty," I said. "What are you doing here?" This was what I loved about living in Ellington. There was always someone I knew near at hand.

"I'm picking up my granddaughter." She pointed at a little blond girl. "We are going to the pool and then out to lunch." Her granddaughter was over helping Carol wash out paintbrushes.

"I have a question for you," I said.

"Shoot."

"It's about the night that Anil and Melba got in the fight."

"Oh, dear, that was awful."

"Do you know what happened?"

"I went to the bathroom. When I got out to the parking lot, Melba and Anil were shouting at each other." She put her hand to her throat. "Rex and Mac had to restrain them."

Mac? Mac had told me he wasn't there. "Did you hear anything? Do you know what they were fighting about?"

"Rex told me it was just the continuing disagreement about the budget. But I'm not sure."

"Why not?"

"Because as I came out, Anil was yelling something about last summer. Mac was telling him to shut up."

Betty's granddaughter ran up to her. "Ready to go, Grandma?"

Betty took her granddaughter's hand. "You bet I am." She turned to me. "If I think of anything else, I'll let you know."

Carol walked over to me. I started helping her straighten up. "What was that all about?" she asked.

"I'm not sure. But someone is covering up something about Melba's murder. I think Anil was right when he told me he was being framed."

"You need to tell the police."

"I will." When I had enough information, instead of just my gut telling me something was wrong. What did last summer possibly have to do with the budget?

"Something else on your mind?" Carol asked.

"Your kids are in the Ellington school system?"

"Why, yes, they are." Carol smiled to soften her words.

"What do you think of it overall?"

"Overall, we're very happy. That's one of the reasons we decided to stay here."

"Did you ever hear any scuttlebutt about the board or Melba?"

"Yeesh. Of course I did. This is a small town, after all. But nothing about murdering someone." She said the word *murdering* with an evil voice and rubbed her hands together.

I laughed. "Don't give up your day job," I said. "What did you hear?"

"Nothing that would lead to Melba being murdered. Sorry."

"Yeah, it's never that easy."

"Actually, a lot of parents were really happy about all the money for the new sports equipment. Everyone is so conscious about concussions now. Which reminds me. Have you talked to Laura? How's Brody?"

"I need to call her. Let me know if you hear anything, okay?"

"Will do."

Chapter 25

My next two attempts at finding the stolen merchandise from the swap were a complete failure. No Mike. Both of the people selling their items were completely legit. In fact, one met me at a police station in Lexington, which was now a safe zone for people who were buying and selling online. So I was now the proud owner of a signed Patriots jersey and a Bruins hockey stick. I had put them up for sale on my virtual garage sale and hoped I could recoup my costs.

After a quick stop home for lunch, I walked over to city hall to see Nancy Elder. The walk was only a few blocks, and the less I had to use Rex's truck, the better. Fortunately, Nancy was in her office.

"I'm leaving in two minutes," she said. She was standing behind her desk, in a red power suit, gathering papers.

"You look nice," I said.

"I'm giving a speech to the Middlesex County League of Women Voters."

"That's great." Maybe she was taking steps to make her move to bigger and better things.

"Have you resolved the situation we discussed?" she asked.

"Not yet. But I'm working on it."

"Then what are you doing here?" She stuffed the papers in a brown leather briefcase.

"I want access to the complete school budget for the past couple of years and all the minutes of the school board meetings."

"Okay. I'm guessing you're here, instead of at the superintendent's office, so no one knows."

"Exactly."

"I'll let you use my office and computer. I'll tell my assistant that you are working on the garage sale for next fall and aren't to be disturbed. When you're done, sign out. And no snooping where you aren't supposed to. I'll have a record of everything you look at."

"Fine." What did she think I planned to do? "Do you have access to their listserv?"

"I do. They loop me in on some things. I'll sign in for you." Nancy's beautifully manicured fingers flew over her keyboard. "I've pulled up two files. The budget and the minutes and signed you into the listserv. I hope this will help you find answers." Nancy picked up her briefcase and headed to the door.

"Kick butt at the meeting."

Nancy paused at the door and smiled at me. "Thank you. I will."

I closed the door after she left, and settled into her comfy leather chair. I opened the first file. Since I wasn't really a numbers girl, I hoped I could make sense of all of it. I didn't even know what I was looking for.

Thirty minutes later my eyes were almost glazed over and I had only finished the first document, the budget from two years ago. I'd concentrated mostly on items relating to the arts and sports, since that was where the recent disagreements seemed to stem from. I decided to switch to the minutes of the board meetings before tackling the next budget. While all of this was public record, I was hoping subcommittee meetings or other documents that were not so readily available might be here.

I read through the listserv between the board members. There had been a flurry of contentious e-mails last spring, that ended in June. I checked the minutes of the July meeting. A line said that the board had agreed to buy new sports equipment across a broad spectrum of sports. Everyone but Anil had voted for the purchase. I wondered why Betty had agreed, because in the e-mail loop, she was pro arts, too.

I went back to the expense reports for the spring and summer of last year. In August there was a bump in the expenses for sports equipment, but it wasn't that big, considering all the things they had agreed to buy. I checked the next several months to see if they'd spread the payments over several months, but the numbers dropped back to the prepurchase amount for September through December.

I leaned back in the chair and swiveled it around to stare out the window. Down the street I could see the police department building and the library. Maybe none of this meant anything and I was wasting my time, or maybe citizens had done fund-raising, like they had for the Astroturf football field. If they had, I'd missed seeing it in the paper—I had been incredibly busy building my business last summer. I swiveled back around to look at a couple more documents.

After I signed out, I thanked Nancy's assistant and started my walk home. Rex bought tons of sports equipment for local teams. Maybe he had some source that kept costs down. I'd check with him when I took his truck back.

Ryne called at one-thirty, when I was almost back home. "The kid's here that came in the other day. If you want to come get a look at him."

"I do. Can you stall him while I drive over there?"

"I'll do my best, but he seems a little antsy. It doesn't look like he has any of the stuff that was stolen from your swap, but maybe he's here on a fishing expedition to see how lax we are about provenance."

"Haggle," I said.

"I know how to do that."

"Duh. After the way you took me at that last sale, I know you drive a hard bargain."

"Just get here as fast as you can. I've got to go, or the kid will get suspicious."

It took me twenty minutes to get there, and by the time I walked in the store, the kid had left.

"Sorry. I did my best. We *haggled.*" Ryne looked at me to make sure the word sank in. I motioned with my finger for him to go on. "I told him I wanted to take a few pictures and show them to my uncle. That my uncle made the final decisions about what we bought." Ryne shook his head. "It must have spooked him. He said there were plenty of places that would take his merchandise. Then he scooped it up and sailed out of here."

"Oh," was all I could manage.

"But I did get a picture of the kid." Ryne opened his phone, found the picture, and handed his phone to me.

The picture was a little blurry because of the low lighting in here. But the boy looked familiar.

"Will you text that to me?" My phone binged when the picture arrived seconds later. "Thanks for trying."

I flopped on my couch when I got home. I realized I hadn't talked to Lance yet about Melba's murder. He ran some kind of business, but I couldn't remember exactly what he did. I opened his bio on the school board site. It said he was a local businessman, but didn't go into the specifics. I did a Google search. Lance had his fingers in a lot of local pies. He had invested in a local restaurant, had been the booster club president for years, had helped develop a new housing area to the north of town that included some low-income housing, and seemed to belong to every local organization there was.

Lance had also had some failures. He'd tried to open an ice cream stand, but the competition from well-established Bedford Farms to the east and Kimball Farm in Carlisle to the west had sunk that project. He and Kelly had opened a gymnastics place, but it had closed after two years. Various other businesses were mentioned, too. Although maybe that didn't mean the businesses had failed, but that he had just been trying to find a passion. I knew people in the military who had switched from one career field to another, hoping to find the perfect fit. I couldn't find a business address for him, so I decided to swing by their house. Maybe he worked from home.

I rang the doorbell at the Longs' house. One of their blond sons answered and recognized me. I asked for Lance.

"Just a minute. I'll get him."

"Wait. Do you and your friends ever have time for some extra projects? Sometimes I need help at the garage sales I run." Maybe this was a way to get in touch with the kid who was selling the sports items.

Lance's son grinned. "We're always looking for a way to make a buck."

I gave him my number. "Will you text me the

names and numbers of kids who might be willing to help?"

"Sure thing."

"Sarah. What are you doing here?" Kelly walked toward me from the back of the house. She was in another tennis dress but was coiffed to the nines, so either she hadn't played yet or she just liked to run around in tennis clothes.

"I wanted to see Lance. I need to follow up on the equipment swap with someone and wasn't sure who to talk to." I wasn't sure where that came from, but it sounded better than saying Nancy Elder had asked me to interview possible suspects.

Kelly looked suspicious for a moment. But it was fleeting. "Have a seat in the living room and I'll get him, if he's free."

The living room had a massive stone fireplace, comfy chairs, and book-lined walls. Books that looked loved and read. A beautiful art deco bar had been set up in one corner, with vintage shakers, martini glasses, and a large selection of alcohol. I had always thought Kelly would be the kind to have a designer house, but every room I'd been in looked well used and comfortable. It gave me a warm, homey feeling.

Lance walked in a couple of minutes later. "Sarah, it's good to see you. What can I do for you?"

"I just wanted to follow up with someone about the equipment swap."

"Even with the unfortunate incidents, you did a great job. Have a seat," Lance said as he gestured to the couch.

I plunked down on one end. Lance sat across from me in a cushy chair. "I'm so sorry that things were stolen. It's so disheartening, when the money from their sale would have helped the local school kids."

"But you kept out some of the most expensive items. We had good numbers, even with those that were stolen," Lance said.

"I'm so glad to hear that." I paused trying to decide what to say next. "And then there's Melba."

"Finding her must have been awful for you."

"It was."

"Everyone appreciates how you emptied the gym so none of the kids present would know what had happened."

"It was instinct."

"Well, you certainly have good ones."

"What do you think about Anil's arrest?" I asked.

"I'm shocked, of course."

He didn't look that shocked, but maybe enough time had passed that any shock value had worn off. "I heard he had a huge fight with Melba. What was that about?"

Lance stood so I did too.

Darn it. No one wanted to talk about that fight.

"The budget," he said.

"I thought I read that they were usually in agreement with each other."

"Until recently, that was true."

"What changed?" I asked.

"Anil. But I never thought he'd murder her."

"So you think he did it?"

Lance looked surprised. "Of course. He was arrested. The police can't have just made up charges."

No. But evidence could have been planted if someone was planning on murdering Melba all along. "Do you know who benefits from her death? Financially?"

"I'm not really sure, but I heard rumors that she left everything to the school system. And that part of the money would fund scholarships for women to attend college."

Kelly came back in. "Lance, honey. You have a phone call."

We walked back into the foyer. Kelly opened the door as Lance trotted upstairs. I stepped out.

"I heard you asking Lance about Melba. This is a difficult time for him. For us. We've known Melba a long time, as a classmate, a teacher to our children, and now as superintendent. Please choose your questions wisely." She shut the door gently right in my face.

I sighed. What did I expect? I sat in Rex's truck, trying to regroup. Mac had lied. Maybe it was time to find out why.

Chapter 26

I stood in the doorway of Mac's office at his grocery store a little after three. He sat behind his desk.

"You can come all the way in and have a seat, you know." Mac gestured to the rickety-looking chair I'd sat in last time.

"I'm good."

"What da ya think? I killed Melba? And so you're afraid to come in?" He chuckled but stopped abruptly. "You do think that, don't you? I didn't. I'm not the one in jail."

"You lied to me."

"About what?" Mac asked.

"You said you weren't there the night of the fight between Melba and Anil. I heard otherwise."

Mac rubbed a meaty paw over his butcher's apron. "Oh, that. Telling a lie doesn't make me a killer."

It didn't take him off my list either. "So what's the real story?"

"Those folks could all be so dramatic. I try to stay

out of that kind of stuff. I have three ex-wives and five daughters. I got enough drama in my life."

"What were they fighting about?"

"Nothing important. Something that happened last summer."

"Please be more specific."

Mac stood up. "It wasn't anything that got Melba killed."

"Why won't anyone talk about it if something important didn't happen that night? Everyone keeps mentioning the budget but won't say anything else," I said.

"Anil went ballistic over the sports equipment purchase. I guess he resented it more than anyone thought, since he killed Melba." He took off his butcher's apron and hung it on a wobbly coat-tree behind him. "Anil killed her, not me. Not anyone else." He smoothed down his brown plaid shirt. "I can walk you out."

Out in the parking lot, Mac stopped and looked around. "Rex must be here."

"Why do you think that?"

"His truck is right over there." Mac pointed to my loaner.

"He very generously loaned me the truck since my Suburban was stolen."

Mac guffawed. "Rex pawned that old thing off on you?"

"Yes, but it's very special to him."

"Did you fall for that story? He's so cheap that he came up with that so his customers wouldn't feel cheated and he didn't have to risk loaning one of his good cars if a customer needed one."

And here I'd been so worried about something happening to the truck. Why anyone thought I could solve a murder when I was that naive was beyond me.

After my conversations with Lance and Mac, I went home. I needed to get the lasagna Ryne had dropped off over to DiNapoli's without anyone knowing what it really was. I grabbed a gift bag and tissue paper out of a stash in my hall closet. I placed the lasagna in the bottom of the bag, added tissue paper, stuck in a bar of handmade soap someone had given me, just in case people were around when the DiNapolis opened the bag, and set out.

The sun beat down on my shoulders as I walked. Maybe I was all wrong about the school board members and needed to refocus on who had stolen the swap items. Mike and Seth were still up to something I didn't understand. Neither of them wanted me to, but I felt like it was somehow connected to the sports equipment swap and maybe even Melba's death. And what the heck had Mike Titone been doing, buying sports stuff on the Web? He had a seemingly successful business. Nothing sports oriented had hung in his store. His black SUV didn't have any team logos on it, like so many cars in this area did. I knew Mike was a big runner. I didn't know that much else about him. The thing that really got my mind racing was it didn't seem very

Mob-like. Unless this had something to do with what was up between him and Seth.

At 3:45 I pushed open the door to DiNapoli's. A few people sat at scattered tables, but no one was at the counter, ordering. Betty Jenkins was at a table with her granddaughter. They were laughing and didn't notice me come in. I handed the bag to Rosalie.

"This is a gift for you. And Angelo." I raised my eyebrows, hoping she'd get the message.

"Oh, you shouldn't have," Rosalie said. She leaned in. "Really, you shouldn't have."

"But you've both done so much for me."

Rosalie patted my hand. The door opened behind me as another customer came in. I decided to say hello to Betty before I left.

"Do you want to join us?" Betty asked when I stopped at their table.

"No thanks. I just stopped to say hello. It looks like you two are having fun."

"We are," Betty said. "She's the last little one in the family. The rest of them are all teenagers. Great kids, but always on the run."

"Are you going to paint another picture tomorrow?" I asked the little girl. She had white-blond hair and big dark eyes.

"Yes. Of a rabbit."

"Oh. I like rabbits."

"So do I. But Grandma doesn't, because they eat her lettuce."

We all laughed. I waved good-bye and walked back home. My thoughts turned back to the stolen sports items. I was borderline obsessed with them. But I felt like they were going to lead me to whoever had murdered Melba.

If Seth had asked Mike to buy stuff, he'd probably do it, but why? *Whoa,* maybe I was going about this all wrong. Maybe I should try selling things instead of just trying to buy them. It might smoke someone out if I listed items that sounded like the ones that were stolen. Minutes later I was home. I quickly set up a new fake account and listed a bunch of items that I supposedly owned. An hour later I had my first bite.

I backed Rex's truck into a space in a parking garage at 4:45 p.m. I could see the small coffee shop across the street. The buyer and I had agreed to meet in Arlington, at the independent shop. I reached over to the passenger seat and took the binoculars I'd brought along out of their case. I was deep in the shadows, and hardly anyone who knew me would expect me to be in anything other than the Suburban.

I had gotten here early and had driven around the block several times to see if I could spot a black SUV like Mike's. Nothing. So now I waited. Five minutes later a black SUV pulled up. I sat still, barely breathing, like somehow I'd be seen. I had told the buyer when I messaged him that I was a dude who'd have on a Boston Red Sox T-shirt.

The SUV sat there for a few minutes before a car

door opened. Through the binoculars, I watched as a man climbed out. I almost dropped them, because it was the tattooed man who'd helped me drag Seth out of his house. After pacing the sidewalk a couple of times, he looked at the SUV and pointed to the coffee shop. He went in but came out a few minutes later, empty handed. Another car door opened, and Mike eased out. I wasn't that surprised. They talked for a minute, before Mike started taking a good look around. I shrank down as much as I could while keeping an eye on them. It felt like he was looking directly at me, even though I knew there was no way to see me here in the shadows.

Both men climbed back in the SUV. I knew I had to follow them.

I noticed a baseball cap partially tucked under the seat on the passenger side of Rex's truck. I snatched it up and jammed it on my head as I pulled forward. I drove like a madwoman out of the parking garage and turned left. I could see them up ahead, driving west toward Lexington. I stayed back. We went down Massachusetts Avenue, crossed the 95, and headed into Bedford. They passed the street that led to where Seth lived. Somehow that made me breathe a little easier.

They turned onto Sweetwater Avenue, which ended at Fawn Lake. Back in the late 1800s, trains brought people from Boston to Bedford for the fresh air. Today it was surrounded by trails and wooded areas. They turned right onto a road that I knew led to a parking area by the lake. It was surrounded by woods. Since I couldn't follow them there without being seen, I continued on. I parked illegally behind a building that in the 1800s had been a pharmaceutical laboratory that used the sweet water of the lake to make concoctions for people. The building had been converted to condos in the 1980s. I trotted along a trail that kept me close to the water's edge and hopefully out of Mike's sight.

Car doors slammed in the lot. I went up a path that looked like it was more for deer than for people, brushing branches aside as I crept forward. Angry voices carried to me. Seth. I snuck up behind a big tree and peered around. Mike, the tattooed guy who'd helped me pull Seth out of his burning house, and Seth were feet away from me. I snapped a couple of photos with my phone. I took the precaution of e-mailing them to myself. The tattooed man's Hawaiian shirt was untucked, but I could see a small bulge under it. Gun.

Chapter 27

The man reached around his back. I couldn't let him shoot Seth. I raced forward. Twigs snapped. He started to turn. I charged him. It was a tackle any Patriots defensive lineman would have been proud to make. We landed inches from one of the rear tires of Mike's SUV. I struggled, grabbing at the man's hand, and finally put my hand around his . . . baseball cap? Where'd the gun go?

I heard a lot of "What the hell?" from above me, and seconds later I was yanked to my feet by Mike on one side and Seth on the other.

"He had a gun tucked in his pants," I said.

The man stood and brushed his jeans off. "She's crazy. All I had was my baseball cap."

I looked at Seth. "He was at your house the night of the fire. He's probably the one who attacked you." I jerked my arms away from Seth and Mike.

Seth didn't look surprised. He knew that this guy was at his house that night.

"If I attacked him, why would I help you drag

him away from the house? I sacrificed my lucky Red Sox shirt to stop his bleeding."

"To make it look like you were a good guy," I said.

Mike stepped forward. "I told you to stay out of this."

I jabbed my finger in his chest. This was becoming a habit. "You don't get to tell me what to do." I jabbed again for punctuation. "Tell me what's going on. Now."

"Just leave, Sarah," Seth said.

"An innocent man is in jail. Someone tried to make it look like he was selling stolen stuff. Mike is trying to buy things and then comes to meet you. I have pictures of you two meeting. If you don't tell me what in the world you have going on, I'm sending them to the *Globe*."

Mike eyed my phone.

"I've already sent them off to a safe place." My e-mail probably wasn't that safe, but they didn't know that.

"Obviously, this isn't a good place to talk," Seth said to Mike. They both looked at me. "Let's meet back at my house." Seth turned back to Mike. "Come in the way you usually do."

Mike nodded and got back in his SUV.

Finally, I was going to get some answers.

Seth's house smelled of fresh paint, with an after scent of smoke. I arrived before Mike and wondered if he was going to show or would do a runner.

Seth sat on his couch, with his head tilted back, eyes closed. A pulse beat in his throat. He hadn't said a word to me since he let me in. I sat in a brown leather chair across from him, feeling awkward, self-conscious, and perturbed. It was five-thirty, and it had been a very long day. A few minutes later Mike and his buddy came in through Seth's back door. Seth pushed himself up with his good arm. I studied Mike's companion.

"This is Two-Toes," Mike said.

Two-Toes? I couldn't help but look at his feet. I grimaced, trying not to think about how he had got that nickname.

Mike noticed my expression. "It's a long story. He was here keeping an eye on Seth because of a situation we're involved in."

"Well, he didn't do a very good job," I snapped at them.

Two-Toes hung his head and nodded. "I heard somethin' in the woods behind the house and went to investigate. By the time I got back, you were pulling Seth out of the house."

"How come you ran off?"

"A known associate of Mike 'the Big Cheese' Titone at the DA's house? How da you think that woulda played in the press?"

He had a valid point. "So mysterious Good Samaritan worked better all the way around," I said.

The men all nodded. Then they exchanged looks. I waited for one of them to start talking.

"The Mob is trying to make a comeback in the sports world," Mike said.

I tried to think of how many Italian athletes I'd heard of on teams around here. *Not many*, was my conclusion. "Go on." It came out frustrated and tense.

"They're betting, trying to influence outcomes, expanding their business beyond racketeering, drugs, and prostitution," Mike said.

"Trying to influence outcomes. Like paying off refs and players?" I asked. New England teams had had their fair share of scandals.

"Bingo," Two-Toes said.

I mulled this over. Why would Mike Titone tell Seth any of this? If it was happening in Boston, shouldn't he be talking to someone in the city? And why would he be talking at all? Wasn't the Mob his bread and butter? My skin prickled. I might be in way over my head.

"Is the Mob also selling sports memorabilia?" I asked.

"Trying to control the market to make things more valuable," Seth said.

"But someone has a decent business in fraudulent items, which is keeping market value low." I didn't know where that thought came from, but it made sense.

All three of the men nodded again.

"We stumbled across them during our investigation," Mike said.

Our investigation? Again, it struck me as odd that the two of them were somehow working together. I kept my mouth shut.

Seth leaned forward. "Someone has a Fagin-like

organization to sell the stuff here in Middlesex County."

"Fagin as in *Oliver Twist*, by Dickens?" Fagin used orphaned boys as pickpockets and took their earnings.

"Only, instead of orphans, we think our Fagin is using teenagers. Kids who need money, for whatever reason."

"But you don't know who's running the operation?"

"They're slick," Seth said. "Layers of people between the seller and the head. The couple of kids we've caught don't seem to know anything."

"That's why you were out trying to buy stuff, Mike?" I asked.

He nodded. "Yes."

"Why does the Mob even care? I don't get it," I said.

"Because it's hurting the value of the authentic items," Seth said. "You hurt their pocketbook, and you end up with a lot of angry people."

"So, on one hand, you're trying to prevent a crime," I mused. "The Mob going after this Fagin character."

"Yes," Seth said.

"And you're also trying to shut down their operations." I rubbed my temples, trying to wrap my head around all of this. Maybe the two different teens who had approached Ryne were part of the ring. Who had access to kids? The school board, that was who. Each of them in their own way. Betty Jenkins had teenage grandchildren. Mac hired them at his grocery store. Lance had teens of his own, and Rex sponsored lots of teams. Anil tutored kids.

I looked at Mike. "If the Mob is behind all of this, why don't you just tell Seth who's doing it? You two seem awfully close."

Mike shoved his hands in his pockets. A move that made me jump slightly. "Jeez, Sarah, none of us are carrying guns." He pulled his hands back out of his pockets. "I don't know who's doing it."

I was so confused. "Explain your connection, then." I gestured back and forth between Mike and Seth.

Mike sighed. "I feed Seth information when I can."

Wow. The people in the Mob are notoriously tight lipped. "Why?"

"I watched my dad pay and pay for protection when he owned the shop. If he didn't have the money, the shop was vandalized or an arm was mysteriously broke." Mike frowned. "Dad never told me this, but you learn a lot sweeping up when you're a kid."

My heart broke for the little kid who watched his dad suffer. "So you joined them?" It sounded like an abuse victim who had turned into an abuser.

"Only to infiltrate and provide information," Mike said.

"Why to Seth, instead of someone in Boston?" I asked.

"Because I trust Seth, and he's *not* in Boston." Mike leaned against the wall.

"How do you even know each other?" I asked. I

wondered why Seth was letting Mike do all of the talking.

"Prep school. Seth was a couple of years behind me. We were both on the baseball team."

I sat back in my chair. I didn't know which bit of information was more astounding, that Mike snitched or that he had gone to prep school.

Mike went on. "My dad wanted me out of the North End. He scraped every bit he didn't give to the Mob to send me off. When he died my senior year, I came back. I wanted my revenge."

"You had to get your hands dirty to do it?" I asked.

Mike glanced down at the floor, and his shoulders slumped. "Yeah. But Seth fabricated some charges against me to make me look like I was doing things I wasn't."

Seth leaned forward. "We're worried that Melba found out who's behind the operation and was killed because of it."

"And you think that's why you were attacked?" I asked.

Seth nodded.

"So things are escalating," I said.

"That's why I told you to stay out of it," Mike said.

"You could have just told me the truth," I said.

Seth and Mike exchanged glances.

"It's dangerous for us and for anyone who knows the real truth. Only Two-Toes here and my brothers know I'm working with Seth. The rest of my guys don't."

"But they helped me out in February, and Seth was there," I said.

"I may have let them think you and I were involved. Romantically," Mike said.

I slumped in the chair. Just what I needed people to think, that I was a mobster's girlfriend.

"They also think Seth is on the take," Mike said. "That I have a DA in my pocket, which is good for everyone."

"That sounds dangerous." I looked over at Seth. "What about your campaign? If that leaks out, you'll never be elected."

"It's a risk I'm willing to take. Finding our Fagin and having an ear in the Mob are more important," Seth said.

"The greater good," I said. Seth was a good man. A smart one who came boxed with model-like looks.

Seth nodded.

Chapter 28

I made my excuses and left. While I drove home, I tried to picture each of the board members as Fagin. It was kind of hard to picture Betty in that role. Leading a tennis camp, yes. Ordering a bunch of kids to lie, not so much. Anil would be telling them all to study. Mac and Lance? They were maybes in my mind. But Rex Sullivan. *Hmmm.* He'd worked with all those kids, sponsoring all those teams, from the time they were little. Maybe it had given him time to develop insights into their personalities, and then he had used that when they became teens.

I jerked my hands from the wheel of Rex's truck like it had shocked me. What kind of monster was I dealing with?

At six-thirty Carol met me at Sullivan Luxury Car Sales so that I could drop off the truck. My Suburban had been returned mannequin free and clean a few hours ago. The dealership was empty again. The pictures of the teams loomed large, and I walked over to study them, as if they could give me some answers. Sadly, pictures didn't talk. I heard a noise behind me and whirled around to find Tim, who'd taken me on the test-drive, standing there, clipping his nails. *Ugh.*

"Did you come back to buy the car?" he asked.

"I wish." I held up the keys to Rex's truck. "Here's the keys to the truck Rex loaned me."

Tim looked disappointed, like he'd actually thought I'd come back to buy something. "You can toss them on his desk. His office isn't locked." He pointed to an office and walked away.

I went into the office and flipped the light on. His glass-topped desk was neat, his filing cabinets were locked, and his computer password was protected. Yes, I checked them all. I turned to leave and noticed an old-fashioned ski pole in the corner. It was just like the ski poles in the two mannequins, and in Melba Harper's chest.

I hustled out of the dealership and leaped into Carol's SUV.

"Are you okay?" she asked.

"I'm not sure."

"What happened?"

I sat for a minute as Carol peeled out of the lot. That ski pole made two matching sets. "I need to stop at the police station."

"Okay. I'll go with you."

"I might be tied up for a bit. Why don't you drop me at my car? Don't you have a class tonight?"

"Olivia is at the store. She can take care of things. I'm not leaving you."

Minutes later we were seated in an interview room, facing Pellner and Ramirez, the state trooper who conveniently was still in town. I would have much rather just told my story to Pellner. Both of the men had wanted Carol to leave, but she'd told them it was either her or Vincenzo DiNapoli.

I explained that I'd seen the ski pole in Rex's office. Ramirez questioned me about why I was at the dealership and specifically why and for how long I was in Rex's office. I left out the part about trying to snoop.

"How can you be sure it's a match to the others?" Ramirez asked.

"I didn't say it was a match. I said it looked like the other ones." I wished I'd taken a picture of it, but I'd left my purse in Carol's SUV while I ran the keys in.

"Did anything stand out about it, Sarah?" Pellner asked.

"Just that it was an older one. Leather loop strap at the top, bamboo pole, leather and bamboo basket. They are nothing like the poles people use today."

Ramirez stood. "Thank you for the information."

The rest of us stood, too.

"Are you going to check it out?" I asked.

Pellner looked at Ramirez, who scrunched his eyebrows together.

"Of course we will," Pellner said.

Ramirez didn't look too happy about that.

* * *

It was almost eight by the time Stella and I sat across from each other at a table at Lucina's in Bedford. We kept giggling every time we looked at each other. Stella had on a pale blond wig that really didn't go with her Mediterrancan skin tone. I wore one that was a brown bob, and it reminded me of the one Julia Roberts wore in *Pretty Woman*. We both had on false eyelashes and more makeup than either of us usually wore. All I needed was a miniskirt and a halter top to look like a hooker.

I held my menu up so I couldn't see Stella, but it didn't help. My shoulders shook with repressed laughter. I had to calm down, or the gig would be up before I even had a chance to order. The last thing we needed was to call attention to ourselves. I did some deep calming breaths before peeking over the menu.

We grinned at each other but managed to bury the mirth. A woman came to take our order.

"Which do you like better, the lasagna or the chicken piccata?" I asked her. This was another attempt to throw everyone off the scent. Lasagna was the special tonight, so there shouldn't be any chance of them running out.

"They're both really good." She said it in a bored tone that made me think she'd been asked questions like this a hundred times and wished people would stop asking it. "But I like the piccata," she said.

Darn it. Now what?

"I want the piccata," Stella said. "You get the lasagna and we can share."

Stella to the rescue. "Perfect," I said, smiling up at the waitress as I handed her back my menu. "I'd also like a glass of the Chianti."

"One for me, too, please," Stella said.

The waitress nodded as she walked off.

We waited and waited and waited. Another waitress finally showed up with two glasses of Chianti and a plate of calamari, which she set down between us.

"We didn't order this," I said.

"It's on the house. Our apologies for the mix-up."

"What mix-up?" Stella asked.

The waitress glanced toward the back of the restaurant. I craned my neck to see what she was looking at, but didn't spot anything.

"We don't have any lasagna tonight." She avoided eye contact.

My eyebrows shot up. This couldn't be a coincidence. "But the specials board and the specials list in the menu say tonight is lasagna night."

The waitress glanced toward the back again. "It's a misprint."

"But it's on your Web site," Stella said. She looked astonished.

"It is?" The waitress cleared her throat.

I took pity on her. None of this was her fault. "I'll have the shrimp fra diavolo."

"Oh, thank you. I'll put a rush in on that." She hurried away so quickly that she tripped over her own feet.

"Do you want to go?" Stella sounded steamed. "I can't believe we're being treated like this."

"I'm hungry. It's fine." I picked up a piece of calamari and ate it. The breading was perfect; the calamari succulent. If the rest of the food was as good as this, their lasagna must be wonderful. I felt bad about letting Angelo down, though.

After we ate, we strolled back toward our parking space. As we passed an alley, I heard a noise that sounded like someone said, "Pssst."

I stopped and looked into the dark alley.

"What are you doing?" Stella asked.

"I thought I heard something," I said.

Stella peered down the alley, too.

"Down here," a woman said.

I still couldn't see her. I took a step into the alley, but Stella grabbed my arm.

"Don't go in there," she said.

"I've got what you want," the woman said.

"What's that?" My eyes were adjusting to the dim light, and I made out a Dumpster but didn't see anyone.

"It's probably a drug dealer. Let's go." Stella tugged on my arm, but I pulled free.

The woman mumbled something.

"I couldn't understand you," I said.

"It's lasagna. From Lucina's. I was your first waitress."

Stella and I looked at each other, mouths open.

"You stay here, Stella, in case this is some kind of setup. I'm going in."

I got my phone out of my purse and turned the

flashlight on. I swung it around, and it landed on a woman just beyond the Dumpster. She was holding a white plastic bag with the Lucina's logo on it.

I trotted over to her.

"I don't know why they didn't want you to have this, and I don't care." The woman frowned. "If a customer asks for a dish and it's on the menu, they should get it." She shoved the bag at me.

"Will you get in trouble?" I asked.

"No. They gave us all some so it wouldn't go to waste." She turned and hurried away.

I walked back to Stella, shaking my head.

Stella just stared at me. "Evenings are never boring with you. And can we take these wigs off now? My head is itching like crazy."

I laughed as we both pulled off the wigs and shook out our hair. "I'm not eating any lasagna anytime soon."

"How do you think they got onto us?" Stella asked.

I raised my shoulders and dropped them. "No idea."

As I walked over to DiNapoli's with tonight's lasagna, my cell phone rang. It was Pellner.

"We went over to the dealership and found the ski pole."

I didn't say anything. I was surprised that Pellner was telling me any of this. I didn't want to break the moment by asking the wrong question.

"Rex denies knowing anything about it. Said that

it wasn't his and that anyone could have put it in his office, which is rarely locked. He has an open-door policy."

I stopped at the light on Great Road and waited for it to change. The night air was hot; the church bells rang out the hour. "It was unlocked when I was there," I admitted grudgingly.

"He claims someone is trying to frame him."

"That's exactly what Anil said." I frowned. "But Rex wanted Melba out. Isn't that motive?"

"It could be but may not be, either."

"Why are you telling me all of this? It's not like you." The light changed, and I crossed the street and then turned right to get to DiNapoli's.

"Because I was hoping you'd reciprocate if you know something you're holding back."

"I came to you today about the ski pole. I'm obviously sharing information." I thought about Seth and Mike's arrangement. But I couldn't tell him about that.

"Okay then. But if you think of anything else . . ."

"You'll be the first to know."

"Sit, sit," Rosalie said, shooing me over to a table. "We'll be right there."

I sat at the table, which rocked a little when I leaned on it. I frowned and pushed on it. Yes, that was definitely rocking. Maybe tomorrow morning I'd hit some garage sales before I went over to the Longs' to put the final touches on their garage sale. I'd noticed that during the summer, more and more people were having sales on Friday mornings. Some were being held midweek even. I could look for a table to replace this one. It would be fun, and I needed some fun. This week had been emotionally and physically exhausting. I dug around in my purse, found a measuring tape, did a quick measurement of the table's dimensions, and typed the information into the notes section of my phone.

I handed off the latest and last piece of lasagna to the DiNapolis as I filled them in on the evening's events. Rosalie and Angelo laughed so hard, they wiped tears from their eyes as I described our outfits.

"You shouldn't have gone into the alley," Rosalie scolded. She looked at Angelo. "No more asking favors of Sarah."

He put his hands up in the air. "I can't make my beautiful wife mad." He crossed his heart. "No more."

"Don't be silly. It was fun and took my mind off things."

"Let's heat this up and see how it tastes," Angelo said. He took the lasagna to the kitchen and put it in the oven.

"How are you doing?" Rosalie asked.

"I feel like someone gave me a bunch of pieces to a jigsaw puzzle, and that if I could fit them together in just the right way, I'd have the whole picture." Sadly, it would be one of someone plunging a ski pole into Melba. "But I've never particularly liked jigsaws. Maybe I'm too impatient."

"Maybe we can help," Angelo said. "Tell us what you're thinking."

What could I say that didn't give away what Seth

and Mike had told me? "It all seems to go back to the swap."

"It does," Rosalie said.

"Someone tried to make it look like Anil was selling stuff that was stolen from the swap," I said.

Angelo and Rosalie both nodded.

"They planned to kill Melba but needed to make it look like someone else did it. Anil told me that Melba called him in the middle of the night, asking for him to meet her at the gym. And that it wasn't the first time she'd asked for a middle-of-the-night meeting."

Rosalie shook her head. "Melba always loved cloak-and-dagger stuff. Movies, books. I think she fancied herself a spy."

"Pfft," Angelo said. "I think she was a lonely woman with a type A personality who worked late at night. She didn't think about other people having lives."

"Maybe it's a bit of both," I said. I didn't want them to get into an argument over the situation. "I'm going to just throw out a couple of theories, and tell me if they ring true." I took a deep breath. "The police probably notified Melba about the attack on me and the robbery."

"That sounds plausible," Angelo said.

"She can't go back to sleep and decides to go over to the gym to see for herself what happened." I looked at both of them, and they nodded their agreement. "While she's there, she notices something is off and calls Anil to come take a look."

Rosalie shrugged. "It works for me."

"But here's an alternate thought. Someone was using the swap to cover something else up. They went over to take care of it. I was a complication, and Melba ended up being one, too." It made me feel very lucky to be alive.

The timer binged, and Angelo got the lasagna from the oven. He brought it to the table with three forks. We all dug in. I went back for second and third bites. So did Rosalie.

"It's not bad," I said.

"Probably was better when it was fresh from the oven," Rosalie added as she took another bite.

Angelo frowned and ate some more, too. "It's okay."

"Maybe we're all just really hungry," I said. Although I wasn't that hungry, because I'd already eaten a big dinner at Lucina's.

"That must be it," Rosalie said as she scooped up another bite.

"Have you had any spies from your competitors come in?" I asked.

"We think so," Rosalie said.

"But we outsmarted them. We don't have lasagna on the menu," Angelo said with a grin.

"We don't have it that often, anyway. Only as a special," Rosalie said.

"And I changed my marinara sauce for our other dishes. This week only," Angelo said. "That way if someone tries the chicken Parmesan, the sauce won't taste the same as at the bake-off."

Rosalie tried to cover a yawn.

I stood up. "Thanks for listening."

"It sounds like you are on the right track," Angelo said. "Watch your back."

That was what I had said to Anil a few days ago. "I will."

Chapter 29

Friday morning at eight-twenty I parked my Suburban in the parking lot of a mostly vacant office building right outside the gate of Fitch Air Force Base. The sun warmed the back of my Boston Red Sox T-shirt and my shorts when I got out of the car to wait for Eleanor. Dressing down was one of my rules for going to garage sales. No one wanted to bargain with someone who was decked out and dripping in jewels. Eleanor pulled up seconds later. Instead of sponsoring me on base, we had agreed to meet here.

"Thanks for letting me know about all the garage sales on base today," I said as I slid into the front seat of her Mini Cooper. I handed her one of the two cups of coffee I'd picked up at Dunkin's. There was a Dunkin's on base, at the base exchange, but the line was usually longer and less efficient than the one at the Dunkin's in town.

"You're welcome. A bunch of people got together

and decided to give Friday mornings a try. It worked for the February Blues sale you ran."

"Yep. More people on base means more buyers." Fitch Air Force Base employed a lot of people. Most of those people didn't live on base, so the base was a lot quieter on weekends.

Eleanor pulled up to the guard at the gate and showed him her military ID. She was considered a dependent since her husband was active duty, and her ID looked different than his. Some days they did 100 percent ID checks, and then I'd have to show some form of ID. Some days the dogs were out sniffing cars for drugs or bombs. Today wasn't one of those days, so we sailed right onto base. It was an acceptable and legal means of getting on base. And sometimes, such as with spur-of-the-moment trips, it was more convenient than filling out all the paperwork. Eleanor was responsible for me while I was here. If I did something wrong, I could be barred from returning. But all I was planning on doing was find a bargain or two.

We drove to one of the older housing areas first. For the most part, enlisted and officer housing was separated. It seemed archaic to me but had to do with chains of command and people following orders. Eleanor parked on a steep hill, and we walked toward the first garage sale. Kids rode bikes and tossed balls, and screams of joy came from a tot lot across the street. Moms and the occasional dad gossiped on corners.

I had to admit that I missed the sense of community I had when I lived on base. Even with all the people rotating in and out, it was easy to make friends, because everyone was in the same boat. In a new place, where they knew no one and had to start over again. I'd been lucky to establish my own small community in Ellington, but it was definitely smaller than the ones I had on the various bases CJ and I had lived on.

The first two places we stopped had lots of kids' clothes and toys. Nothing I was interested in, but Eleanor picked up some things for her sister's kids. Eleanor didn't even try to negotiate a better price.

"Um, Eleanor. That's not how garage sales are supposed to work," I said as we walked up the hill to the next sale.

"What are you talking about?" Her big brown eyes were wide.

"Ask for a better price."

"But it was already a good price," Eleanor said. "Have you seen how much toys cost at the store?"

I laughed. It was hard to argue with that.

We stopped at a house that had a table out that might work for the DiNapolis. I gave it a shake. It rattled like a skeleton, so I flipped it over. I could fix most things with carpenter's glue and bolts. But the wooden legs had splits in them. There was no way to fix that without buying new legs, which would be more work and money than this table was worth.

"Oh, look at this," Eleanor said. I walked over to find her holding a bee figurine on a spring, so the bee bobbed around. It had a happy expression that reminded me of Eleanor.

"It's cute," I said. "How much?"

"Fifty cents. It's a bargain."

I took the bee from her and approached the man watching over the sale. "Will you take a quarter for this?" I asked.

He frowned. "It's only fifty cents."

"Everyone wants a bargain," I said.

"It is a bargain. Look, the sticker's still on the bottom. It cost five dollars and ninety-nine cents."

A non-bargainer. Garage sale goers didn't like that.

"I'll take it," Eleanor said. She whipped out a one and handed it to him. "Keep the change."

I laughed. "Paying more than they asked? You are never going to live that down."

We walked back down the hill to Eleanor's Mini. She carefully placed the bee and the things for her sister's kids on the floor behind her seat. "Let's head over to the other side of base."

"Okay," I said.

It took only a few minutes to get from one side of base to the other. It would be less if any of the roads we traveled had a speed limit higher than twenty-five. We cruised along at just below twenty-five. Speeding on a base was never a good idea. If you got caught speeding too many times, you could get your base driving privileges taken away.

We parked in front of a sale with lots of tables crammed with stuff. It didn't look that well organized, but the number of items was impressive.

Sometimes these kinds of sales were the most fun, because you could find buried treasure. As we approached, I realized a lot of the stuff was sports equipment. I strolled around the sale. Everything looked clean, although some things had been thrown on tarps on the ground. That was a last-resort move, in my book.

Finally, I saw a table that looked like a good possibility for DiNapoli's. I shook it, and it seemed fairly sturdy. I looked underneath. This one I could fix. After measuring the table, I called to one of the people running the sale. There wasn't a price on the table.

"How much do you want for this?" I asked.

"I don't know. How about fifty?"

I usually priced everything at sales. If you didn't, you came off sounding hesitant, like this person. The hesitant person was the best person to bargain with.

"I can give you ten."

"Twenty-five?" she said.

I gave it a shake. "Look how loose it is."

"Okay. Ten it is."

"I'm going to look around before I take the table, if that's okay with you."

"Sure. Have at it."

Eleanor was talking to a woman over near the sports equipment. I wandered over and picked up one of the baseball helmets. It was heavy. Heavier than I remembered Brody's being. I looked inside and saw it had a lot of thick padding. It didn't look that different than the one Brody owned. I scanned the rest of the equipment. It all looked about the same as Brody's. Some was more worn, and other pieces looked almost new.

The woman Eleanor was talking to looked up. "Can I help you with anything?"

Eleanor introduced us. "I wondered about the baseball helmet. A friend of mine's son had a helmet with a big dent in it. This one seems sturdier. Where did you get it?"

"Rex Sullivan paid for the equipment. You'd have to ask him."

"This looks new," I said.

"My husband's fault. He convinced our daughter to try softball, but she'd rather be reading a book or playing with her friends. The whole experiment was a disaster."

"You didn't have to turn the equipment back in?"

The woman frowned. "I never heard we were supposed to. I probably should call someone and check. Were you interested in buying something?"

"No. Thanks. Just curious," I replied.

Eleanor helped me carry the table to the car. She put the backseats down. We shoved the table in the back of her Mini. It fit if we left the back open.

"I don't want you to get in trouble by driving across base with this thing sticking out," I said to Eleanor.

"We should be fine. We aren't going that far," Eleanor said as we took off.

We cut across back streets but eventually had to

pop out on Travis. We'd gone about a block when we heard the *whoop-whoop* of sirens behind us.

Eleanor pulled over to the curb. "Rats. My husband is going to kill me." In the military, an egregious breaking of rules could result in one's spouse being notified or even his or her commander.

"Oh, no," I said. "I'm sorry. I'll take the blame."

We both looked behind us as the security policeman stepped out of his car and snapped his beret on his head. *James.*

I bounced out of the car. "James. I haven't seen you in a long time." James had worked for CJ, hated to be called Jim, and was a hard worker, always willing to lend a hand.

We hugged. I held a hand up to shade my eyes as I looked at him. He seemed more rested than the last time I'd seen him. "Why did you pull us over?"

"That table is about to fall out the back of the Mini," James said.

I turned toward the back of the Mini. The table did seem perilously close to tipping out.

"We just have to drive off basc. My Suburban is parked at the office building on the left." I pointed. You could see it from here. I went to the back of the Mini and shoved the table back in as far as it would go.

Eleanor peered at me from the driver's seat. "Is everything okay? Am I getting a ticket?"

"I don't think so." I turned back to James. "That should last until we get to my car."

"Okay," James said. "I'll just follow you off so you don't get in trouble."

When we pulled into the parking lot of the office building, James pulled into a space and got out.

"Let me give you a hand with that," he said.

I ran over and opened the Suburban and, with James's help, got the table tucked securely in the Suburban, legs up. I hugged Eleanor. "Thanks, Eleanor. That was fun, even if you don't know how to drive a bargain."

Eleanor laughed and waved before she took off.

I turned to James. He looked good. He'd always been cute in a rugged way, but he also looked more relaxed than I'd seen him in a while.

"How are you?" I asked. In the spring James had told me he was seeing a therapist off base. It was against military rules to go off base for medical or psychological help without your commander knowing.

"Good. I know you were worried about me seeing a therapist off base."

"I was. I am. But you look more relaxed than you did. That's a very good thing."

"I went to the base chaplain and told him about it. He went with me to my commander when I told her."

I'd heard that she was a tough woman. "What happened?" I looked quickly at the rank on his uniform. All his stripes were still there. He hadn't been demoted.

"She wasn't happy. But the three of us worked through it. She put a letter of reprimand in my folder, with the promise that she'd remove it if I toed the line for the next six months."

I smiled. He'd gotten off light. "You are a good line toe-er."

"I am under normal circumstances, and with the help of a good therapist."

"Excellent."

"I also met someone. I like her a lot." James turned a little red around his ears.

"Do I know her?"

"She's new on base. I met her at one of thc fun runs a few weeks ago."

"I'd love to meet her sometime."

"Thanks," he said.

"For what?"

"Being a good friend." James gave me a hug and slid back into the patrol car. He sketched a salute as I waved to him, smiling.

I went to slam the back of the Suburban shut and took a second look at the table. "Oh, no," I muttered. I dug through the glove compartment until I found a small magnifying glass. I took it back to the table and looked it over. The underside of the table had lots of tiny holes, which could be woodworms. I should have examined it more closely at the sale. Woodworms weren't worms but the larvae of beetles that burrowed into wood. There they had families and made more holes. To get rid of them, you either had to use chemicals or an expensive freezing technique. The table wasn't worth it.

"Arrgh." I said it out loud and glanced around to see if anyone had heard me, but I was alone. If it was woodworms and I introduced them into DiNapoli's, they could spread from this table to chairs to other tables. Soon enough all that would be left was a pile of dust to sit on and eat off. Okay, so that was a little dramatic. It would take years to accomplish that. But it was the last thing anyone needed. I should have noticed at the sale. I sighed, slammed the back doors shut, and resolved to make a trip to the dump.

Chapter 30

On my way home I decided to drive by a couple of sales in Concord I'd seen listed online. I liked this new "garage sales on Fridays" trend. Maybe I should try doing some. The first neighborhood was filled with lots of swing sets, basketball hoops, and bikes. It was probably a great place to buy stuff for kids. If I wanted antiques or vintage things, I'd look for a neighborhood with older people living in it. I slowed in front of the first house but didn't see anything that appealed to me. I didn't bother to park.

My stomach growled as I drove the few blocks to the next sale. I parked and took a look around. The lawn was large and shaded by beautiful maple trees. It made shopping actually pleasant on a hot summer morning. The sale had lots of interesting knickknacks and quite a bit of vintage jewelry. Most of it looked like it was from the forties, fifties, and early sixties. Vintage jewelry was popular, even if it wasn't made of precious metals and gems or didn't have a designer signature. Lots of crafters bought it to make other things out of it. The prices were really reasonable. I started picking up pieces and soon had a handful.

"Here, would you like a bag?" A silver-haired woman offered me a quart-size plastic bag.

"Thank you." I almost told her she had some beautiful pieces, but stopped before I said it. Complimenting a seller's items made it harder to bargain. By the time I looked over all her jewelry, I had filled the bag and had a handful. Instead of trying to haggle over each piece, I offered her a lump sum.

"Perfect," the woman said. She handed me another bag. "And go fill this one. On the house. I really need to get rid of all of this."

As I looked over the jewelry, I realized some of it tried to be something it wasn't—fancy and expensive—while some of it was unapologetically fake. It made me think about Melba's killer. Maybe it was someone who appeared to be one thing but was really another. Rex was the first person who came to mind. He appeared to be a benevolent benefactor by supporting all those teams and getting lots of kudos for doing so. While it was generous of him to loan me a truck, why did he have to lie about it?

Mac and Lance also seemed to present one kind of image. Mac was the laid-back cigar lover, but his brother had been fired as superintendent and Melba had taken over. Lance was Mr. Friendly but then had insisted I sign the papers saying I wouldn't sue. Anil and Betty seemed to be the most genuine.

I picked out the pieces I liked the best, wondering

what I was actually going to do with all of this. When I'd filled the second bag, I waved at the woman and strolled back to my car. Ripples of heat rolled off the hood of the car as I set off for home. The rolling hills, low stone walls, and woods were peaceful. I wished my mind was peaceful, too.

After a quick fluffernutter sandwich at home, I pulled up to the Longs' house at twelve thirty. I resisted the urge to pound my head on the steering wheel after catching a glimpse of the setup in their front yard. "The customer's always right," I muttered to myself. The tent Kelly had ordered looked like something out of *The Arabian Nights* as its sides ruffled gently in the breeze. If harem dancers, genies in bottles, or magic carpets appeared, I'd know I was hallucinating, that my injuries the other night were worse than I'd imagined. But no such luck. The tent stayed put.

Kelly Long waved frantically and met me at the bottom of the drive.

"What do you think?" she asked. Her black, wavy hair danced in the breeze. Her exotic brown eyes glittered with anticipation.

I'd better not answer that the way I wanted to. Which was something like, "Are you completely bonkers?"

"Isn't it amazing?" she asked.

"It certainly is," I said.

"This sale will be better than any of those you see on HGTV." She bounced a little as we went up the drive. "No one's ever seen anything like this in Ellington."

"They certainly haven't," I said. Kelly wasn't one to interpret sarcasm.

"I'll be the talk of the town."

"Oh, you will be," I agreed.

"The electrician has been here so now it's up to us to make it perfect," Kelly said.

"Oh, good." I'd finally realized that Lance was just defeated and was giving in to Kelly's whims. I could only dream of having the kind of money to do that.

My concern was that if this sale was a dismal failure, Kelly would blame it all on me. Which wouldn't help my business. I put on my game face. "Are you sure you want to put all your things in the tent this afternoon?" I asked.

"Absolutely. I want to make sure it will be perfect for tomorrow."

"What about overnight? I'm worried about people taking things."

"Between our sons and their friends, our rottweiler Daisy, and my Glock, I don't think we have a thing to worry about."

Oh, good heavens. "Okay then. Let's get to work."

The good thing about Kelly was she had the energy of three hyper toddlers rolled into one. She also wasn't afraid of hard work when she felt passionate about something. The two of us dragged a Jenny Lind–style double bed frame into the tent first. Jenny Lind beds weren't a brand but a classic style of bed with wooden spindles. The real Jenny Lind was a Swedish opera singer who toured America in the 1850s and supposedly slept in a spindle type of bed.

It was hot in here. When we'd started working, we put three sides of the tent down so no one could see in from the street. Only the back side stood open. Sweat had pooled in almost every spot on my body that was available for pooling. Fortunately, Kelly had brought out two large window fans. They helped a little bit.

I positioned the bed in the corner. This one was painted white. I'd love to see it in turquoise, but it wouldn't go with Kelly's vision. She'd explained that to me when I mentioned painting it the first time I had seen the bed in her garage. Next, we carried out the box spring and mattress. Kelly brought out a new expensive brand of sheets with a high thread count. I hoped for Lance's sake they'd been on sale. We made the bed and covered it with a beautiful white chenille bedspread. It was a twin, but twins worked on a double because back when they were originally made, the bedspreads hung to the floor. Now that everyone used dust ruffles, a twin came right to the bottom of a double mattress. We folded an old quilt across the bottom of the bed and then added ten throw pillows made out of vintage dish towels.

We stepped back to admire our work. "It looks inviting," I said.

Kelly smiled. "Told you."

We worked companionably for the next couple of hours. The sturdy frame of the tent allowed me to hang her five chandeliers, mirrors, framed paintings, and photographs with U hooks. A combination of Oriental and rag rugs covered the driveway. Painted dressers were tucked in corners. I decorated their tops with lace runners and Depression glass. The pale pinks and greens complemented each other and the furnishings. If this were a store, I'd want to shop in it. Or if it were a house, to live in it.

"Where did you get all this stuff, Kelly?" I'd been curious, but she'd never mentioned it when I was over here pricing earlier in the week.

"Most of it came from an aunt of Lance's in York, Maine."

Lance stepped into the tent. Kelly and Lance were such a contrast to each other. He had silver-blond hair. His eyes reminded me of the pale green sea glass I used to pick up on the beach near my home in Pacific Grove, California. Together they were the definition of light and dark. He looked around. "Where's the sports equipment going to go?"

I held in a groan. *More sports equipment?* I'd had my fill. Besides, we hadn't allocated any space for sports equipment. The only space we had left was going to be our kitchen corner. We needed to bring out the Hoosier cabinet. We planned to fill the shelves with Pyrex and Fire-King, which were wildly popular and increasingly hard to find. Kelly also had the assortment of utensils with wooden handles. Plus, vintage tablecloths and dish towels. I moved to a corner of the tent, pulled out my phone, and tried to look busy while they worked it out.

"I told you, I didn't want to sell the sports equipment at this garage sale," Kelly said, hands on hips.

"And I told you, I didn't want to hire her"—Lance jerked his head toward me—"for a second sale. No offense, Sarah. We're going to be in York for most of the rest of the summer."

It seemed to me that people from Massachusetts all fled to Maine, the Cape, Martha's Vineyard, or Nantucket for most of the summer. One parent would take the kids, and the other would work and commute on the weekends. It was vastly different than the way I had grown up. My dad didn't see any reason to take a vacation, because we lived in Pacific Grove, right next to Monterey, California. Whenever my mom suggested going someplace, he'd grumble and say, "People come here for vacation. Why leave?"

"Sarah, what do you suggest we do?" Kelly asked. Her foot tap, tap, tapped away as both she and Lance stared at me. It was more of a glare, but I chose to ignore it.

"Why don't we put a couple of tables on one side of the tent for the sports equipment?" I said.

Kelly's face turned red.

"I promise I'll make it look good," I added. "I have a lot of recent experience dealing with sports equipment."

Tap, tap, tap. Lance and I waited, trying to see if this compromise worked for her. Kelly finally gave a quick nod. "Okay, but I'm. Not. Happy."

Lance just nodded and left. I was guessing he heard that a lot.

After Kelly and I finished with everything in the tent, I would take a ton of pictures for my Web site. I might not have wanted to do a sale this way, but I did want to take advantage of the fact that I had.

I swiped at my forehead just before sweat dripped into my eyes, cursing the closed tent. From what Kelly had told me about her vision, in the morning there'd be a large crowd gathered at the bottom of the driveway. Together, we'd slowly open the tent flaps and tie them back as the crowd gasped and congratulated Kelly on her masterpiece. I hoped it worked out like she'd planned.

We carried the Hoosier cabinet out and angled it in a corner. That was the last piece of large furniture that we had to move. Kelly said she had some errands to run. So I continued to work on my own. I ran a damp cloth over the nooks and crannies of the Hoosier cabinet. It was painted a pale green, probably to cover up the fact that it was made out of more than one kind of wood. Kelly's only had one minor chip in the porcelain top. I followed the damp cloth with a dry cloth, just to make sure I didn't cause any water damage. Then I arranged all of the other kitchen items Kelly was selling.

I hung a chandelier I'd created for Kelly over the cabinet. It had been an old wreck of a thing that Kelly had wanted to toss out. But I'd searched through a box of junk she had and found a bunch of old tin sifters. I drilled holes in the sides of old sifters to use as lampshades. I'd painted the sifters bright red on the outside and bright silver on the inside. The chandelier had come out cuter than I had imagined. My throat was parched, so I searched for my water bottle and found it tucked in a corner near the bed. I drank deeply, even though the water was warm. I checked my phone. Kelly had been gone for a couple of hours.

I slipped out of the tent, through the garage, and knocked on the door leading to the house. It seemed rude to just barge in, even though I'd been in and out all afternoon. No one answered. I stood there like an awkward teen, trying to figure out my next move. Then I heard voices coming from the backyard and smelled smoke. I opened the door at the back of the garage and peered out at the backyard. Lance stood over a grill, in a flowered bib apron. Kelly stood next to him with a martini in hand.

"Stay for dinner?" Lance called to me, waving a colorful wicker fan over the coals in an attempt to encourage the fire.

"Martini?" Kelly asked, raising hers.

I wondered when she'd returned. Under other circumstances, with other people, I would have jumped on the opportunity not to have to fix food for myself. "No thanks," I said. "I wanted to take a look at the sports equipment that you want to sell. If it's all right with you, Kelly, I'll come over in the morning to set it up." Since Kelly wasn't an early riser, we weren't starting the sale until ten. Kelly had decided that way people could go to breakfast, other sales, and still make it here for the planned grand opening.

Kelly downed the martini. "That would be fine."

"I'll show you what we have to sell," Lance said.

I followed him down to their basement. A teenager's dream. We passed by a home movie theater with big comfy chairs; an arcade full of old pinball machines and foosball, air hockey, and pool tables; and another room with another giant TV, where a group of boys played some game. They worked their controls with the focus of a diamond cutter. Some of them looked like the kids who had been at the hospital with the baseball coach the night Brody was injured. I tried to see if any of them looked like the kid who'd shown up at Ryne's uncle's shop. But Lance moved too quickly for that.

Lance took a key out of his pocket, unlocked a door, and threw it open. The room was almost bigger than my apartment and was crammed full of everything from bikes to golf balls.

I must have gasped, because Lance whipped around to look at me. "You want to sell all of this?" I asked. If so, I'd be here all night, pricing.

Lance smiled. "No. Just the stuff over against that wall. And I already priced it."

"Great," I said. I felt better knowing all I had to do was arrange it. I picked up one of the helmets. It reminded me of the ones with the thick padding that I'd seen on base this morning. "I'll bring some baskets and old buckets with me to arrange things in so Kelly won't be upset."

"If you can keep Kelly from being upset, that will be a first," Lance said.

I didn't know what to say. "I'll see you in the morning, then."

Chapter 31

As soon as I was back in my car, I sent a text to Laura. Where did Brody get his baseball helmet? The one that I sent to you. I'd been thinking about this since this morning at the garage sale.

Laura sent a text back. From the school. Why?

I didn't want to go into the details of why right now. A friend was looking for one for her son.

I think the school uses AA Sporting Goods in Woburn.

Can you send me a picture of Brody's helmet? The inside, too?

We tossed it. It wasn't safe any longer with the dent in the side.

Darn it. How's he doing?

Good. Still has an occasional headache.

Are you getting settled in?

Sort of. We're surrounded by boxes.

Good luck. Miss you. I closed the texting app.

* * *

The drive to AA Sporting Goods in Woburn didn't take as long as it might have. Usually, highways on Friday evenings were a nightmare, as everyone scrambled to leave town for their vacation homes. If they weren't leaving, they were heading into Boston for a Red Sox game or a night on the town.

I walked into AA a little before their six-thirty closing. I'd looked at their hours online before I left and drove up here. The store was narrow, with shelves exploding with items. Bins burst with balls, bats, and face guards. I'd been a bit worried about my disheveled appearance and noticeable sweaty odor. It didn't seem to matter here. A lone man stood at a counter near the door. It looked like he hadn't played any sport in quite some time.

"Help you?" he asked without looking up from a computer he was typing on.

"My nephew plays baseball and needs a new helmet."

"Second row on the left. We're closing in five minutes."

I wandered down the row and looked at all the different types of helmets. None of the ones here looked like Brody's. I went back to the front of the store. The man now stood behind the counter with keys in his hand.

"Didn't find what you needed?" he asked.

I tried to describe Brody's helmet. "I heard that

Ellington's school district bought their equipment from you. That's where the helmet came from."

The man was shaking his head before I finished my sentence. "Used to buy their equipment through me."

"Why'd they stop buying from you?"

"Because I'm not about to compromise the quality of equipment I sell to people."

"And someone else was?" The thought chilled me.

The guy rattled his keys as he stepped toward the end of the counter. "I didn't say that."

He'd implied it, though. "Do you know who they bought from after you?"

The man just stared at me. I pulled a twenty out of my purse and put it on the counter. He just looked at it, so I took out another one. He scooped them both up. I couldn't believe this ploy actually worked. Although he hadn't told me anything yet.

"I heard they used an auction company that someone on the board had a connection to." He came around the counter and held the front door open. "We're closed."

I went home and took a long cold shower. Then I stood in front of my meager little desktop fan, trying to cool off. At least I didn't have to go somewhere to eat lasagna tonight. In fact, I didn't have to go anywhere or see anyone. I checked my emotions. *Wow.* I was okay with that. It had to be progress. Or maybe it was exhaustion or dehydration. I thought about CJ. I realized I was okay being alone. It surprised me. I could finally let go of CJ as my partner in life. I'd always care about him, but I no longer needed him.

I sprawled on the couch and started researching local auction houses. Although no one had said it had to be local. I tried variations of the board members' names and the word *auction*. Nothing popped up as an immediate answer. I went to the school board Web site and looked through the budget reports. They didn't show where things were purchased. But these weren't the in-depth budgets I'd studied when I went to Nancy's office. There was a note on the site inviting anyone who was interested to go to the superintendent's office to see the full budget. I guessed not many people did that. And even though I'd been running around questioning the board members, I really didn't want to picture any of them as a murderer. Each of them seemed likable in their own way.

I came across some articles about sports helmets. Last year a company had knowingly sold helmets that didn't meet safety standards to school systems. There were tons of lawsuits pending. It burned me to the core that someone would do this. I thought of Brody and his dented helmet again. I thought about the Red Sox game I'd watched a few days ago, where the batter was hit by a wild pitch. He'd just trotted down the baseline to first base, as if nothing had even happened. Quite a contrast to seeing Brody lying in the hospital. One good helmet and one bad.

The frustrating thing was I couldn't find any

connection between the helmets, an auction house, and the Ellington school district or board. At some point, I drifted off to sleep. A buzzing noise woke me up. I swatted to get the fly away from me but realized it was my phone. I located it between the back of the couch and the cushion. By the time I'd dug it out, I had one missed call. From Nancy Elder. She left a voice mail asking me how I was progressing and reminding me I had only a few more days to meet the deadline she'd imposed.

I sat up and rubbed my temples. It was only seven-thirty. I still didn't know what had caused the fight between Anil and Melba. Anil was still in jail, so I couldn't ask him. Melba obviously wasn't available, either. Maybe Anil's wife knew. I looked up their address and made a deal with myself. If I could work up the nerve to go over and question a woman I'd never met before, I could go get ice cream at Bedford Farms after.

Fifteen minutes later I stood on the small stoop of a neat ranch house on the side of Ellington that bordered the base. Two tall evergreen bushes stood sentinel on either side of the porch. Their scent spiced the air. A tired-looking woman in a beautiful red sari answered the door after I knocked repeatedly.

I stuck out my hand. "Mrs. Kapoor, I'm Sarah Winston. Anil asked me to help find out what really happened to Melba."

Her face lit up. "Yes, he told me. Come in. Call me Prisha. You've solved the case?"

She looked so happy, I hated to say no. I followed her into the neat but sparsely furnished room. We sat on opposite sides of the couch. I moved one of the colorful pillows scattered across the back. Her dark eyes watched me as if I had the answers to life. The room was very warm, and it wasn't just from the discomfort I felt.

"Are your kids here?" I didn't want them to overhear what could be a difficult conversation.

"No. They are in Mumbai with their grandparents. They go every summer, but we are especially happy they are there now. Since you haven't answered my question, your answer must be no."

"It is for now. But during the course of my investigation . . ." I paused. Jeez, that sounded like a line from a B movie. The whole week had seemed like a bad movie. "I heard that Melba and Anil had an altercation at the school and that the police were called. Do you know anything about that?"

Prisha tugged at a corner of her red sari. "Anil was horribly embarrassed about that evening. He is not a man of temper. He'd never kill someone because he was angry."

I nodded. I hadn't known Anil long, and I didn't know him well, but if he was the kind of man I believed him to be, he was a gentle, studious soul.

"Did he tell you what happened?" I asked.

She picked up a bright turquoise pillow and played with the long silk tassel. Her nails were painted hot pink but were chipped. She remained silent.

"If I'm to help Anil, I need to know this. The police might be using the incident against him."

She set the pillow aside but continued to let the tassel slide through her fingers. "Anil was unhappy with how purchasing was being handled."

"Purchasing of what?" I asked the question to confirm what I already expected to hear.

"Equipment for the school."

Bingo. I leaned toward her. "What kind of equipment?"

"Everything from desks to sports equipment."

"What exactly upset him about it?"

"They were cutting corners by not following the proper purchasing procedures of accepting bids. Anil didn't realize it until he studied the budget, scouring places to save money without hurting academics. It was buried very cleverly."

"So he confronted Melba about it?"

"Yes. She denied all of it." Prisha shrugged. "Maybe she didn't really know."

"Maybe digging into it is how she ended up dead." That would explain why someone was in Melba's house the night Stella and I drove by. I pictured the person running from the house and down the street. They wanted to find out what evidence she had.

Prisha and I stared at each other for a moment before I stood.

"Thank you for talking to me," I said.

"You'll still help my Anil?"

"Yes. Of course. I don't understand why the police aren't investigating this."

"Because he hasn't told them."

"Why not?"

"After he visited you, there were threats. Phone calls. E-mails. Come with me."

I followed Prisha out the back of their house. It was still warm out, but at least there were some puffs of air. We entered their detached garage through a side door. It was a small garage. Most of the space was taken up by a silver van. The air smelled of gas, oil, and damp wood. Prisha flipped on a light and pointed to a dark corner. A mannequin sat there, with a ski pole through its chest.

Chapter 32

I skirted the van and walked over to the mannequin. The ski pole was old, like the other three. Until recently, I'd never realized how chilling an inanimate object could be. Dolls and clowns in scary movies? Yes. Mannequins in real life? No, at least not until one was sitting in my apartment.

"He wanted me to leave town with the kids, but I refused to go."

"You need to tell the police. They need to see this."

"What if they think we are the ones doing this? Anil's uncle owns a dress shop in South Boston. We have access to mannequins."

"Has Anil at least told his lawyer?"

Prisha shook her head.

"He has to, Prisha. And you should go stay with a friend." I gestured to the mannequin.

"I feel safe enough. Since Anil's arrest, there haven't been any further threats."

"You can't let whoever is doing this win. Anil could be convicted of murder."

"He's counting on you."

"He needs to put his faith in his lawyer and the truth. Not me." Prisha and Anil's trust in me made me feel like I was wrapped in thick chains.

"I will talk to him," Prisha said.

I sat on an empty bench outside of Bedford Farms Ice Cream. The Almond Joy ice cream in my small cup was melting almost faster than I could eat it. Almost. I'd opted for a small, which had two softball-sized dips, instead of my usual kiddie size. The parking lot was full; kids wore baseball uniforms, teens flirted, and parents chatted with each other.

I shared the bench with two squirmy boys and their mom. Melted chocolate ice cream dribbled down chins, coated fingers, and flew around like water out of a water pistol. I was too tired to care if any landed on me. However, I stood when a very pregnant woman waddled over with her cone. She sat, looked at the boys next to her with alarm, and rubbed her stomach.

Great Road ran in front of the store. Cars raced by. I kept an eye out for Seth's car, because I had called him after leaving Anil's and asked him to meet me. This was as professional a place as I could think to meet on a Friday night. Anyplace else would involve alcohol or personal spaces. I wanted to avoid both when dealing with Seth.

He pulled in, parked, and loped over to the window to order. I tried to view him neutrally—just another handsome man wearing a white T-shirt over jeans. The sling gave him a vulnerability that probably had every woman's hormones in a five-mile radius going. Even the pregnant woman beside me seemed to have forgotten her ice cream to enjoy the view. When he walked up to me with a frappe—or, as the rest of the world called it, a shake—in his hand, I felt a lot of eyes on us.

Seth must have noticed it, too. "Let's go talk over there." He pointed to the massive chestnut tree on the other side of the parking lot. It was a little calmer over there.

I scraped the last bit of my ice cream out and sucked it off the spoon. As we passed a trash can, I dropped the cup and the spoon in it. The tree provided a little shade but couldn't stop the humidity. My hair was normally straight, but I could see little bits curling around my face.

"What's up?" Seth asked.

I'd been vague on the phone, worrying that my theory was way off. "I think there's a connection between the swap meet, the murder, and the stolen items, and"—this was the big one—"I think someone bought defective helmets for the school."

Seth frowned. "Why do you think the helmets were defective?"

"The school nurse told me there'd been a lot more complaints about concussions this year. And my friend Laura's son got a concussion when he was playing baseball. I had his helmet, and it wasn't nearly as sturdy as others I've seen. It had a dent on the side where a ball hit him. It didn't seem as heavy as others I've seen." I filled him in about the man from the sporting goods store and the possibility that the equipment had been purchased through an auction house.

Seth didn't laugh in my face or walk away. I took that as a good sign. I handed him my phone after I uploaded the article I'd found about the helmets, and waited impatiently while he read it.

"Someone came to the gym to steal the defective helmets," I said when he was done reading. "They must have replaced some of them with better helmets. I would have noticed if all the helmets had gone missing. They covered that by stealing some of the auction items, too. I think your Fagin and the person who attacked me are one and the same."

"Why go to all that trouble? Why not let them scatter at the swap?"

"My guess is they didn't want them out there or traced back to whoever bought them in the first place."

"Do you know who's behind all of it?"

I went through each of the board members, their access to teens, and their possible motivation for wanting Melba out of the way. Rex and Mac seemed to have the most powerful motivation. Seth nodded as I talked.

"Did you narrow it down?" Seth asked. "Do you think Rex is behind all of this?"

"I've thought it was Rex for a long time. He had the best reasons for killing Melba. She didn't give his kid a grade he thought he should have. They might have had an affair. He wanted her job."

"But you don't think that anymore?" Seth took a long pull on his frappe.

"I think it's Lance. I did some checking into his businesses a few days ago. He's had some successful ones but also some failures. One of the recent failures was a retail store, which would give him access to mannequins."

"Anyone can order a mannequin online."

"True, but why bother? There are other ways to threaten people." I paused. "I asked his son one day if he or his friends would be interested in helping with garage sales. He said they were always looking for ways to make a buck."

"Aren't all teens?"

"Yes, but I think one of the kids who came into Ryne O'Rourke's antique store, trying to sell things, was a kid I saw at their house. I've got a couple of photos." I found the photo I'd taken at Ryne's uncle's shop and the one Ryne had taken. "Maybe you can check with the kids you caught selling stolen merchandise and see if they connect these two back to Lance. And ask Mike to see if Lance has any reason to go up against the Mob." I paused. "Check out auction houses and his finances, too." Lance and Kelly certainly appeared to be wealthy, but maybe they weren't.

"Okay. I'll see what I can find out. Your information is a good start."

* * *

I pulled up to the dump at seven-thirty on Saturday morning. I wanted to get rid of the table in the back of my Suburban before I headed over to Kelly's house. A man waved me through the gap in the chain-link gate, and I pulled around to where they were unloading things. I looked at the tall pile of trash. A few years ago, before I'd moved to the area, a young woman's body had been dumped here like it was a bit of trash. They'd eventually identified her as a woman from Cambridge, but the case remained unsolved. It was probably the reason I really didn't like coming here.

I hopped out. The odor of rot hit me in the face and slapped me around. I tried mouth breathing as I opened the back of the Suburban. It didn't help. Another man came over, and we unloaded the table.

"This looks salvageable," he said.

The dump had recently opened a store where they recycled things people brought to the dump. Some people thought it was gross, but I thought it was a great way to literally turn trash into treasure.

"It does look fine, but see these holes? It's woodworms." I explained what woodworms were, and the man thanked me.

I looped my car around and gave the trash heap another glance. Were those spots of blue? I braked, shoved the car into park, and slid back out. I made my way over to the trash heap, trying again to ignore the smell of rot. It seemed alive, like it was going to wrap me in its stinky arms. Intermingled with the trash were blue helmets. I tugged on the metal brim of one. Someone shouted at me to stop. But I worked it free. It was just like the one Brody owned.

"Do you want to bring the whole pile down?" The man who'd helped me get the table out stood with hands on hips.

I looked at the heap towering over me with a leery eye. "No. Sorry. Is there any way to find out who left these helmets here?"

The man snatched the helmet from me. "Bunch of teenage boys. Pulled up with about thirty of these in the back of an SUV a couple of days ago." He squinted at my Suburban. "Looked a lot like yours."

So my Suburban hadn't been stolen just to send me a message, but they'd actually used it to haul the helmets.

"Why didn't you put the helmets in the store?"

"Boys said they weren't no good. Kinda like you did with your table."

"Do you know any of the boys?"

"Naw."

"Would you take a look at a picture for me? See if you recognize this kid as one of them?"

"If you hurry. Ain't got all day. Other people got stuff to dump, too."

Technically, he did have all day, since it was so early, but I didn't think pointing that out would help my case any. I retrieved my phone and flipped through pictures until I found the one I'd taken of the teen who'd brought the stuff to Ryne's uncle's store. I held my phone out to him. He squinted at it.

"Could be," he said. My heart thumped a little harder. "Might not be."

"You must have security cameras. Could I look through the tapes?"

"If you come back with a warrant."

That wasn't going to happen. I got back in the Suburban and sent Seth a quick text before I left. I might not be able to come up with a search warrant, but he should be able to.

Chapter 33

I arrived at the Longs' house at eight. I'd never been more on edge before a garage sale. I had talked to Seth and Pellner on the phone multiple times last night. They had tried to convince me to cancel the garage sale. But there were still some missing links that I hoped would be resolved today. Mike Titone had finally told Seth that he'd have someone watch out for me. It wasn't much comfort since Two-Toes had been watching Seth when he had been attacked.

I tried to put all of that out of my mind as I bustled about, trying to make Lance's sports equipment look as nice as possible. I'd ended up bringing several battered card tables with me and started setting them up. Kelly gasped with displeasure when she saw them.

"Wait," I said before she had a hissy fit. "I brought some vintage tablecloths to cover them." I flicked one open, and the breeze caught it before it fluttered gently onto one of the tables. It was decorated with slightly faded American flags. I'd pinned a NOT FOR SALE note to it in two different places. The tablecloth was unusual enough that I didn't want to part with it. I hoped that breaking one of my garage sale rules—everything at the sale should be for sale—wouldn't come back to haunt me. Kelly was having fits and was rearranging behind me almost as fast as I was arranging.

I set the baseball bats in an old apple basket and balls in a square wooden box from the early nineteen hundreds. Gloves comingled with helmets—lovely sturdy helmets—on one of the card tables. It ended up looking very nice, and even Kelly managed to agree. Time was ticking away, so I hastily set up the other items, like golf clubs and skates, on two other tables. Fortunately, Lance called Kelly in so I could finish up in peace. By nine-thirty everything was all set. I went back into the tent for one last look.

Kelly bustled in with a grocery bag. "I almost forgot all of this."

I worked up a smile and repressed a groan. She set the bag on the bed.

"Where should we put this?" she asked.

It was a bunch of toiletries, some opened, some not. Who would buy this stuff? Then I reminded myself that every time I'd thought that in the past, someone would purchase whatever it was I'd written off. I'd sold a bunch of half-empty bottles of nail polish for fifty cents a pop at one sale. A mother with three tween daughters had snatched them up.

I looked around the tent. Every space was crammed with artfully arranged items. Adding to it now could ruin the effect. Kelly watched me expectantly.

"I have an old champagne box in the Suburban. I'll go grab it, and we can put everything in it." I ran down the driveway and down the block to my car. It was going to be hot today, and the air hung heavy with humidity. I hoped it didn't make the pretzels on the pretzel bar soggy. They looked so cute in an assortment of old glass jars. I had found cute pink- and green-striped bags for people to use for the pretzels. At least the Italian sodas, already sweating in the ice-filled washtubs, would be popular. A couple of teenagers were in charge of all of that.

After I grabbed the champagne box, I hustled back. A small crowd was starting to gather at the end of the driveway. Kelly had two of her boys blocking the way and offering bottles of water to those waiting.

I set the box on a nightstand and filled it with an assortment of lotions, fingernail polishes, perfumes, and aftershaves. I grabbed a piece of linen stationery and wrote a sign that said ALL ITEMS 50 CENTS.

"We'll set up the vintage TV tray that's folded against the wall between the bureau and nightstand," I told Kelly. It wouldn't show off the wooden TV tray, which was painted with flowers, as much, but there really wasn't any other spot for the champagne box. I set up the tray and angled the champagne box so that part of the top of the TV tray still showed. After smoothing the bedspread where Kelly had set the bag of toiletries, I looked at her.

"Is Lance going to help today?" I asked.

"I told him to go golfing so he'd be out of our hair."

Usually, the more the merrier, but it seemed like a lot of her boys' friends were around to help.

"Ready?" I asked.

She nodded. We went to the front of the tent. We each grabbed a bottom corner of the canvas and slowly unveiled the contents. I actually thought I heard someone gasp, but then the crowd surged forward, and there was no time to even think for the next several hours.

Things were going amazingly well. Kelly drove a hard bargain, and so I followed suit. When someone offered half, I'd counter with a couple of dollars under the asking price. One woman wanted the chandelier that I'd thrown together using the sifters as lampshades. I'd priced it at fifty. She offered me ten. I countered at forty-eight. She offered me ten dollars and one cent. I countered at forty-seven dollars and ninety-nine cents. Under different circumstances, I would have never, ever acted like this, but something about this woman got my dander up.

Someone else came along and watched us. "I'll take it for fifty," she said.

"Butt out," the other woman said.

The second lady folded her arms across her chest. "Fifty-five."

The first woman gasped. "She can't do that."

I shrugged. "I don't see why not. We couldn't settle on a price."

"I wasn't done. You know as well as I do that haggling is part of the fun."

I did indeed know that, and it was fun most of the time. I nodded. "She's offered fifty-five. Do you want to bow out?"

The woman put her hands on her hips. "Sixty."

The two went back and forth. People quit shopping to watch. I'd rarely seen anything like it at a garage sale.

"Ninety-five," the first woman said.

The other woman threw up her hands. "Fine. It's yours."

The first lady looked smug and turned toward me to pay. Behind her back the other woman winked at me and slipped away in the crowd. I suppressed a laugh as the lady counted out her ninety-five dollars.

I noticed another woman filling her arms with the lotions, aftershaves, and perfumes that were in the champagne box. I grabbed a plastic bag, hustled over, and said, "Here. Let me help you."

Someone jostled her from behind, and several of the items slipped from her arms. A dark green glass bottle just missed hitting an Oriental rug. It broke open like an egg on the cement. Others rolled harmlessly to one side or the other.

"I'm so sorry," the woman said as she bent to pick things up.

"No worries," I said. "I'll clean it up. Don't cut yourself." The musky smell of the aftershave hit me before I took another step. It shot my memory back to the Ellington High School gymnasium. The person who'd attacked me had been wearing this scent. The whole incident played itself out in my head.

"Sarah, are you all right?" It was Kelly asking, but she wasn't the only one looking at me with concern. "You're very pale."

"I'm fine." Was I? "I'll get something to pick up the glass."

Kelly nodded. "Go through the garage door into the house. There's a broom and dustpan right inside the door."

The scent seemed to follow me. Maybe some had splattered on my shoes or clothes. I tried to take a deep breath in the garage, but it didn't help. As I went in the house, I gave myself a talking-to. I had to get through the rest of the sale. I couldn't crack up now. This was another link in my chain of evidence pointing to Lance.

As I hurried back outside with the broom and dustpan, I glanced around to see if I could spot whoever was supposed to be watching me. No luck. They were either very good or gone. In the far distance, a rumble of thunder sounded. I ignored it, concentrating on cleaning up the mess. I noted the brand of aftershave. Nothing I'd ever heard of, but then again CJ had never been one to wear the stuff.

What brand it was didn't seem as important as the fact that it was here. I took the mess out and dumped it in the trash, but the scent lingered like an unwanted friend for the rest of the afternoon.

Toward the end of the sale, I heard car doors slam. Two groups of people piled out of two separate cars. I went over to Kelly.

"We need to keep an eye on them." I jerked my head toward them as they swarmed up the driveway.

"Why?" she asked.

Before I answered, I made sure the zipper was closed on the fanny pack I wore around my waist. It bulged with money. "I've seen groups like them before. They try to distract and overwhelm. Then they steal. I'll stay by the jewelry. See if you can get a couple of the boys to stand over by the sports equipment. And someone to help you in the tent."

Kelly put two fingers to her lips and let out a whistle that raised the hairs on my arms. Teens came running over to her from various locations. The hairs on my arms almost stood straight up as I watched her tell them what to do. Not one protested, like most teens would. It was like Kelly had some kind of control over them. She looked over at me.

"What? Did my whistle startle you?" she asked.

I snapped out of it. "It's certainly ear piercing."

I stood over the jewelry as the two groups roamed the tent. Five of the newcomers came over to where I stood, but I managed them and kept them from taking anything. The whole time I kept wondering if I was wrong about Lance. If Kelly was actually the mastermind, the Fagin-like leader.

If it was her in the gym, she could have worn the aftershave to literally throw me off the scent. Then decided to get rid of it here at the sale. But why would she do it? I looked around at the tent, the house, the kids, at Kelly herself, who always looked impeccable. In fact, she'd changed outfits midway through the sale, after the other one became sweat stained. Appearances were important to her. So much so that she was willing to kill someone to keep them up?

The two groups seemed to have grown weary of the number of us watching them. They trudged back down to their cars, slammed doors, and took off. If they made off with anything, it wasn't something of great value.

Kelly came and stood beside me. It took everything I had in me not to leap away.

"Thank you for that. For knowing those people were up to something," she said.

I almost choked. "It's part of my job. It's why people hire me."

"It's something I didn't realize when I hired you. You are very different than you appear." She gave me a long look and then smiled.

So are you. Or maybe I was wrong about everything and was overthinking. Thankfully, a woman came up and wanted to buy the Jenny Lind bed, one of the last big pieces we had left.

By three o'clock, the official end of the garage sale, a wind whipped up, causing the tent to slap itself. The noise was unnerving. The rumbles of thunder were closer now, and a streak of lightning brightened the sky. Not much was left. The sports equipment was mostly gone; the inside of the tent had only a few scattered pieces. Kelly had gathered the teens to help get everything put away. I hadn't seen Lance all day and wondered if he was still golfing.

I snapped a few pictures.

"What are you doing?" Kelly asked.

"I want a record of how well the sale went." I knew that would play to Kelly's ego.

"Oh, great idea. There's hardly anything left."

What I really wanted was to get pictures of the teens to send to Seth so he could find out if there was any connection between these kids and the others who'd been selling stolen merchandise. After I finished taking pictures, I counted out the money with Kelly in the garage.

She'd made well over fifteen hundred dollars. But once I took my 40 percent and the hourly fee she owed me, and she paid for the tent and the electrician, her cut wasn't that much.

Kelly looked around with satisfaction. "You'll put the before-and-after pictures up on your Web site?"

"Yes. On social media, too, if that's okay with you."

"Of course it is. Is this your most successful sale ever?" she asked.

It wasn't, so I tried to dodge the question. "I've never had one like this. It was extraordinary." When Kelly's smile broadened, I realized this sale was never about the money, but it was about appearances. *Very interesting.*

"The local newspaper promised to cover it," she said. "I saw someone taking pictures with a professional-looking camera."

I was not sure a garage sale was newsworthy, but it would be a boon to my business if they did. "That's great." Another flash of lightning streaked across the sky. A house-shaking boom of thunder followed closely. "I'd better run," I said. I tucked my tablecloths under my arm and grabbed a card table in each hand.

Kelly grabbed another one. "Let me help you."

We scuttled toward the end of the driveway. A couple of the boys helping with the tent deserted their posts and took the card tables without being asked. As we got to the Suburban, huge raindrops splattered down around us.

"Go," I said. "I can get these in on my own." But Kelly and the boys stayed to help. One even slammed the rear doors back together before he dashed off. The rain pelted down.

"Thanks again," Kelly yelled. She took off running, arms pumping.

I stared at her, mouth agape as goose bumps broke out on my arms. She ran just like the person who'd been at Melba's house the night Stella and I went over there. Thoughts flashed through my mind faster than the raindrops hit me. Kelly turned at the top of the driveway and saw me standing there in the rain, staring.

Chapter 34

It was almost ten when I made the phone call. My fingers shook, and I hesitated over each number. But I finally punched in the last number and held my breath as I listened to the rings. Kelly picked up on the fifth one.

"I know what you bid last summer," I said. "A low bid on defective helmets." My voice was more even and calm than I could imagine. "But that's not the only thing you did. You killed Melba to keep her from talking. I'll give you until noon tomorrow to turn yourself in so you and your family can have some dignity. Not that you deserve it, but your kids do." Then I ended the call before Kelly could say anything.

The storm that had started that afternoon still pounded against my windows. I took a shaky breath and looked up. Pellner, Awesome, and Ramirez, the state trooper, stood around me in a semicircle.

"Well, that's done," I said.

Besides the three of them, there was a cop parked

down the block and another lurking in the alley behind the house. He was the one I felt sorry for, as he was hunkered down outside in the storm. It had taken almost from the time I'd left the garage sale to now to reach Seth, suggest the plan, and get everyone to agree to it.

There had been much protesting about my involvement. Ramirez hadn't even wanted me to make the call. He had just wanted to use my phone. I had insisted that Kelly would know if it was my number but not my voice. Pellner hadn't wanted me to be in the apartment. After the beating Kelly had given me in the gym, I felt I deserved to see the look on her face when she was caught. I'd won, since they needed my cooperation for this to work.

Part of me hoped that she wouldn't take the bait. That I was wrong, that the kids who'd talked to Seth during the day were wrong. Seth had done a lot of digging while I was at the sale. Kelly had an uncle who ran an auction house. The school board had bought the sports equipment through it. If our theory was correct, at some point Lance and Kelly realized the helmets were defective. Melba had somehow found out. Kelly killed her before she told anyone, and worked to frame Anil in the process.

Kelly had used the Sportzfan moniker among many others. That's how she knew I was trying to track the stolen items. Stealing the stuff from the high school gym helped cover up what was really going on. Lance and Kelly were in deep financial trouble because of all the businesses Lance had failed at. It seemed like Kelly would do anything to keep people from knowing. The kids Seth had interviewed had said Kelly was using the money from selling the stolen items to buy replacement helmets as well as to keep the family afloat. I'd thought back to the swap and how shiny the helmets had looked right before the sale.

The apartment was stuffy with the windows only cracked open. I turned on the TV and the light in my bedroom. The spare key was back in its place on the door frame. It was Ramirez who had suggested I try to keep something of a normal routine, in case Kelly decided to watch my apartment before making a move. An hour later I brushed my teeth and changed into a T-shirt and gym shorts. My usual summer sleepwear wouldn't be appropriate with all the men in the house.

I turned off the TV and shut off the light. I lay down on what I still thought of as CJ's side of the bed. I couldn't use my regular side, because it was occupied by a Rescue Annie mannequin used for training EMTs in CPR. There was some sweet irony in using it. Stella had loaned us a wig that approximated my hair. The mannequin was tucked under a light blanket and was lying on its stomach, so little of it showed. Minutes ticked by slowly, and an hour in I started worrying that she wasn't going to come.

Five minutes later Pellner came into the room. "Someone's coming," he said softly. We both slipped into my closet, and Pellner left the door slightly ajar. I'd cleaned it out so that there was room for both of us and so we wouldn't knock anything over. Awesome was behind the shower curtain in the bathroom, and Ramirez was hiding in the attic space off my living room.

It was hard to hear anything over the sound of the rain, but at last there was fumbling at the door and soft steps in the hallway. A person dressed in black crept into the room and then to the side of the bed, ski pole in hand. The person lifted it and plunged it over and over into Annie. I watched my fake self being killed.

"You were supposed to die with Seth in the fire. One fire two birds. You told Lance you'd be there. But you messed it up," Kelly said when she finally quit.

Pellner pushed me aside as Awesome flicked on the light. I stayed in the closet as instructed, not wanting to put the police in harm's way any more than necessary. Kelly fought them, kicking, lashing out with the ski pole, and biting. I'd warned them about how strong she was. When she was finally cuffed, I stepped out of the closet. I realized my room smelled like the aftershave I'd noticed the night I was attacked and that Kelly was the one wearing it.

We made eye contact as Ramirez read Kelly her rights. I didn't feel victorious, as I had expected. I just felt sad, not only for me but for the kids she had manipulated into selling stolen goods, for the ones who'd been harmed by the faulty helmets, and for Melba. Minutes later they hauled her out of the house and everything was quiet. Even the storm had moved on.

* * *

An hour later I sat alone in my living room. My filmy curtains billowed in the cool breeze. As tired as I'd been earlier, I was awake now. I'd heard Ryne climb the stairs a few minutes ago and unlock his door. The police had asked him to leave the building for the duration of an operation they couldn't risk explaining. He'd cooperated.

Stella had been in Boston. Awesome had asked her to please stay there until he let her know it was safe to come back. No one wanted anyone to get caught in the cross fire, if there was any. Outside, a car pulled in beside the house and a car door slammed. I could hear Stella singing as she came up the steps. I met her at my door.

"I got the part. I'll be in the fall production of *The Phantom of the Opera,*" she said.

I threw my arms around her. "Let's toast to that."

Stella followed me into the kitchen. I popped open a bottle of prosecco and poured the bubbling wine into two glasses.

"To new beginnings and hitting the high notes," I said.

We clinked our glasses before settling in the living room.

"I would have never guessed that Kelly Long was so crazy," Stella said.

"Or that Lance was such a doormat. He couldn't say no to her, even though her schemes were getting them deeper and deeper into debt."

"And in legal trouble. Why did she attack you that night at the gym?" Stella asked.

"So Melba would show up at the gym. Kelly went there to replace some of the defective helmets. Some part of her didn't want anyone to get hurt by using them. But she also wanted the auction items to sell." I sipped my prosecco. "My being there made her plan to kill Melba easier."

"How so?"

"The police notified Melba about what had happened. After they left the gym, Melba stayed behind and called Anil. Of course, she didn't realize Kelly was hiding somewhere in the school."

"Is Kelly the one who attacked Seth?"

"Yes. She thought getting him out of the way would stop his investigation into her theft ring." I bit my tongue so I didn't mention Mike's involvement.

"What a mess," Stella said.

"It is, but it's over. Tell me about your role."

We ended up talking into the wee hours.

Chapter 35

Sunday afternoon was the big lasagna bake-off. At four o'clock I stood in the Bedford town hall, along with Stella and Awesome. We'd gone from booth to booth, looking at the lasagna. They had sampled something from each booth, but the thought of eating any more lasagna had turned my stomach. I was off lasagna for a good long while.

The judges filed in and sat behind a table on a platform. One was a celebrity chef from Boston. I didn't recognize the other two. Plate after plate of lasagna was put in front of them. They looked at them, sniffed them, and tasted. I could see Rosalie and Angelo across the room. Angelo was drumming his fingers against his thigh, and Rosalie was biting her lip.

The judges made notes and drank water after each plate. The room filled with more people, and it grew hotter and hotter. The judges huddled together. Then they called for fresh seconds of a few of the lasagnas. They retasted and talked some more.

This couldn't be good for Angelo. I'd hoped he would be the clear winner. I spotted Tony from Billerica smiling and shaking hands, not a care in the world. But he didn't stand a chance. I didn't recognize any of the other chefs in the crowd.

Finally, the celebrity chef from Boston stepped to a microphone and flashed his megawatt smile. "Hello," he said. The mike screeched. "I'm so happy to be here in the lovely city of Bedford."

My knees started to shake. *Just get it over with.*

"We ate so many wonderful lasagnas today. You made our decision nearly impossible." He looked down at the notes in his hand. "The first runner-up is Angelo DiNapoli of DiNapoli's Roast Beef and Pizza. And the winner is Chef Ben from Belliginos."

Belliginos was the restaurant in West Concord that I went to with Ryne. If anyone had to beat Angelo, it should be Chef Ben. I tried to clap as I looked around for Angelo. Chef Ben leaped up the few steps and onto the stage. I finally spotted Angelo. He had a smile pasted on that looked so fake he might as well have been a mannequin. Just as Chef Ben reached for the large trophy, which looked like a bronzed piece of lasagna on a tall pedestal, one of the other judges whispered in the celebrity chef's ear.

The celebrity chef turned really red and said something back. The judges huddled again. Chef Ben stepped back, while another judge stepped forward.

"Our apologies. We got that twisted around

somehow." He glared over his shoulder at the celebrity chef. "The winner of the lasagna bake-off is Chef Angelo DiNapoli of DiNapoli's Roast Beef and Pizza."

A big cheer went up. I did my concert hoot and wormed my way forward. Angelo climbed onto the stage, pulling Rosalie along with him. They handed him the trophy, and he held it up over his head before stepping to the mike.

"I know for a fact that Chef Ben makes a very good lasagna." Angelo looked out at the crowd, spotted me, and beamed. Chef Ben had the good graces to laugh. "I'm honored to be in such good company. I wouldn't be here if it wasn't for my lovely wife, Rosalie. She's the real star of DiNapoli's Roast Beef and Pizza at one hundred Great Road in Ellington. Best lasagna in town." He held the trophy up again and gave it a kiss.

I waited my turn to congratulate Angelo and Rosalie. Angelo kissed me on both cheeks. "Thank you. We're having a party at the restaurant at seven. Be there."

I got dressed up for the party. A light blue sundress, open-toed wedge sandals, a swipe of mascara and lip gloss. I walked over to DiNapoli's with a bottle of good champagne in my hand. I crossed the town common on my way over. People were out strolling, kids were chasing each other on the lawn, and someone was playing fetch with their dog.

I couldn't stop smiling. The sign on DiNapoli's

said CLOSED, but I pushed through the door, anyway. The restaurant was packed with people. I found Rosalie and gave her the champagne.

"I guess you'll have to save this until later," I said.

"It was lovely of you. And for what you did for Angelo . . ." Her voice caught. "He's a character."

"But he's your character. How can I help?" I gestured to the crowd.

Rosalie handed me a bottle of Chianti. "Refill glasses?"

"Of course." I moved around the room, filling glasses for friends and strangers. Carol, her husband, Brad, Stella, Awesome, Pellner, Nancy, James and his new girlfriend. It seemed like half the town was here.

I went back for a fifth bottle and opened it.

Angelo stopped beside me, beaming. "Quit working. Enjoy." He pinched my cheek.

We both looked at the trophy standing on the counter.

"Well done, Angelo." I poured two glasses of Chianti and passed one to Angelo. "To lasagna," I said.

"To family," Angelo said. "You may not be blood, but you are definitely family."

We clinked glasses and took a drink. I knew the warmth spreading through me wasn't from the wine as I looked over all the people jammed in here. People I loved, people who loved me. The door opened again, and Seth walked in. His sling was gone. He wore a white shirt and black dress pants. He scanned the room, looking for someone, until his eyes locked on me. We stared at each other.

Keep it professional, Sarah.

A slow smile spread across Seth's face as he watched me. A definitely unprofessional smile. I refrained from fanning myself. If hearts could sing, mine was.

"Can I have your attention, everyone?" Angelo yelled above the crowd. "Thank you for supporting Rosalie and me through the years. Lasagna is on the house!"

I wanted to thunk my head on something. *Nooo, not more lasagna.*

Garage Sale Tips

Lots of people sell food at their garage sales. Some even say they make more off selling food and drinks at the sale than they do selling their belongings. Here are some things to think about:

1. First check with your city or county regulations to make sure you can sell food. Regulations vary widely from place to place.
2. If you want to sell water, soda, or other drinks, make sure you have a way to keep them chilled (or warm, if it's cool out).
3. Think about what the weather is going to be like. If it's hot out, avoid things that melt easily. Even chocolate chip cookies can make a mess, so a gingersnap or oatmeal cookie might be a better choice.
4. Some people go so far as to sell hot dogs or hamburgers. Personally, I worry too much about having a hot grill out where strangers are milling.
5. You will need an extra person to deal with food and drink sales while you deal with selling the garage sale items.

Setting Up a Pretzel Bar

What you'll need:

Bowls for the pretzels
A scoop
Paper lunch bags or single-serving plastic bags
Assorted pretzels
Cooking spray (optional)
Seasonings and toppings

Put a friend or family member in charge of scooping the pretzels into the bags. You can spritz the pretzels with cooking spray once they are in a bag to help the seasonings and toppings stick, but you don't have to. Let the customers add their own seasonings and toppings.

For your seasonings, you don't have to look farther than your spice cabinet. Popcorn seasonings work especially well and come in a wide variety of flavors. For toppings, you can use everything from sweetened cocoa powder to jalapeños. Just keep in mind the messiness factor, especially on hot days. Have fun!

Acknowledgments

To John Talbot of the Talbot Fortune Agency, thank you for your support and for believing in me.

To my editor at Kensington, Gary Goldstein, you are one of a kind! Thanks for working with me.

To my Wicked Cozy Authors blog mates—Jessie Crockett, Julie Hennrikus, Edith Maxwell, Liz Mugavero, and Barbara Ross—who knew when we started this that our friendships would grow and strengthen like they have?! I love each of you and your uniqueness. And Wicked Cozy Accomplices Sheila Connolly, Jane Haertel, and Kim Gray, thank you for your friendship and creativity.

Ashley Harris (no relation, but a dear friend and former neighbor), yes, I stole some of your garage sale stories.

Michelle Clark, medicolegal death investigator, thanks for talking me through using a ski pole to kill Melba!

Eleanor Carwood Jones, please don't pay more for things at a garage sale than is asked.

Barb Goffman, independent editor, you are a master at finding and fixing plot holes.

Clare Boggs, your editing skills have sharpened

with every book. Sometimes I think you know Sarah as well or better than I do. You are always willing to read at the last minute. Thank you.

Mary Titone, you read for me, you set up events for me, and you go on adventures with me. Thank you for all three!

My daughter, Elizabeth, thanks for bringing me chai, fixing me breakfast, walking Lily, and making me laugh when I'm stressed.

Bob, my patron of the arts, partner, and love, I can't imagine life without you.